THE EBONY CROSS

EARLY 20TH CENTURY DONEGAL.
A SAGA OF FAMILY, ADVERSITY AND TRIUMPH

Best Wishes

Anne C W 29/11/22

First Published in Great Britain 2022 by Mirador Publishing

First edition: 2022

Any reference to real names and places are purely fictional and are constructs of the author. Any offence the references produce is unintentional and in no way reflects the reality of any locations or people involved.

ISBN: 978-1-914965-41-8

Mirador Publishing
10 Greenbrook Terrace
Taunton
Somerset
UK
TA1 1UT

The Ebony Cross

Early 20ᵗʰ Century Donegal.
A Saga of Family, Adversity and Triumph

By

Anne Cassidy Waters

Dedication:

For Pat. Thank you.

Chapter 1

The train rolled into Amiens Street station with a rattle and squeal of brakes. Exhaling a final puff, it shuddered to a halt. It was the first time Bridie had travelled to Dublin and she felt very alone. Gingerly, she picked her way through the crowded train station and out into the cold, dank evening, her woollen shawl offering little resistance to the biting wind. Gaslight barely penetrated the mist rising from the River Liffey, not attempting to encroach into the sinister corners and alleyways of the silent street.

Movement in the shadows startled Bridie, and she jumped as a huddled wraith emerged, with outstretched hand. 'A penny, luv, can you spare a penny, just milk for the babby?' A mewling sound came from within the ragged bundle clutched tightly to her breast. Too weak to squirm effectually, the baby's flailing arm, like a blown twig, was a gentle plea for help. Bridie had barely a shilling herself in loose change, but the desperation that was apparent in the young woman's eyes, made her halt her hurried stride, and release a penny from her precious hoard. 'T'anks, t'ank you,' the figure whispered, and, in the gloom, her retreating steps softly echoed, 'blessin's of God on ye, ma'am, blessin's of God.'

Bridie rushed on and reached the lights and bustle of Sackville Street without further incident. Her destination was the genteel suburb of Rathmines where, thanks to Fr. Michael, the newly arrived curate in Donegal and friend of her prospective employers, she had been fortunate to secure a position as a housemaid. Used as she was to the hills of Donegal, the length of the walk was not a problem, but the exact location of the house was an issue. By the time she finally came across the imposing residence of number 26, Munster Terrace, she was thoroughly soaked, hobbling on blistered feet, from totally unsuitable shoes.

No 26, was a three-storey, over basement, redbrick mansion, set in a quiet terrace of understated elegance. Bridie had never encountered a servant's entrance in Donegal, so her natural inclination was to climb up the steps to the front door, but exhaustion, sore feet and all-pervading dampness, accorded some common sense. She descended the basement stairs and knocked on the door.

'You are late, we are already serving dinner,' was the peremptory greeting, from an inhospitable and censorious voice. Uncaring, Bridie stepped inside without uttering a word, too wet and fatigued to argue or appear contrite. To her immediate left stood a young girl in the black and white uniform of a maid. 'Rosie,' the autocratic tone continued, a voice Bridie could now see belonged to a frosty-faced housekeeper with a visibly heaving bosom, 'take her upstairs and show her what's, what.'

Bridie quickly followed Rosie, who appeared to be about eighteen or nineteen, a little younger than her own twenty-three. Bridie's speed was not to escape the housekeeper's accusatory tone but because she desperately needed to relieve herself after such a long journey. She tugged at Rosie's sleeve, 'I need the toilet, is it back outside?'

Rosie smiled. 'Nooo… We're very modern here. It's in the house, in the attic where we are going. It's the only one you are permitted to use.' This convenience was Bridie's inauguration to modern city living.

Upstairs was a floored attic containing six beds, each adorned with a bedside locker from a haphazard selection of discarded but good quality furniture. The room was clean if a little sparse, with grey walls and two windows, dressed with elderly lace curtains. Although her own home had lacked many necessities and was scarce in luxury, Bridie had only shared a bedroom with her sister, Josie. Slightly dismayed at the thought of living and sleeping in such close proximity to five strangers, yet knowing she had little choice, she wearily sat down on her allotted bed. Fatigue threatened to overcome her, to the extent she disregarded the wet patch seeping from her sodden clothing and smearing the bedspread. Not for long, however, as Rosie calmly informed her that the attic bedroom was out of bounds until seven o'clock in the evening, and there would be *'hell to pay'* if the housekeeper saw the stained bedspread.

'At all other times, ye must remain in the kitchen, in case ye're needed for duty,' explained Rosie.

Wearily, Bridie stood up and opened her suitcase, but the misty rain had penetrated the cheap cardboard and dampened the clothing inside. She withdrew a worn tweed skirt and stockings displaying a darn too many, but at least they were reasonably dry. Slowly, she trailed after Rosie, undecided whether the kitchen or the inhospitable, hard bed, was the better option. Bridie was set to work immediately, washing dishes and scouring pans, and welcomed her bed when ten o'clock arrived. Yet, that first night it was difficult to sleep. The bed creaked every time she turned, in unison with all others in the room. Snores, both lusty and soft, and the absence of her own space, prevented her from drifting off except for a few minutes at a time. She thought of her niece Ellen in Donegal. Although her sister Josie had three older boys and two girls younger than Ellen, Ellen held a unique spot in her heart. From the moment Bridie gazed into the smiling eyes of her tiny goddaughter, she was lost. She knew she would miss her and their daily walks and chats together and resolved to write as often as possible.

The five young women with whom Bridie shared the attic were pleasant and all too aware of their place within the hierarchy of the house. This *'sense of place'* was unsettling for Bridie. The isolated farmhouse from which she hailed had been little more than a barn but owning land, however rocky and barren, conferred a certain status. This minor status did not mean the tinker or journeyman who passed by were ever treated with disdain and respect was freely awarded for their trade. The imposing edifice where she now found herself was unsettling as, for the first time, she encountered the rigid social boundaries of class.

Mr and Mrs Bailey were imperious but polite and that was reasonably acceptable. The main irritation was the two children. The seventeen-year-old daughter and the fourteen-year-old son were arrogant and demanding. 'Fetch my coat,' from young Julian or the dismissive wave from arrogant Miriam, guaranteed a reprimand for Bridie from the housekeeper, Mrs McConnell, 'Your manner is not in keeping with your position in this house. Remember, a servant must present a humble manner to her betters.' Only Bridie's flashing eyes betrayed how her hackles rose at this remark, but defiance was visible in her stance. Her face flushed daily with anger at the expectation she bow figuratively, if not physically, to the younger members of the family. Their attitude rankled, perhaps unreasonably, as they were reared to believe deference was their right.

The first month dragged slowly by as Bridie was not accorded any wages or free time. It was considered instead, that as she was receiving training for a lifetime's career, she was quite privileged enough. Her duties were not so much arduous as dull and tedious with long hours standing at the kitchen sink or hauling water up and down the stairs. Weeks alternated, from an early start at 5am with only short breaks until 7pm in the evening, to an 8am start until 10pm at night. On certain occasions, all staff had to work much later. Service in the dining room was handled by the butler, Mr Corcoran and the housekeeper, Mrs McConnell, but if there was a dinner party, the kitchen staff had to be on hand until all food was served and the kitchen tidied for the following day. Understanding the magic of utilising a myriad amount of cutlery for even the smallest snack needed to be learnt and, within the first week, she was initiated into their mysteries.

Finally, her first free afternoon arrived and, with the comforting tinkle of coins jangling in her pocket from her very first wage packet, she made her way as soon as lunch was completed into Dublin city centre. Any capital city can be full of adventure, but for a young, impressionable girl from Donegal, it was magical. As she became more accustomed to her surroundings, she realised Rathmines was an easy walk into Grafton Street and Georges Street.

It was February and the weather was still cold and damp, but Bridie relished the solitary quiet of a ramble through St Stephen's Green before wandering the streets, inhaling the atmosphere. Soon, the unfamiliar aroma of coffee brought her hesitantly into Bewley's café. Curiosity, and her natural determination overcame any sensation of awkwardness and she ventured inside. Coffee was unknown in Donegal and Bridie wallowed in the scent and the luxury of sipping a cup of the heady brew, contemplating how best to describe such a treat in her next letter to Josie. The discomfiture she felt at being alone dissipated once she saw the number of unaccompanied women, apparently comfortable and relaxed, in the establishment. It soon became a regular haunt after an hour of window shopping. Entry to many of the finer shops was facilitated by a doorman sporting a top hat. Their scrutiny and dismissive looks were initially intimidating, and it was some time before she garnered enough courage to enter these hallowed bastions. Where her Donegal dress might have seen her entry barred, her housemaid's attire made her acceptable. The entire uniform, supplied by her employers, the cost, of course, deducted from her weekly wage, was a flag of respectability.

The conspicuous opulence on display in the large department stores and jewellery shops was overwhelming and a great source of material for letters home. In Bridie's experience, such luxury was entirely unknown in Donegal. Although there was absolutely nothing she could afford to buy, the glimpse into a rarefied world of wealth was an eye-opener. Gradually, as she became familiar with the city and wandered further afield, the distinctions within became more apparent and the dingy and seedy underbelly impinged on her consciousness. She witnessed how ragged children begging at street corners were such an accepted part of the landscape, they were rendered invisible. Bridie was perturbed, and especially so, considering such a daily waste in the kitchens of the house in Rathmines. Vast amounts of food were prepared every day and all the staff, in addition to the family, ate well, but such abundance developed a carelessness. Once it was dark, a rustling could be heard from the area where the bins were stored. Depending on who was on duty, the scavengers were either ignored or sent packing.

It was now late March with a bitter wind blowing and the smog in the air dirtied every visible surface. Her new coat offered little protection and she felt chilled from the harsh, unceasing gusts, swirling off the River Liffey. The fascination of the city began to pall as the disparity between rich and poor, where the excesses of one and the deprivation of the other became ever more apparent. The abundance of jewels and carriages and the richness of clothing on display at every turn, erected boundaries that reinforced class difference.

Gradually, Bridie began to explore further downtown where she felt more in touch with the ordinary Dubliner. This new awareness of the blatant poverty in other parts of Dublin, hardship that should have been offensive to any right-thinking person, affected her vision of the city. She wandered along the quays, towards Christchurch Cathedral and down towards Thomas Street. Much of the housing was dilapidated but still very much occupied. She was continually appalled at the sight of young children in threadbare dresses and shorts scampering along the streets, apparently oblivious to the biting cold. Her admiration for how these children managed to laugh and play, despite adversity, was boundless. There were quite a few affected by Rickets but undaunted by bent limbs and bare feet, they joined in the fun. She would later learn that the slums of Dublin were considered some of the worst in the world, with a death rate comparable to Calcutta. Donegal was a county that had more than its share of poverty and she recalled many children wrapped in sparse clothing, often without any shoes. Yet, they had melded into the background and Bridie realised with hindsight, that she too had been blind. The poverty had not impacted on her, and she felt a momentary sense of shame. Perhaps it was the vastness of Donegal that enabled the hardship to be hidden. It merged seamlessly into a scenery so familiar that she had accepted its existence, without a qualm. By contrast, the concentration in Dublin made it impossible to ignore. She realised there were layers that remained invisible if one chose not to look beneath the surface.

That night she chatted to Rosie, questioning her knowledge of Dublin city. They were alone in the attic, fortunate to have the evening off together but, nevertheless, careful to whisper lest they were overheard. Rosie reluctantly revealed her background. The fifth child of fourteen, the family lived in a two-room flat in Henrietta Street. She said they felt lucky to have two rooms as many families had to share. She was glad to leave and loved the comfort of her job. She went home weekly but more out of duty than love. Conditions remained unchanged. There was never enough food or heat. Her father had no work, and her mother was ground down with childbearing and rearing. Rosie resolved that that life would never be hers.

'What was your hometown like?' asked Rosie.

'Well,' responded Bridie, thoughtfully, 'I grew up on a farm. It was called "Droimreagh" …'

'Drim what?' interrupted Rosie.

'It is pronounced "Drumrea". It is a Gaelic word. It was a small farm with a cottage attached. There was no running water, so we carted water every day from the well nearby. I hated that job. My muscles ached and I spilt half the water on the trudge to the house, that meant I had to go back again.' Bridie paused, wistfully drawn back to memories of childhood, before continuing. 'We were lucky because if you had some land, you could grow food and there was always turf for heat. If you were a labourer in the fields or quarries or, even a fisherman, then employment was seasonal. Many men and young boys had to travel to Scotland for months at a time when there was no work. Women stayed behind and scrounged and grovelled to sustain themselves and their children, as best they could. Some dug potatoes and others weaved or knitted.'

Rosie snapped back, 'Ye were well off so. Where I grew up, it was tough. Tea and bread were all we had some days. I often went to school with no food. When I got home, it would be a watery stew from old rotten vegetables.' Rosie paused, inhaled a long, slow breath, and calmed down.

'Sorry, it is not your fault, but I hated those tenements, and still do. Women begging for scraps, bits of meat that no one wanted, like pigs' feet or fatty bacon, trying to feed a family of eleven or twelve, or even more. And that was when me ma had a few pennies. I remember days when she didn't have that and would pack us all up to walk to Dollymount strand. We had an oul pram to push. There was always a little one in it for a ride. Dependin' on your age, you either minded the youngest ones and stayed at home, or went with me ma lookin' for cockles, winkles, mussels, or whatever ye could find. Me brother Jem, he would sneak into a garden that had vegetables and nick a few onions or carrots. That meant a decent stew when we got home. Sometimes he clambered up a wall and stole some apples. We packed everything into an oul flower sack and stuffed it anywhere in the pram we could fit it.

'The walk home was hard, what kept us going was knowing we had some food for Ma to cook. But I remember chapped knees, roaring red, and chilblains nearly on every toe. Do ya know, many women also worked, even with large families to care for. They worked at market stalls, selling fruit or flowers. I remember me ma takin' in la'ndry to make a few bob. Our clothes were other people's cast-offs. Men, begging for work and getting rejected for no reason, other than the way they looked. If you were more desperate than that, there was the Vincent de Paul or another crowd who examined ye and decided if you'se were worth helping. Misery and cold is all I recall from those tenements, and I am never going to live in one again.' Rosie's tirade abruptly stopped from lack of breath and almost panting with vehemence and the strength of, for her, an unusual rant, she then slowly continued.

'I remember Christmas being a sort of happy time. There was the excitement beforehand, decorations in the window, big streamers, and candles. There were no real toys but there were usually some sweets or fruit and then, there was always porter. Afterwards, me mother would be hiding from the moneylender coming to collect. Me da would be shoutin' at her, askin' why she couldn't manage, and he the one who took most of the money for drink. That is why there are two things I promised meself. The first is never marry, just work here, and the second is give me ma a few pennies each week, as long as I can, so she is no longer hungry or scared.' Rosie turned away to hide her tears, angrily swiping at her reddened cheeks.

Bridie drew the girl towards her and lightly massaged the thin, bony, shoulders. 'Rosie, how did you get the job here anyway?' whispered Bridie, continuing her massage. 'A priest in Donegal helped me.'

Rosie, nervous about how voices could carry in the silent house, turned, and whispered in Bridie's ear, 'It was Mrs McConnell. I know you are not too fond of her, but she has a soft heart.'

'Oh, don't mind me, Rosie, I just hate the idea I am less than anyone else and she reinforces that, daily,' responded Bridie, with a dismissive shrug.

'Anyway,' muttered Rosie, so quietly Bridie had to struggle to hear her, 'I was helpin' me ma sell flowers on a Saturday, and she was buyin' some. She asked did I want some work. I think she felt sorry for me 'cos I was standin' in the freezin' cold and shiverin', 'cos I had no coat. She said they needed an extra chambermaid as there was some sickness in the house and if I was interested, to call at nine on Monday and ask for her. I was trembling that mornin'. She told me to make meself presentable, but sure I was wearing most of me clothes that day and didn't know what else to put on. '*Make sure you go downstairs,*' she said. '*Ask for me and don't talk to anyone else, and if you are squeamish, don't bother coming*'. This was before they had the indoor plumbin' installed. I thought they would let me go when they eventually got it in, but they kept me on in the kitchen.'

The following week, Bridie wandered down Henrietta Street, mainly out of curiosity. The Act of Union in 1801, merged the parliaments of Ireland and Great Britain and, Henrietta Street, built during the 1720s, was populated by the wealthy establishment. The demise of the Irish Parliament after direct rule was implemented from London, meant much of the establishment departed from Dublin. Their departure initiated a gradual decline in the fortunes of the street and by the mid-19th century, many houses had fallen into disrepair and, through neglect, slowly declined into tenement dwellings. At one point, 835 people lived in just 15 houses. The once, elegant, cobblestone street, was now crumbling and instead of shock, anger surged within Bridie at the conditions she encountered.

One end of the street was dominated by the graceful and dignified Kings Inns who controlled the entry of barristers into the justice system. The incongruity of rats openly scavenging at the other end of the street was not lost on Bridie. The cacophony of babies crying and the aura of decay and despair, not to mention the pungent stench of overflowing sewage, was overwhelming. A number plate, long since discoloured, revealed that she stood outside the house where Rosie's family lived. With her interest piqued, Bridie wandered inside. Immediately, she was engulfed in lines of washing and had to fight her way through a hallway that was once a fashionable entryway. The discarded wealth, left to moulder, a very poignant reminder of the inequality existing in

Dublin. A high, decorative ceiling graced a stairway that had once been carved with pride by a master craftsman. Balusters were missing leaving dangerous gaps, providing a magnet for playing children and an assured cause of death or injury. The walls were a patchwork of blue and red that she later learned were called, "rickets blue" and "raddle red", supposedly, disinfectant paints but, relatively ineffective. The smell was a mixture of urine and bleach, combined with the stench of rotting refuse.

As Bridie turned to leave, a voice behind her probed, 'Miss, Miss, are you lost, luv? Who do you want? Mind that nice coat on the red raddle, it'll stain it, and it don't come off easy.'

Bridie looked down and tugged her coat closer to her as she responded. 'Thank you, no, not lost, just wandering around.' Turning, she greeted a thin, wizened woman, of indeterminate age. She may have been fifty but, equally, seventy-five.

'Where are ye from, it's not Dublin anyway, yer not from these parts.'

'Donegal,' replied Bridie, as the woman prattled on.

'I heard of there, alright. My, but it's a cold, oul day. Do you want a cuppa tea, luv? I'm Mary.'

'Well, aye, yes,' responded Bridie, 'thank you, Mary,' and she followed the woman into a spacious room that, at one time, would have screamed, opulence.

The decorative plaster that held high sway in the hallway was impressive but, in this room of dank walls and torn curtains, eyes were instantly drawn above. A gracious ceiling of sculpted flowers and cherubs, yellowed now with smoke that spewed from a sputtering fire, was still breath-taking in its sorry splendour. The smoky fire sported an old shoe and a solitary piece of splintered wood, in a vain attempt to produce heat. Bridie was directed to sit on a battered tea chest and gratefully sipped her brew. She was mindful of the hospitality, knowing that provisions were scarce and sparse. She may just be a housemaid, but with it came some luxury, such as reasonable, and regular meals. One corner of the room was cordoned off with a tattered net curtain and, through a gap, Bridie saw a bed strewn with old coats. A mattress, similarly, dressed, lay in another corner.

'I let poor Maisie sleep there,' nodded Mary. 'The poor créatúr, sure she has nowhere else to go. Sure, we all have to help each other.'

Bridie recognised the sense of community that Rosie had alluded to, a spirit of kindliness and genuine sharing. She could tell, just from this small encounter and the chatter of this woman, that if there was someone in need, a neighbour was at hand to help despite their own desperation. Bridie turned to leave but could feel her treasured sweet, that weekly treat shift in her pocket, almost leap into her palm. 'Here, Mary, a wee gift, thank you for the tea.' Wide-eyed, Mary hesitated then gratefully took the chocolate.

The walk home was introspective, and her swirling thoughts struggled for a pattern. Money was always tight so, usually, Bridie ignored the singing tones of young lads with newspapers for sale. Distinctive flat caps and threadbare scarves encased determined faces full of resolve. Gnarled toes and calloused feet, shabby and dusty with skin as durable as leather but offering little protection against the wind and rain, gave testament to long hours tramping the streets. Today, however, she stopped and listened, finally purchasing a copy of James Larkin's newspaper, *The Irish Worker and People's Advocate*. Instinctively, she knew to hide the newspaper when she entered her place of employment. The first item she read was an advert for a 'Social and Dance,' in Liberty Hall on Sunday evening. As she read, she realised that there were a lot of events held in Liberty Hall, choir practice and Irish dancing to name just two. In her innocence, she assumed she could plan her days and evenings off carefully so she could attend at least one function, every so often. That choice was not accorded to the servants in Rathmines. Although, whenever an opportunity arose, she frequented Liberty Hall, it was only on a rare free afternoon allotted by the housekeeper.

Bridie's interest in events in Dublin continued to grow as tensions increased in the city between unions and employers. Jim Larkin had set up the *Irish Transport and General Workers Union*, and membership was growing at a rapid rate, much to the consternation of employers. By 1913, membership had risen to approx. 10,000 and, Bridie, unbeknownst to her employers, applied for admittance to the *Irish Women Workers Union,* formed by Delia Larkin, a sister of James Larkin. Bridie's consciousness of the inequality existing, not just in Dublin but within the whole country, was becoming more marked, as her reading widened and matured and as she contemplated all around her. Rosie was the reluctant beneficiary of many of Bridie's burgeoning thoughts on trade unions and workers' rights. Rosie was very pretty and fair but wafer-thin. An obsequious and deferential manner somewhat marred her ethereal appeal. By contrast, Bridie was dark-haired with a presence that could not be ignored. Not especially pretty, she was nevertheless extremely striking, with green eyes that flashed excitement and interest in all her surroundings. Bridie's expression also challenged and so put her at variance with the housekeeper and her ideas of how a maid should conduct herself. Rosie was terrified to stir up any rancour within their employment, lest she lose her job. She urged Bridie, both to be quiet and to be careful, but this was now next to impossible.

Emmeline Pankhurst and the demand for women's suffrage had lit a new spark within Bridie. The nuances of many of the ideas within the articles she read required a lot of thoughtful consideration. Currently, the vote was confined to men of property, wealth, and status. There appeared to be a willingness to extend the franchise to all men, regardless of position or education, but a reluctance to even consider women. All women were therefore excluded, based on gender alone, and any contribution they made to society was largely, unacknowledged. There was a blind spot among many men of power, and the struggle for voting rights for all women, would not be easily won. The death of Emily Davison at the Epsom Derby, in June, was a source of sadness and frustration and Bridie searched for a movement in Ireland with comparable aims. *The Irish Women's Franchise League* was formed by husband and wife, Hanna and Francis Sheehy-Skeffington. They also founded the first Irish feminist newspaper *The Irish Citizen*. The first copy purchased by Bridie, the 1913, 8th April edition, headlined the death of Marjorie Hasler. She was a tireless advocate for women's rights in Ireland. She had been imprisoned with Hanna Sheehy-Skeffington in 1912, for breaking windows in Dublin Castle, in a vain strike for women's suffrage. Marjorie Hasler had also suffered injury at the hands of the police whilst supporting Emmeline Pankhurst in London in 1910. This injury resulted in continual headaches and combined with the debilitating effects of imprisonment, she succumbed to illness on, 31st March 1913. She became an inspiration for Bridie and a catalyst for action.

Meanwhile, as tension continued to rise between employers and unions, the employees of No 26 were told, in no uncertain terms, that sacking would be an immediate consequence if anyone dared to join or appear to sympathise with the ITGWU. Incensed, and determined not to be bullied, Bridie continued with what had now become a clandestine activity. Before entering Bewley's café, Bridie bought her newspapers, particularly *The Irish Citizen*. Each edition headlined the following words, and they alone inspired her, "For men and women equally, The rights to citizenship. For men and women equally, The duties of citizenship". Once coffee was ordered and served, she took a moment to savour the aroma, before she read each paper from front to back, sadly, discarding them on the way home lest the housekeeper detected them.

Countess Markievicz, who was to later become the first woman elected to the British House of Parliament, was now a figure on Bridie's radar. An Irish Republican and activist who could have led a life of ease but, instead, devoted herself to the Irish cause and the Irish poor. The conflicting demands of nationalism and women's rights were highlighted through the vilified cartoon published in the May 1913 edition, of *The Irish Citizen*. The cartoon depicted John Redmond, an Irish Nationalist MP, demanding Home Rule but with his foot leaning on a woman. The question of what took precedence or could both demands coalesce side by side was an ongoing debate. Bridie found her steps leading her regularly to Liberty Hall in her search for satisfactory solutions. At this point, in July 1913, Bridie was conflicted by her need to earn a living and her desire to have more meaning in her life, a desire that went beyond the expectations of her gender at that time. In particular, the continuing poverty that she witnessed each week and the comparison with the waste and extravagance in her place of work, gnawed at her, generating a continual quest for information and answers.

Chapter 2

T he 'Dublin lock-out' began in August 1913. Thousands of workers united under Jim Larkin, in a bid to secure better pay and conditions. The employers also united, securing their premises so workers had no access, in an effort to force them to acquiesce and relinquish membership of the trade union. This bitter dispute continued until January 1914, with a pyrrhic victory for the employers. Many faced bankruptcies as a result of the dispute but, on the surface, it appeared the right to unionise had been broken.

Bridie gave the workers her full support and was hopeful that reason would prevail, and the dispute satisfactorily settled within days. But as the days passed into weeks, hope began to fade. On her day off, she offered her assistance in the soup kitchens as so many people were now, not just hungry, but starving. Growing up in the insular world of Donegal did not offer an opportunity to meet with those of a faith other than Catholic. Interaction with members of other religions was also frowned upon by the clergy. As such, Bridie had never spoken to a Protestant woman before she met Countess Markievicz. Working alongside such an inspirational woman, Bridie could forget for a while the haggard children who clamoured for food on the street outside. Children, with dull, blank expressions and fathomless eyes, eyes that held bottomless pits of despair and emptiness.

It was in Liberty Hall that she first encountered Dr Kathleen Lynn, another Protestant woman, whose compassion, and dedication was an inspiration that impacted Bridie her entire life. She was another woman who forsook a life of comfort to help those less fortunate.

Kathleen Lynn had trained to become a doctor despite the difficulties such a path entailed for a woman of her time. She stood alongside James Connolly as his equal believing Ireland's future lay in independence from Britain. Bridie realised, contrary to her previous experience, that not all those born into a higher class were necessarily disconnected from the average citizen without any understanding of their plight. Of equal importance, was a dawning recognition that religion was no barometer of empathy. An understanding of inequality was based on a social affinity and rapport and not religious ethos. These women did not discriminate on account of social status. They only saw people in desperate need of assistance. They were also women who overcame boundaries and achieved their own goals despite the gender barriers that existed. The attitude of her own, supposedly Christian Church, astounded Bridie and confused her.

Tentatively, because of her upbringing, but with determination born from her newfound awareness, Bridie quietly queried the Church's stance from the local priest. 'Father, why does the Church stand with the employers when so many are hungry? Did Jesus not preach compassion and love for the poor?'

His disdain diminished Bridie, and her now reddened features turned a rich crimson. 'How dare you question the Church and your betters. Such effrontery!' expostulated the curate, almost tongue-tied in his effort to voice his displeasure and contempt. His anger was a physical force that forbade further questions and Bridie left the church more confused than ever. Endless questions tumbled through her brain, but no answers were forthcoming. How could her Church instruct those with nothing to return to a life empty of all but hopelessness and drudgery? As the strike escalated, those questions reverberated continuously.

On 31st August 1913, Bridie was walking as per usual, to the headquarters of the ITGWU. Despite the difficulties that would ensue should her employers learn of her activities, Bridie felt compelled to assist. Unwittingly, she walked into a violent scuffle that, subsequently, became known as "Bloody Sunday". Dozens of police baton-charged strikers who had gathered in Sackville Street in support of Jim Larkin. Police had arrived to arrest Larkin and according to many onlookers, they had charged into the crowd without any provocation. They indiscriminately struck the now fleeing horde and Bridie received a blow that knocked her to the ground. She eventually stumbled to the union headquarters where Dr Kathleen Lynn attended to her.

Rosie was aghast when Bridie arrived back at the house in Rathmines. There was no hiding the injuries to her face or how they were received from the housekeeper and subsequently, the lady of the house, Mrs Bailey. On the 1st of September 1913, Bridie was sitting forlornly in Bewley's café, sipping her final cup of their unique coffee and contemplating her future. Her meagre belongings were in her cardboard case on the floor beside her, her paltry savings in her handbag. Her eyes welled with unshed tears as she contemplated her future. Returning to Donegal was not an option and wearily she gathered her belongings and trudged on down to the awaiting boat, at Dublin docks.

Bridie disembarked from the boat in Liverpool at about 5.30 in the evening. Fortunately, as it was August, the evening was still bright and sunny. The journey had been uneventful, but Bridie felt queasy and was glad to be on dry land. She had found a seat beside two women, but it was impossible to engage in conversation as the younger woman sobbed continuously onto the shoulder of her companion.

Probably desperate, like myself, mused Bridie, *leaving home and family for the unknown.* Nevertheless, she was glad to sit near them as the boat was full of young men, many the worse for wear, from too many pints of beer. It was a lonely few hours with a frightening future ahead. Images of Donegal floated through her mind making her question what she was doing. She physically shook her head, as if that action alone could dislodge Donegal's mountainous splendour and wild, windswept landscape, permanently from her memory. Unbidden images crept in instead, warm evenings by the fire toasting bread as the gales howled outside shaking the rafters. A sneaky tear escaped to slip slowly down her cheek and created a kinship with the sobbing woman beside her. She continually questioned her decision to travel to Liverpool but knew there was no alternative. There was no future for her in Donegal.

The passengers were all now ashore and the two women, the younger no longer crying, were greeted warmly by friends on the dockside. Bridie anxiously searched in vain for any sign to indicate the direction she should head. Finally, she followed the two women and their companions assuming they knew where they were going, eventually locating a signpost for the city centre.

Incredibly and, for the first time, Bridie had experienced Mrs McConnell's soft heart, the one Rosie had insisted was hidden beneath her exacting and forbidding demeanour. Mrs McConnell's sister was a nun in a convent in Liverpool and she slipped the address into Bridie's hand as she left the house in Rathmines. 'They are constantly in need of hired help,' she whispered and was gone before Bridie could thank her.

The convent was supposedly near the city centre so Bridie trudged along behind the group, finally reaching a section where she could ask for directions. The summer evening was still bright but after the trauma of leaving Dublin and the long journey on the boat, she was drained. After a few false turns, she came upon a bleak, imposing and austere, grey building. It was, in fact, a private academy for girls.

As maids were always needed, she was hired immediately which obviated the need to look for lodgings that night. She was shown to a room not dissimilar to the one in Rathmines, but this one held more than ten beds. Evening sunlight streamed through the small attic window highlighting the dust motes dancing overhead. Sleep was not elusive that first night as, overcome by exhaustion, Bridie sank into welcome oblivion within seconds of lying down. She was put to work immediately the following morning, labour that was physical and exacting. Each morning, Bridie rose before dawn at 5am, and she was more-or-less on her feet until eight at night. Her first unenviable task was cleaning bedpans. The pungent odour assaulted her nostrils and clung to her clothes. It was a full two weeks before she ceased gagging as she scrubbed the foul mess from inside the pans. It was a relief to spend the rest of her working day attending to endless laundry. Bedsheets had to be pristine white and were inspected at regular intervals. Her hands were red raw from bleach and her eyes constantly stung while sweat rolled down her cheeks in a continual stream. Her back ached and her feet were swollen and there was no more welcome activity than to sink gratefully into bed at night.

The ethos in the school was Roman Catholic but the culture was very British. The class-based prejudice, overseen by the nuns in the convent, was palpable. Their discriminatory practices aggravated Bridie and it was with supreme effort she shrugged off an irritation that threatened to constantly niggle. Among the schoolgirls themselves, there was a hierarchy depending on the occupation of their fathers and this hierarchy was also implemented religiously by the nuns. Together, the girls were a community apart, a tribe of their own, with needs catered for by invisible hands. Cloaked in pale blue dresses with starched white pinafores, they automatically followed a routine coded by generations before them. Bridie was both intrigued by the rigid boundaries that set the girls apart and irritated by the inculcation of a conformity and regulation that forbade any questioning of their allotted gender role. Their moulding into a position of superiority with no recognition of how they, in turn, were subordinated, ensured a continuation of class discrimination and domination that included their own. She fantasised that all the servants who maintained the smooth running of the school were sylphlike spectres attending to the pupils' needs, unseen and unappreciated. Regular meals, clean clothes, and spotless surroundings were an expected norm of their social status, with no thanks required.

In early November, she was permitted an afternoon off and with Mary, another laundry maid, travelled into Liverpool town centre. Her body had become, if not used to the robust physical regime, more accommodated and, for the first time, she felt able to indulge in an activity other than sleep. Time-off was strictly rationed, so both Bridie and Mary were fortunate to be awarded the same free afternoon. Mary was eighteen and had lived in the convent since she was twelve. Although it was a school, education was not extended to the servants, so Mary was barely literate. She was more excited than Bridie at their outing and she positively glowed at the now festive appearance of the city as it prepared for Christmas.

Liverpool shocked Bridie with its similarity to Dublin. A land that was supposed to promise a future looked remarkably like the one she had just left, with the same vast gulf between the "haves" and "have nots". Shop doormen opened the doors of carriages to assist fur-clad women to enter and browse for Christmas presents with servants trailing behind to carry purchases. In doorways and alleyways, spectres, obviously cold and hungry, huddled together for warmth and children, shoddily and scantily clad for the icy winter, begged pitifully at corners for scraps. Mary traipsed blissfully by, gazing in open wonder at the colourful, festive windows on display while Bridie shrugged off disturbing images of Henrietta Street. They both bought small trinkets and sweets for the big day as Christmas for the servants in the convent was, supposedly, a cheerful time with less work. The students, in the main, returned to family for the holiday so there were only the nuns to cater for and the few remaining girls whose parents were abroad or unable, for a variety of reasons, to return home. Bridie's connection with religion was now tenuous at best, stretched by the clergy's disregard for the hungry children during the lockout. Living in a convent did not allow for absence from religious services and there were quite a number over the holiday, but services were, at a minimum, an escape from the laundry.

The work in the convent school was both disheartening and thankless. It was not how Bridie visualised her life and she was anxious to move on in another direction. Yet she lingered, as winter of 1913 turned to spring1914. She knew that at home in Donegal her letters gave the impression that her life was exciting and glamourous. Josie even hinted that she was right to refuse an early marriage and look for adventure before settling down to have children.

Inside, Bridie railed against her current circumstances, but lethargy had taken hold preventing her from deciding to move in another direction. News of what was happening in Ireland was sparse, but she understood that the strike had failed and that conditions for workers were as bad, if not worse, than before. Perhaps, if she had been still living in Dublin, she would have been more involved and active, but the depressing nature of her current circumstances and the monotony of the work, made her feel listless and worthless. There was also a distinct anti-Irish sentiment prevalent in

Liverpool, its origins stretching from the days of the Irish Famine. A significant influx of immigrants into the poorer sections of the city, bringing both disease and conflict, had stirred discontent and hostility. Consequently, many Irish were banned from accommodation and employment. Racism can be overt, with blatant discrimination excluding immigrants from lodgings and work, thus hindering them from forging a new life. The most insidious can be subtle, an ignorance or a disdain for another culture, with covert exclusion from integration and a general lack of respect for other identities. There was no particular incident, but Bridie internalised a lack of esteem and of value, and a belief she had little to offer, settled on her like a mantle, stunting her ambition.

The summer of 1914 saw international tensions reach a new height and everywhere there was talk of war. There was even discussion of the effect war would have on women and where their contribution might lie. Women were still without the right to vote. Yet, it seemed from all reports they would be considered capable of working in traditionally male-dominated areas for the duration of the conflict. Such illogical and conflicted thinking was exasperating but also the catalyst that sparked Bridie to take an interest in where she was going and what she wanted for the future. She knew she had more to offer than the ability to work in a laundry and, by chance, she stumbled across an article on the Voluntary Aid Detachment, an association of volunteer assistant nurses and for short, called VAD's. The latent admiration for Dr Kathleen Lynn and her work with the poor inspired Bridie to enquire further, only to be rejected on the spot. It may have been because she was Irish with only primary education, it may also have been because the average VAD was middle or upper class, more than likely a mixture of both. Whatever the reason, Bridie was determined in a manner that had been missing since she left Dublin, to become a volunteer nurse and not to be put off by the initial rejection. The imminent war, despite the jingoism, was bound to see an upsurge in the need for medical aid. She could not leave her job as she had to earn a living. Still, she began to read in earnest, mainly first aid pamphlets or any relevant material that might give her an edge should an opportunity arise. The school matron was Mrs Hardwick who occupied that awkward space that positioned itself as a bridge between the nuns and the servants. She was always quite pleasant, and Bridie decided to approach her with a proposition.

'Mrs Hardwick, I was wondering if you could help me with something. Provided I attend to my chores would you allow me in my spare time to assist on the school sickness ward?'

'Why?' asked Mrs Hardwick, blunt and to the point.

Bridie was reluctant to say why but knew she had no choice, 'I want to improve myself, maybe train as a VAD, but I need some experience and knowledge.'

Mrs Hardwick pursed her lips thoughtfully. 'Have you spoken to Sr Genevieve?'

'No,' stammered Bridie, 'I thought you first, then maybe if you agreed...' Her voice trailed off.

'I'd expect you to work late, be here during the night if required.'

'Yes, of course, anything. I just want the chance.'

'Well, it so happens I could do with some help, especially in the evenings. I will talk to Sr Genevieve and get back to you.'

A week later, Bridie began her new role. At first, she was only allowed to make beds and bathe the sick children, the practical basic duties, that did not require any specialist nursing skill. In a time when vaccinations were unknown, there were continual outbreaks of childhood illnesses. Gradually, she sat with children through the night as they raged with fever or were too weakened to reach the bucket. It was exhausting because there was no quarter given for her daily duties. At times, she staggered through a day with no more than two- or- three hours of sleep but with an exhilaration and a purpose she had not felt since Dublin and Liberty Hall.

'Thank you, Bridie. I know you must be tired from all those nights by the children's bedside, but you were needed. I could never have managed it alone.' Mrs Hardwick's simple thanks conveyed a respect that Bridie had not felt since leaving Donegal.

An outbreak of measles in the school cemented this sense of esteem and proved, time and again, how capable and invaluable was her contribution. Mrs

Hardwick patted her back, with instructions to rest. 'I will have a word with Sr Genevieve. You go to bed now. Laundry can wait.'

Opportunity arose once more with the outbreak of war and the first influx of casualties. In general, VADs did not go to the front as a belief existed that volunteers were from a "particular" class of women and from too sheltered a background, to be able to endure the horrors they would encounter. A change came in November when a committee was formed to set up the Liverpool Merchants Mobile Hospital. The hospital was to be stationed in France and staffed by VADs. This was Bridie's chance, and she approached the school matron for a reference. That reference was duly supplied and in 1915 Bridie was on board a vessel to the frontline standing proud and tall in her starched uniform. She was not without nerves but there was also a tinge of excitement at her venture into the unknown. She felt part of a team with a purpose and, at long last, felt she was achieving something worthwhile.

Chapter 3

Bridie's war had a slow, vague, almost spurious start. The field hospital, without any patients, was pristine and the image of efficiency. Bandages were rolled and instruments sterilised, drugs counted and carefully placed in order. War seemed a distant illusion, but that myth was shattered all too soon. One Tuesday evening in February 1916, Bridie was given a reprieve from duty and looked forward with relish to a few hours by herself. Her rest was short-lived as she received instructions to prepare to move. The Battle of Verdun had commenced, and Bridie was thrust headlong into its centre and into the unending stream of wounded and dying. Some were dazed in shock, and some gazed in despair, many were without hope, all bore a cloak of dejection, some questioning Bridie for answers she did not have. Her training had not prepared her for the long hours and the constant cries of anguish but sometimes, the bleak silence was more poignant. She gently washed mud and blood displaying wounds that were so crude and raw, her helplessness to assist was laid bare. Come morning, as life slipped away from one poor soul, another took his place. She knew her nights would forevermore be haunted by lifeless eyes, shattered limbs, and agonising whimpers.

The frantic hours and days melded into one as did the ceaseless torrent of wounded. Bridie operated on automatic, hollowed inside, as though she had no place anywhere, not on the war front, not in the hospital in Liverpool and, still less, a place in Ireland. The stench became bearable, scarcely noticed, as her mind numbed to the daily horror. It was as though in her search for her own path, she had now become frozen in time and lost her way. Conversely, when news of a rebellion in Ireland trickled through, her natural exuberance was piqued and curiosity at what had occurred at home, could not be contained. On 24th April, Padraig Pearse, a schoolteacher and Irish Republican, read a Proclamation from the front entrance of Dublin's General Post Office and formally declared Ireland a Republic and Independent State. Bridie was in full sympathy with this aspiration, and it was essential to discover more of what had occurred around the country but, especially, in Dublin. Her questioning caused some colleagues to query her loyalty to the King and she became a target for accusations, of "traitor". As the weeks progressed and the leaders of the Rising were executed, her distress at what was happening in her home country became apparent but, in no way did it affect her desire or ability to assist the soldiers in need of nursing care. Despite her meticulous and painstaking attention to the wounded, Bridie became ostracised by a few who should have known better.

By July, Bridie had been moved again but this time to where the Battle of the Somme was now raging. She held the hands of too many as they passed away in agony. A mere boy of sixteen clutched her feverishly as he begged for his mother, a twenty-year-old sobbed quietly knowing he would never see his new-born son. She was drawn to a quiet, reserved man named Harry, and learnt he was from a rural area near north Liverpool that she assumed might be akin to Donegal. It was a vague, but welcome reminder of home and as he also knew Liverpool city well, they found they had a connection in common. He was blind and, regretfully, the prognosis was such that the blindness seemed irreversible. Whenever Bridie had a few moments to spare, she read to Harry, and when her own eyelids began to droop and her words faltered, Harry sensed she was drifting away and recited his poetry with a soft cadence and passion she envied. They both looked forward to a stolen escape from the chaos around them. Whilst Bridie transported Harry to an imaginary world when she read a few pages from a well-thumbed novel, his soft tones and gentle burr allowed Bridie to drift home to Donegal, if only for a few minutes.

He lightly folded her hand in his own as he whispered of spring meadows and fragrant flowers and of love, faithful and forsaken. When he was shipped home to England, Bridie felt part of her go with him, but he promised to wait for her return and offer a haven from conflict. The war continued unabated and without an end in sight. Sometimes Bridie's moments with Harry intruded, grounding her for a short while. Still, even the memory of Harry began to blur, as she struggled to keep the focus on her own survival.

By October 1917, Bridie had been at the front for nearly two years, and with palpable relief, she read new orders sending her back to England. She was assigned once more to the hospital in Liverpool but, initially, was given two weeks welcome leave. Her dearest wish was to return to Ireland, especially Donegal, but in the current conditions, it was impossible. The first few days of her return to Liverpool were spent resting and acclimatising as best she was able, to civilian life. She contented herself with sleep, bracing walks and reading. Slowly, it dawned on Bridie that, although it was impossible to be alone in such a busy hospital, she had no close friend in Liverpool. There was an urge to confide and try to rationalise the mayhem of the war, but her solitude hindered that basic need. On an impulse, Bridie wrote to Harry, not sure if she expected or even wanted a reply, but he was her only contact in a senseless world. Would Harry, she questioned remember her, as all he had felt was the touch of her hand and all he had known was the sound of her voice?

While Bridie struggled to forge her own path, Danny, brother of her childhood friend, Annie, had no such issues. Genial and affable, Danny loved a pint, a cigarette, and a chat. As he was also fond of his food, he had a generous waistline which he patted comfortably when engaged in humorous discussion. His dark hair, a shade too long, not from any style but mere laziness, topped a smiling face without guile. He expounded on many topics usually without a lot of knowledge, but with roguish blue eyes gleaming, he would stir the pot to generate debate. He also had an eye for the girls, especially the friend of his older sister, Annie, but so far, Bridie just saw him as an irritation. The one topic he shied away from was politics, believing it was best left to those with more education.

He avoided Liam McShane and his ilk whenever he could, as they were too serious by far and too anxious to engage in political debate. Liam might be Bridie's nephew and raised in the same household but, dour and intense, he was the antithesis of the smiling, cheerful friend of his sister.

Danny's decision to follow Redmond's call to join the British Army was more a reflex than a conscious choice. At twenty-one, Danny was still a drifter and he floated into enlisting, not out of genuine belief, but because his family had always been Redmond supporters and, he supposed, he was one too.

John Redmond was an Irish politician and Member of the British House of Parliament. He was instrumental in securing the passage of the Home Rule Bill for Ireland, but the outbreak of the First World War delayed the Bill's implementation. In a major speech, in September 1914, he urged young Irish men to fight and support Britain with the prospect that, after victory, there would be Home Rule in Ireland. There was some encouragement from Danny's family to follow Redmond's call, but overall, a sense of adventure spurred him on. Also, a realisation that Donegal offered no future for those without land.

Scotland was the next port of call and he had witnessed many friends drifting over there, looking for work, struggling to keep wife and family together. Danny would not have described himself as ambitious, more self-preserving, and that required the forging of a new path away from his home county.

The reality of war was not yet a real concept for Danny. 'Sure, it will be over by Christmas,' he was fond of saying, echoing a widely held sentiment. The war was ephemeral at most and viewed more as an opportunity with steady pay, while he found his way forward. Nevertheless, he took his time deciding to enlist and it was the summer of 1915 before he joined the 16th Irish Division as a volunteer. He was accepted into the army with alacrity, but to his surprise, when he first donned the British Army uniform, the signifier of Empire, a niggling doubt surfaced. With a purposeful effort, he was able to despatch that doubt to the back of his mind, but it lingered there, prodding him, when he least expected it. The initial rigidity and regulation of the first few months he found mind-numbing. In retrospect, Danny wondered if he would have lasted were it not for Mick and Shay, both from Tipperary, providing some human and much-needed companionship.

The two Tipperary lads had enlisted together, pals from school days. Their motivation for enlisting was the basic need to earn a living. Mick was heavily built, a lumbering giant with an easy smile. Shay was thin, almost skeletal, and ate enough for two. Playing endless card games and continuously smoking blunted the monotony of the days but the change came all too quickly—a tsunami of terror that took them all by surprise. Mick went in the first week. One bullet into his head and he was no more. Shay took longer. His final journey was not to the field hospital where he could die on a relatively clean sheet. Instead, poor Shay lingered for three days where he fell, muttering incoherently until he gasped his last torturous breath.

Danny's war continued unabated, but he was a different man. He still shivered when rotund rats crept unhurriedly past, sniffing possible tasty morsels, confident in their place. He ceaselessly scratched at bites from swarms of hungry flies and, fruitlessly plucked at the lice that found a haven in every nook in his body.

Faces of the dead and wounded crept upon him furtively, when he was least aware, beseeching him for mercy. Anguished cries of pain and yearning jerked him awake from an already restless stupor. Danny raged inside at the folly around him, and a lazy mind drifted no more. As the dying and the dead mounted each day, he fumed at the waste of men. Men he now viewed as pawns from poverty and pawns through misplaced patriotism, but in the end, all chess pieces of the powerful. What was soon apparent were the number of soldiers who were expressing disillusionment at a war that continued to claim thousands of lives, orchestrated by those who never had to fight. Similarly, to Danny, they all continued to stagger on because there was no alternative. Wearily, he dragged his body from one day to the next surprised to awaken whenever he managed, against the odds, to fall into a slumber.

George now lived alongside Danny in a muddy home deep in the trenches. A quiet, introspective man, he read constantly from a conglomeration of notes and leaflets, hidden within his inside pocket. Danny guessed George was from Scotland by his accent, but he did not respond to small talk. When he did speak, it was contemplative and reflective, remarking on the conditions in which they found themselves and pondering reasons why. He never suggested answers, only posed questions. He revered a man named Keir Hardy who had passed away in 1915. Hardy was an ex-miner, active union leader, and founder of The Scottish Labour Party. He inspired George and, he in turn, inspired Danny.

When the attack call came, as it invariably did with regularity, George carefully replaced his documents, checked his rifle and with no hesitation climbed out of the trenches. On a sunny spring morning he landed back beside Danny in three broken pieces. Danny blessed him in the only way he knew with the "sign of the cross", whispering beseeching words to a God that appeared to have forsaken them. Hesitantly, Danny removed the sacred literature, spattered with blood but intact, and vowed to read it and understand it, as a tribute to a quiet, unassuming gentleman that he would never forget. George had given Danny pearls of wisdom in their short time together and had stretched Danny's mind to the point he now had numerous questions of his own. He felt a compulsion to put pen to paper lest he forget his burgeoning ideas. Paper was at a premium and a precious commodity for trade. He bartered whatever he possessed, as the urge to write down his churning concepts, became overwhelming.

There was a mixed reaction from the companions and comrades who fought alongside Danny when news of the Easter Rising in Dublin, came through. Admiration came from some quarters, but for others, especially those from Mainland Britain and the North of Ireland, it was viewed as a betrayal and treason. Danny continued to fight and survive and ignore the racial taunts he encountered, especially vicious, as further details filtered through. He was unsure himself how he felt. He had answered Redmond's call but now realised it had been a rash and thoughtless decision. Why had others felt so differently that, in Dublin, they were prepared to put their lives on the line, rising against a Crown that was surely going to win? Whether they were right or wrong to rebel was one question, but while so many Irish men were fighting on the "war front", their subsequent execution, in such a callous manner, appalled him. In particular, Danny found the execution of James Connolly, a man so severely wounded he was strapped to a chair, especially upsetting. As more news filtered through, the details incited a surge of anger and momentum within him. He read the Proclamation in a newspaper secreted into the trenches. The inspirational words, guaranteeing equality and opportunity for all, uplifted Danny and focussed his thoughts in a manner that had never previously occurred. Yet, for a while, all his introspection had to be put aside as the fighting got underway in earnest. Untold numbers died beside him, while others were destined to return home, wounded and scarred for life. Why or how Danny survived was a mystery to him, as the mayhem and massacre of the Somme decimated all those around him. More than one million men were killed or wounded at the Somme. Overall, it is estimated about fifty thousand Irish men died in the First World War.

Danny stepped onto the quays in Dublin, astounded he was still whole. Although he was free to return to Ireland in December 1918, he did not return a soldier, a Redmond acolyte, or even a definite supporter of the Rising. Danny returned, grateful to George, whose quiet unassuming influence had inspired him to think and to question. That influence, in turn, incentivised Danny to become an avid reader of Connolly, a man he had come to admire and respect. That path led inevitably to Karl Marx, as Danny determined to source an avenue for his fledgling ideology. Danny's journey from a congenial, jaunty, and unconcerned young man, had now consolidated into a determined and focussed activist.

Once Danny was settled back in Dublin he emulated his new mentor, James Connolly, and daily frequented the library. James Connolly stirred something in him, a kinship perhaps, with a fellow Ulster man, albeit the second generation, or maybe it was because they both had served in the British Army and were now treading the same path. Either way, Danny read avidly, discovering how Connolly's parents had emigrated to Scotland and he had been born in the impoverished area of Cowgate in Edinburgh. The more Danny read, the more he recognised how he had lived a blinkered existence before joining the army. To his dismay and slight shame, Danny realised that in 1912, when he was a thoughtless nineteen-year-old, James Connolly, was uniting Catholic and Protestant workers against employers under the banner of *The Irish Transport and General Workers Union*. Connolly's interest in politics and how the working class remained subordinate, inspired him to form the Irish Socialist Republican Party, in 1896. He helped found the Irish Citizen Army, a small unit of trained volunteers whose purpose was to defend demonstrating workers against the, at times, unfettered brutality of the police. The Irish Citizen Army eventually played a part in the 1916, Easter Rising. As an ardent advocate of rights for all, regardless of gender, James Connolly went on to be one of the architects of the Irish Proclamation and, subsequently, commanded rebel forces in the GPO during the Irish Rising. Wounded, and unable to stand, he was later executed, strapped to a chair in the Stonebreakers Yard, Kilmainham Jail.

Inspired by Connolly, Danny spent his days reading, informing, and developing his own, often confused, thoughts. He was amazed that he could have been so ignorant, sailing through life while so much was occurring in his capital city, only his experiences at the Somme giving him pause. In an attempt to better understand the influence of power and class, he turned to Karl Marx. It was difficult processing certain ideas and concepts but gradually he began to understand how the information we are fed can frame how we think, view and see others. He submitted a few articles to the press, but they were all rejected, his ideas smacking too much of Communism. Danny promoted the idea that accepted moral codes kept people in their "place" and, as such, were a weapon for class interests. This viewpoint was far too radical for the conservative powers that held sway and were in a position to prevent publication of his ideas. Any article that challenged the new emerging powers, influenced by and under the stranglehold of the Catholic Church, was suppressed.

Christmas 1918 was now approaching and Danny, despondent at his lack of success publishing his articles, packed a bag to return to Donegal. He was to spend his first Christmas with his family in four years. The trip would be more of a pilgrimage because of his mother's death while he was away. The journey itself was arduous as the train only travelled as far as Sligo. Fishing boats from

Killybegs were often in the waters off the coast and, with luck, he might be able to board one for the balance of his journey. Otherwise, it would be a series of uncomfortable lifts in a variety of carts and carriages. Killybegs to his home was an easy trip once he managed to arrive there.

Danny was fortunate to board a vessel and, surprisingly, as they neared the dock, he spied his older brother Gerry sitting patiently, waiting on the pier with the ancient donkey and cart. In honour of Danny's return, Gerry was wearing his best-tattered suit and greying white shirt. Cap slightly askew, he puffed contentedly on his father's old pipe, contemplating the world, while he waited for Danny's arrival. For a moment, Danny felt a pang of what he could only describe as jealousy, at such an image of serenity, a fulfilment with his world that was continually eluding Danny. Never a tactile family, they awkwardly danced around each other for a few minutes, clapping each other on the shoulder. Unshed tears of relief at Danny's safe return and unity in grief over the death of their mother, glistened in both brothers' eyes. After a few unintelligible grunts, Danny clambered aboard.

Chapter 4

War breaks down existing barriers as men and women bond with a common purpose. Bridie soon learnt that when war is finally over, those boundaries reassert themselves, some in a different format, but rarely classless.

Harry was pleasantly surprised to receive Bridie's letter. He had often thought of her during his long recuperation and wished he had been able to tell her his sight had been partially restored. He recalled the soft caress of her hands upon his face and the hypnotic resonance of her Irish brogue as she read to him each night. Remembering Bridie was a welcome escape from his mother, Sophie. She was a woman with aspirations and wished her eldest son to marry well, without question, money, but a title, however minor, was a definite asset worth pursuing. Every time Sophie produced another suitable match, he escaped by letting his mind drift to France and Bridie. Much to her annoyance, he could not bring himself to show much interest in the string of inane young girls Sophie produced with regularity. Harry was sensible enough to know she had too much influence over him but found it impossible, especially since his return from the front, to challenge, let alone defy her. There was no way she would approve of Bridie, but he was determined to see her and prepared himself for battle.

After dinner that evening, he broached the subject while clutching the letter for courage, cognizant by the puckering of her lips, that an argument was about to ensue. 'Send her a polite thank you, Harry, that will be sufficient.'

Harry drew in a breath and responded nervously, 'I want to meet her. I never actually saw her, and you cannot overestimate how she helped me through those dark days.'

'Well, we all did our bit for the war, so no particular thanks needed, beyond the card,' was the short retort. 'She is not our sort anyway, so best not to pursue a friendship.'

Nonplussed, but determined for once to stand his ground, Harry insisted, 'I want to meet her, and I am going to ask her for tea.'

Harry's mother raised her eyebrows. 'Well go ahead then, but if she is uncomfortable, don't say I didn't warn you.' With that final barb, she left the room.

Two weeks later Bridie received an invitation to tea in Harry's home. She would have preferred to meet him at a neutral venue, perhaps a hotel in the centre city, but his insistence on inviting her to his house left no option for refusal. She was to take the train and he would meet her at the station on her arrival. *It's possible his sight forbids him to travel far,* she mused. Yet, travelling alone to his home seemed intimate, implying a relationship that was, at best non-existent, at most, only fledgling.

Despite her misgivings, the following Sunday morning saw Bridie anxiously scouring the train station for a sight of him. Harry had written that some of his sight had returned but she knew he had no idea of what she looked like. She instantly recognised the tall, slim man looking slightly perplexed at the number of possible young women alighting from the train. His appearance took her by surprise, dressed as he was in casual clothes consisting of a stylish, tweed jacket and upturned trousers. He appeared very much at ease and totally unlike the man she remembered. She had dressed as well as she was able in a neat, black skirt, but frowned anxiously at her boots that had seen better days. Her pink lace blouse, however, was new and her black jacket had been hardly worn, purchased shortly before she left for France.

Nevertheless, there was Harry, and Bridie walked towards him, hand outstretched, her face alight with a beaming smile. 'Nice to meet you, Harry.'

'And finally, to meet you, Bridie,' he smiled and bent forward to lightly kiss her cheek. 'It is so lovely to see you at last and to be able to thank you for all you did.' The kiss brought a most unexpected blush to Bridie's cheeks, but it also broke the ice. He then led her to his mother's *Wolseley*, first introducing her to Charlie, the elderly chauffeur, before assisting her into the car. Bridie was too stunned at the sight of the car and driver to do other than nod and hope he did not notice her boots.

They fell into an easy, relaxed chat during the short drive to Harry's home which was a small but impressive manor house set in lush, rolling countryside. Harry told Bridie of his plans and how he intended to focus on farming on what was now his land. His father had died at the turn of the century, and he had inherited the estate which had been in the family for countless generations. 'It isn't that big an estate,' he said, 'but it has great possibilities.' Harry became animated as he expounded on his future ideas and how, once the war was over, he intended to focus on cattle and horses. He always liked to ride but all their horses had been given to the war effort, and anyway, it was only now he was well enough to consider getting into the saddle once more. His enthusiasm and pride reminded Bridie of many of the farmers in Donegal but there the comparison ended. Their smallholdings could not compare to the house, now appearing, at the far end of a wooded drive. Small it might be to Harry, but it still dominated the landscape and had no similarity to any farmhouse Bridie had entered before. Harry continued to chatter, and Bridie only half-listened as she absorbed the subdued, understated, charm of the house in the distance. 'I have two younger brothers,' he said, 'one currently stationed in Belgium and the other in Dublin.' That news gave Bridie some pause for thought and she hoped there would be no awkward mention of Ireland over tea.

Harry held the door for Bridie to enter an elegant drawing room comfortably but expensively furnished. She composed herself as she sat near the blazing fire, determined not to allow any feelings of inadequacy to show on her face. This careful poise was dented slightly when Harry's mother joined them. Haughtiness preceded her as she rustled across the room in grey silk that hung beautifully and paid homage to expensive corsets. She was tall, almost regal, with greying hair, and managed to be both pleasant and mannerly, while remaining cool and slightly condescending. The hand proffered to shake was so limp that Bridie was taken aback. The effect was such that her own hand, originally outstretched with warmth, became flaccid and even more lacklustre than that extended by Harry's mother.

'Welcome, Bridie. Harry has told me so much about you.' Intoned Sophie, as she indicated with a wave of her hand that Bridie should take a seat.

'Please tell me all about yourself. I understand you are from Ireland. Maybe we have some acquaintances in common?'

'Probably not. I am from Donegal, a rural area.' Responded Bridie, with a glance of enquiry at Harry.

'Really? And your father, what does he do?'

'He has passed away now, but he was a farmer.'

'Like Harry here? How interesting. How large is the estate? Did a brother inherit?'

Sophie's questions continued and afternoon tea became a test of endurance, highlighting an ever-widening social divide. Bridie could sense that Harry's mother viewed her with disdain but saw her also as a threat and an adversary. It was impossible to ascertain whether it was through a misguided belief of an existing or possible relationship with her son, or simply contempt for her background. Both women eyed one another across the table and the more Sophie tried to patronise Bridie, the more Bridie determined to relax and refuse to be intimidated.

Harry frowned, perplexed, as tension crackled between the two women who fought for politeness, as they endeavoured to keep a veneer of cordiality in the room. He had depended on Sophie far too much since his return from the war and, because of the problems with his sight, had ceded a lot of his independence. He found it impossible to regain control and remove the power she had over him. She was a formidable woman and there would be battles ahead if he wanted to continue to see Bridie. Already, his mother had pronounced her, 'unsuitable, poor, uneducated and Irish and, undoubtedly, Catholic.' Likewise, Bridie had decided in no uncertain terms, '*she would never return to his home again whilst his mother treated her in such a condescending and impolite manner.'*

It was a friendship at first, a haven for Bridie, who still felt very isolated in Liverpool. Harry's insistence on seeing Bridie was, perhaps for him, a first stab at becoming his own man. Bridie's unequivocal gaze and forthright manner struck a chord within Harry. Probably in some hidden recess he recognised a strength similar to his mother's. He travelled to see Bridie once a month, initially escorting her to tea, but, eventually, dinner. She fascinated Harry with her opinions and outspoken attitude. He had always conformed and believed there was a code that had to be followed. His admiration for her grew as she recounted her journey from Donegal to become a VAD in France. Exploring other ideas with Bridie gave him an illicit thrill and he returned home after each visit enveloped in thought. It had never occurred to him before to consider the reasons for such a gap between rich and poor, the subordinate position of women, or the factors that contributed to inequality in society, in general. He understood that Bridie made him think outside of the circle within which he was reared. He, in turn, gave Bridie the gift of books that had little to do with the life she had led. There was no connection with Donegal or the daily grind on a farm. Instead, they opened a window into a rarefied world that represented "the other", the life from which she was excluded. Yet, there were tenuous connections with some of the women depicted, and their struggle for identity struck a familiar chord. Harry and Bridie, for a time, found a missing link with each other as they endeavoured to move on after the horrors of war.

Sophie watched her son, covertly. She genuinely felt Bridie intended to trap him into marriage and she determined to use all the wiles at her disposal to prevent it. At the same time, she felt powerless, as with Harry's sight reasonably returned, his need for her was diminished. He had a new swagger about him and a reluctance to follow her direction, even in small matters. Sophie, intuitively, sensed when their relationship had taken a new turn and her acerbic comments took on a more stringent tone. 'Well, Harry, I assume you are sleeping with her, the little Irish tramp?'

'Be quiet, Mother, don't speak of her like that.'

'How will I speak of her, Harry? An Irish nobody determined to trap you. She'll be pregnant next.'

Harry marched away in a fury, as he had done almost every night in the past week. Sophie watched him speculatively. She was under no illusion, her son thought he was in love with Bridie, and she would have to be more subtle, or she would lose him entirely to that girl.

Harry had always kissed Bridie when they met and when they said goodbye, but as the weeks and then months progressed, his kisses became more ardent. Both became reluctant to end their evenings and agreed meeting once a month was not enough.

It began as a beautiful April day, in 1918, and they travelled by coach to Oakley Village, just outside Liverpool. By three o'clock the rain had come down in sheets soaking them both through. Their efforts to remain dry by sheltering had stalled their departure, leaving them with too little time for the last coach and, therefore, stranded. Harry turned questioningly to Bridie, hapless as always, and she pointed to a small hotel. 'Should we see if there is a room available?' Harry looked puzzled and then agreed. Amused, Bridie responded, 'Well, Harry, I think, perhaps you'd better try and buy me a ring first. Anything will do. I will wait here for you.'

Harry rushed off, as always, agreeable to any decision. They entered the small hotel nervously, but nothing was indicated by word or action that anyone thought they were other than Mr and Mrs Wickham.

Once inside their room, the large bed was like a beacon, signalling their unstated intentions. There was a certain hesitancy, as it was the first time for them both. Harry had some limited experience with women from his sojourn in Belgium, but Bridie's experience with men was confined to Harry. He now wandered the room, nervous and hesitant. Bridie sat on the bed, and after some thought, Harry sat down beside her. Although only inches apart, there was a gulf that seemed impossible to bridge until Harry's fingers reached for Bridie's. That slight, tentative movement eased the awkwardness. He pressed Bridie's fingers to his lips, enquiry, always a constant feature of his expression. Bridie turned towards him and gently stroked his face, before rising to stand before him. More by instinct than knowledge, she took the lead.

Slowly she unbuttoned her blouse. Harry's stare was unfaltering as the soft swell of her breasts was revealed. Tantalising, Bridie now turned and, conscious of her allure, she bent forward and removed her stockings. Mesmerised, Harry stood, and drew Bridie towards him, gently caressing her nipples before he lay her on the bed. Bridie relished the feel of Harry's weight upon her as, with taste and touch, he discovered secret places of pleasure she never knew she had. Harry, for his part, gloried in her body and all thoughts were banished from his mind.

Three times they had travelled to a different destination, posing as husband and wife. Breaking such a Church and societal rule did not bother Bridie, the war had changed her perspective on many things, but she was nevertheless, always anxious. That yearning to awaken with his warm body tucked into hers, or to feel one hand gently caressing her hip, even that shiver, from fingers as they tingled tracks along her spine, was not enough to satisfy. If there was no real love between them, if she genuinely believed she would never marry Harry, then their physical relationship had to end. Besides, she worried about pregnancy or if the hospital discovered her subterfuge. Either event was a reason for instant dismissal. Her achievements had been too hard-fought to waste for a fleeting physical pleasure and her latest quest to train as a qualified nurse had not been shared with Harry. She kept putting off that discussion because, if her application was refused, it would have been an hour of wasted explanation and recrimination.

Bridie had long since refused to go to Harry's house preferring, instead, their agreed rendezvous. Yet, twice, she had broken her resolve not to visit his home. The first time was before their relationship had taken its new turn. Harry had pleaded that his mother was aware she had been less than welcoming and wanted to start afresh. Tea, once again, had been an excruciating affair with feigned politeness. Undoubtedly, the invitation from Sophie was a ploy to deliver a warning. When Harry left to fetch their coats prior to departure, leaving both women alone, Sophie went on the attack. 'I know you think you can catch Harry, make him marry you and, if I were in your shoes, I might try the same. But believe me, I will stop you in any way I can from trapping my son.'

A scathing look was Bridie's only reaction before she left with Harry. The second time she had reluctantly acquiesced to Harry's pleadings was because of his brothers. They were both due home in mid-June and there was to be a small dinner party. Bridie flatly refused to go to the dinner party but compromised by agreeing to another afternoon tea.

April and May 1918 were a time of great unrest in Ireland. Relations with Britain were reaching a new low over the proposal to impose compulsory conscription, to fuel the now decimated British armies in Europe. There were numerous rallies in Ireland against conscription followed by a general strike, on 23rd April. Except for North-East Ulster, there was unified support across the country and thousands signed anti-conscription pledges. Antipathy to the British proposal came, as expected, from Nationalists and the clergy but, surprisingly, also from staunch Unionists such as Edward Carson and the Chief Secretary and Lord Lieutenant. It was considered that conscription would not only fuel Nationalist sympathy, but would also provide training, which would subsequently be used against the British Crown. In May, it was alleged that Sinn Féin was conspiring with Germany, and a substantial number of Sinn Féin leaders were arrested. It was at this time, out of necessity to fill the vacuum, that Michael Collins began to emerge as one of the more inspiring and prominent leaders.

Against this fractious backdrop, Bridie travelled to the manor house in late June for the agreed afternoon tea with the recently returned brothers, Anthony, and George. The table was set on the terrace. If it were not for the company, Bridie would have enjoyed the view of a tranquil lake, complete with lethargic swans, partially hidden in reeds that swayed gently in a soft breeze. As tea progressed, one brother attempted to subtly goad her by denigrating the Irish, but Bridie refused to rise to the bait. The ordeal was almost at an end when Anthony, who had been stationed in Ireland, posed a question that tested Bridie's endurance, ultimately denting her resolve. 'Well, Bridie, as an Irish woman who found work and advancement in England, I assume you oppose the havoc your fellow countrywomen are causing? Their opposition to conscription and the chaos they precipitated on 9th June, cannot be condoned by any right-thinking woman.'

'I assume you mean Lá na mBan?' responded Bridie with raised brows. 'I think they are to be admired. Sending men to be slaughtered in Europe, to fight for a Britain that refuses to grant Irish freedom, is not to be countenanced. I fully support those women and because I could not be there to take part, I wrote to Cumann na mBan and registered my vote. That might not be acceptable, but at least it was a gesture.' Bridie contemplated in astonishment the red flush that suffused Anthony's face. It was almost unnerving, but fortunately, she instead found it satisfying, almost humorous.

'Are you saying,' he postulated in a rush, 'that you agree with the sudden surge to glorify the instigators of that traitorous rebellion at Easter, two years ago? You will tell me next you don't think those rebels should have been executed.' An earnestness now tinged both his appearance and his delivery, as leaning towards Bridie, he patronised, 'You must see the only way forward, to keep Ireland under control and civilised, is to eradicate the so-called Nationalists. They are a threat to the stability of our union and an insult to the Crown.'

Bridie bristled at his tone, mindful this was no idle question but one to test her loyalties and possibly demean her. 'As you say, Anthony, I am an Irishwoman. As such, I cannot agree with the execution of any Irish person.'

Bridie stood to leave but was halted by Anthony's response. 'So, you feel it was in order to gun down our soldiers in the cause of freedom for ruffians, who were too cowardly to fight for their King?'

'Don't forget, Anthony, I was at the Somme, and I nursed many English men but also many Irish. Those Irishmen and women who fought in Dublin in 1916 and those still fighting, are looking for the freedom you readily believe Belgium deserves, yet you deny it to Ireland. He is your king, Anthony, not mine or any Irish person.' With no further word, Bridie walked slowly away. Harry, in a quandary, scuttled behind her, glancing apologetically back at his family.

Once seated on the train, Harry eventually ventured to ask, 'Bridie what was that all about? What did you write about? I don't understand.'

'Well, Harry, I assume you know that Britain attempted to impose conscription in Ireland and there was tremendous opposition to it, including a general strike. The various women's clubs and societies, led by Cumann na mBan...'

'Cum, eh, sorry, a what?' interrupted Harry.

'Cumann na mBan. It is an organisation of Irish women dedicated to the Nationalist cause. With the Irish Women's Workers Union, they organised a day of resistance. Just recently, women converged on City Hall in Dublin and in various locations around the country, to sign a pledge stating that conscription was tyranny, and they would not, *'fill the places of men deprived of work through enforced military service.'* Over 40,000 women signed this pledge in the Dublin area alone. I just had to show some support, so I sent a letter requesting my signature be added.' Harry had no response, which was as expected, and further generated the now almost continual doubts about their relationship.

Today, however, Bridie was thoroughly out-of-sorts. Despite Harry's mother and the added disapproval of his brothers, they had continued to meet, at least one weekend a month, more when feasible. The physical side of their relationship had almost ceased but their shared war experiences brought comfort to both. She had been looking forward to their trip to Greenmount Park, quite a pretty and genteel area, not too far from Liverpool itself. It was to be their last outing before Christmas and her planned trip to Donegal. Now Harry had cancelled again, at the last minute, and she knew it was Sophie, it was always Sophie. Her disapproval of Bridie was now so blatant that Harry was unable to satisfactorily sanitise her remarks. He was gentle and kind, an oasis after the ravages of the war, a much-needed friend, but there was no denying he was also weak and dominated by his mother who continued to use a variety of methods to break up the relationship.

The letter was clutched in Bridie's hand and thoughtlessly, she twisted and crumpled the missive as she pondered its contents. Another cancelled outing was giving her more than a pause for thought. It was not just Sophie's interference or Harry's ambivalence that made her hesitate. Their actions just cemented her realisation and confirmed that it was past time to end their relationship, enabling them both to move on. She intended to go to London and although Harry had pleaded with her to stay, he had given no indication he wished their relationship to become more permanent.

Not that I would have said yes. I fully intend to become a nurse in London, mused Bridie. They had no future and were just stalling the inevitable separation. With a heavy heart, she sat down and wrote to Harry, knowing he would be hurt but hopefully he would gradually come to understand. They had been a security blanket for each other, a comfort after the war, but now they both needed to follow different paths.

To say Harry was devastated when he received Bridie's letter would be an exaggeration. Nevertheless, he was disappointed because he did love her in his own way. However, he was not surprised. Beyond a general passing reference, Harry had made no mention of marriage. The idea of living in the same house with Bridie and his mother did not bear contemplation, but that was not what held him back. He was unsure if she was his future. He hated the thought he might resemble his mother but lately, to his chagrin, he had become more conscious of how their accents and clothes accentuated their social difference. On one occasion, he believed a hotel owner had looked askance and, although it may have been his imagination, he had still cringed with embarrassment. The pressure within his family over his friendship had soured his relationship with his brothers as well as his mother and he was not a man who could handle any tension. As always, he was the last to reach a decision, but he knew within himself, Bridie was right. It was time to go separate ways especially now the war was over. There was a future ahead with new beginnings. He folded the letter and placed it in the drawer beside his bed. Bridie would always occupy a special place and that letter would help preserve and store memories to savour at some other time. For now, he dressed carefully as he was escorting his mother to a dinner party where the Honourable Louise would be seated beside him for the third time in as many weeks.

Chapter 5

It was with great difficulty that Bridie arranged passage, but five days before Christmas, 1918, she finally arrived in Dublin en route to Donegal. She had three precious weeks of leave before she needed to return to the hospital. There was a general air of jubilation that women had finally achieved the right to vote, and on 14th December, women in their thousands had cast their first ballot. There were limitations as the franchise only applied to women over 30, but the first step had been taken. By contrast, all men over 21 were given the vote, gender the only prerequisite, so male patriarchy was still an ongoing battle. Nevertheless, achieving the vote was a small victory and with the war finally over, Bridie was happy to be back in Ireland. The Irish political landscape was changing and the push for independence from Britain was the constant conversational topic. The election result saw John Redmond's political party lose its dominant role and Sinn Fein representatives, doing better than expected, secured 73 seats, propelling them into a position of power. As such, Bridie was glad to escape to Donegal as tension in the city was palpable and not conducive to assuaging her inner turmoil over Harry.

She alighted, cautiously, from the train in Sligo, sniffing the air, tentatively glancing from right to left. Although there was still quite a journey ahead before she reached the farm, she instantly felt at home. The sweet scent of turf assaulted her senses and the crisp tang in the air, sweeping down from snow-capped mountains, made her realise how she had missed the wild, barren beauty of the county of her youth. But scenery does not feed or clothe and as she travelled from the train station, she gazed around with a new perspective. She noticed the encampments at the side of the road, patched tents that offered little shelter from December's cold and wind. Smoke rose from small cottages, or "botháns", that housed a dozen or more children. Bridie wore a warm coat and bonnet and felt a class apart. She was greeted with deference by some, but envy by others, huddled under threadbare shawls and blankets, stamping feet to keep out the cold.

While she had been away the new farmhouse had been constructed and her old home was now being utilised as a barn. She was curious to see the new house but was already conscious that an indoor toilet had not been included in the design. That was an inconvenience she would have to endure over the holidays! It seemed the entire family were in the farmyard to greet her, and Bridie was engulfed in the open arms of her sister, Josie, while the rest of the family clamoured around. Bridie hugged Josie tightly as they whispered nonsense to each other in the Irish language of their childhood. Her taciturn brother-in-law, Donal, gave his usual nod before striding off to return to his chores. Bridie glanced after him, recognising there was little change in the puzzle that was Donal. She could never decide if he was intensely shy, or just so self-contained, he did not need to communicate with more words than those deemed necessary. Now, as he sauntered away scratching his reddened nose, with his remaining few strands of wispy, grey hair waving jauntily in the soft breeze, he reminded her in some ways of her father. Stoic in the face of the many hardships encountered in life, all endured without complaint, but above all, steadfast in his love for Josie and his children. She surmised there was a deep well of hurt arising from his difficulties with his eldest son Joe, but she was not one to whom his inner thoughts would be revealed. At times, he appeared to be on the periphery of the family, a steady rock, unmoved by all the fuss around him. There were only a few occasions she could recall when she had seen Donal become animated. That was when a fiddle was placed in his hands. She remembered how he could make that instrument sing as another spirit took hold of his body, at least until the magical tune was completed.

The sisters had been born eighteen years apart, their mother having suffered numerous miscarriages in between. When she died shortly after giving birth to Bridie, Josie had become as much a mother as a sister to Bridie and the separation of years and miles could not affect their bond. When Josie had married Donal at age twenty, for a time they had all lived together in the old farmhouse. Their father had been, not just appreciative of Donal's help but had enjoyed some male companionship before he too, passed away. Whilst Bridie was tall and dark, Josie was small, slight, and extremely fair. Yet, Josie had given birth to six children. Bridie's gaze now fell on Ellen the eldest girl, standing slightly awkwardly to one side. The warmth of Bridie's smile and the intensity of her hug melted away any shyness. Despite her excitement, Ellen had felt a slight trepidation at meeting Bridie. She knew they had been close, but she was only ten years old when Bridie left. Bridie engulfed her in a smothering hug and gleefully shouted, 'You have grown so much and are so, so pretty.' Such affection rekindled their old closeness in an instant. Standing behind Ellen was Sarah, quietly confident even at such a young age. Bridie stretched out a hand to each girl and together all three walked towards the new house. Its construction had been described in detail in Josie's letters, but it was exciting to see it now, fully built.

The farmhouse was erected only a few years previously by Donal with help from their three sons Liam, Sheamus and Ciaran. Walking proudly ahead, Ellen showed Bridie around. There was one main central room dominated by a brick fireplace for cooking and heating. Four smaller rooms, two on each side of this large main room, were bedrooms, one of which was now for Bridie. Sitting at the table, sipping tea, was Joe with his young son, Brendan. The family dynamic was intricate. Donal, Josie's husband, had been married and widowed at a young age and Joe was his son from that marriage. As such, Joe was a half-brother to Josie's six children. Joe, in turn, had a son Brendan, and history, as it so often does, repeated itself and Joe himself was now widowed. Joe was not often seen at the farmhouse as relations were, at best, strained, but Bridie's return demanded his presence, if only for the sake of form. He doffed his cap in acknowledgement but remained silent. Bridie's greeting commanded more and reluctantly, he commented, 'Looking well, Bridie. England agrees with you.'

'Thank you, Joe, you're looking well yourself, as are you, Brendan.' Brendan's face creased with a smile of genuine welcome.

Standing shyly in the background was little Kathleen, the youngest child, just turned eight years old. Opening her arms, Kathleen limped across and hugged Bridie. Bridie looked questioningly at Josie, who shook her head. 'It happened while you were away. Well, you know Liam's horse, Manabán?'

'Of course, the white stallion that he reared from a foal, of course, I know him,' replied Bridie.

Josie continued, 'Poor Liam has never gotten over it. It was an accident and Kathleen is coping well, yet he blames himself.'

'Tell me all about it,' demanded Bridie.

'Oh, it was November, four years ago, and there was such rain and wind. Kathleen was always Liam's pet, and he saddled Manabán to collect her from school.'

'Already in school from four years ago?' interrupted Bridie, turning towards the youngster.

'Oh yes, for a number of years now,' responded Josie. 'Well, around here, they can start at three, you must remember that. It keeps the school full, and it helps the mothers.' Bridie nodded. She did indeed remember. 'Anyway,' continued Josie, 'Liam often collected her when he could spare the time but especially, if the weather was bad. They were nearing the bridge over the stream and Manabán would not cross. He reared and reared, and Liam lost his hold on Kathleen while he attempted to control the horse. She tumbled to the ground, almost at the same time as the bridge collapsed. The river was running so swiftly, and they would have been swept away in an instant if they had fallen into the water. Knowing it could have been so much worse is how we cope with it, but Kathleen's leg was badly injured, and it seems she will always have a limp. We got Johnson immediately, and no one could have done more. His hands are a gift from God, so we have a lot to be thankful for.'

Bridie looked taken aback, 'Do you mean old Johnson, the bonesetter? I thought he only looked after animals?'

'Oh, no,' responded Josie, 'he is better than any doctor.'

Bridie thought the wisest course was to say nothing more.

Kathleen smiled and shrugged her shoulders, knowing they were talking about her and enjoying the attention. She piped up, 'I am fine, Bridie, I can still do everything I want.'

'The problem,' continued Josie, 'is Liam. It eats away at him that she was injured in his care. Knowing it could have been worse is no help. She is his pet, and he harbours such guilt. I believe she is improving, that her walking is getting better, but he thinks I am making that up to ease him. Sure, you know Liam, always his own man and what he thinks is always right.' This was said with a smile. Liam was Josie's firstborn son, and they were close with that special connection that mothers, and sons enjoy.

Bridie felt quite strange carrying a lantern once more into the dark night to an outside lavatory before retiring for bed. Yet, she smiled to herself, feeling grounded and content, aware of where she came from once more. She shivered, a rustling from possibly a rat, more likely a cat, as it scurried past. She opened the door, but the lantern was unable to scan the corners, so the spiders sat in wait, undisturbed, ready, in her imagination, to pounce. Hastily completing the necessary, anxious to return to the warmth and light of the farmhouse, still, Bridie paused momentarily to glance at the barn. It was her old home and stood, shrouded in darkness, looming silent and empty, the keeper of memories of her past. Despite the contrast in comfort between the two homes, Bridie had a pang of nostalgia for the house of her childhood. With a sigh, she entered the farmhouse planning to spend some time in the barn the following morning.

'Josie, is the barn unlocked, can I go in?'

'Now, Bridie, when did we ever lock any door around here?' replied Josie with a laugh. 'Of course, it's unlocked.'

Ellen stood up and took Bridie by the hand and together, they entered the barn. The scattered farm implements did not take from the essence of what was once a warm sanctuary for Bridie. The old stone fireplace still stood proud, displaying its cast iron pot, complete with the ladle. Bridie was surprised to see them still there, slightly rusted, abandoned and discarded. The circular bench, where they had bent studiously over schoolwork, was also still intact. Evenings by a glowing fire, cuddled up to Josie, with their father puffing on his pipe, were conjured in an instant. She could almost smell her father's tobacco and feel the rough, tweed, of his jacket. When surrounded in that family glow, it was natural to speak Irish and the gentle cadence of the language contained them in their own private world. Outside of those moments, English had to be spoken, the language of advantage, the passport for work when they were of an age to leave school. Shaking herself, banishing ghosts that threatened to consume, she forcefully returned to the present. Bridie tugged her shawl tightly around her and murmured, 'It's getting cold, Ellen, let's return to the house,' surreptitiously wiping the few tears that trickled down her cheeks. The ease that rekindled between aunt and niece was such that Ellen and Bridie became constant companions until the time came for Bridie to leave.

That evening the house filled up with neighbours as, one by one, they came to call and welcome Bridie home. At these impromptu parties, a whistle was always produced from some pocket and a fiddle magically appeared out of nowhere. Donal played the first jig but not with the flair Bridie recalled, as fingers, twisted with the onset of arthritis, hampered his past ease with the instrument. Despite that, his lively tune soon had a group of friends whirling around the floor. Food was plentiful because everyone arrived with an offering. As the beer and whiskey flowed, confidence surged, and so did the songs. Ciaran sang loud and lustily although, always, out of tune. Nods of approval were evident, once Liam took his turn. His haunting rendition of some of the old ballads, such as "Boolavogue" watering many a reddened, whiskey eye. Shouts for more erupted when he launched into, "The Rising of the Moon" and the chorus echoed, vehemently and vigorously, in the still night. Sheamus, on the other hand, was nowhere to be seen. Josie laughed at Bridie's question, and smiled, 'In the barn, I assume, with some young one.'

Yet, despite the gaiety, and the constant music and dance, Bridie sensed an undercurrent, an unspoken tension. It was noticeable that some of the neighbours Bridie had expected to see were absent. *What about Annie or Danny Walsh,* she wondered, she had naturally expected them to be here. Annie had been a good friend and her brother Danny had been the slightly younger, irritating pest, with an obvious crush. She noticed many of the young lads stood in groups, apparently, in heated debate. Their angry faces and pointed fingers an indication of strongly held opinions that could not be altered or dissuaded. She also felt somewhat out of place. She was not sophisticatedly dressed but living in England gave her access to fashions that were unknown in Donegal. Yet, she knew that many of the covert looks that glanced her way were not related to her dress but were unsettling nonetheless, in their vaguely, concealed animosity. This gave her pause for thought and the reason for their perceived hostility, puzzled and gnawed at her throughout the entire evening.

The following day, Christmas Eve, Ellen joined Bridie and Josie on their walk to the local graveyard. Sarah declined to accompany them, but Kathleen happily alternated between running and skipping, causing Bridie to comment. 'That leg doesn't seem to bother her much.'

'No, just really when she is tired, or does a sustained amount of running around. I am thankful she wasn't more seriously injured.'

On this note, they reached the family plot. It was the tradition to place some holly on the graves of loved ones and Bridie carried a wreath for her parents. Her mother had died shortly after her birth, but through her father and Josie, she felt she knew her well. Her father had a special place in her heart. Hard-working, with a quirky sense of humour, he had raised his two girls with love and a gentle hand, that always contained a pipe. All four bowed their heads as Josie led them in reciting the "Lord's Prayer" in memory of that special man. At night, Josie and Bridie had knelt with their father by the fire as he recited the ancient prayer with the supplication changing each evening, depending on the season and who was to be remembered, whether through death or need. The invocation by the graveside was a personal tribute and special thanks to him.

They rambled back and Ellen could not contain herself, rhapsodising about the party. Bridie listened quietly, beginning to wonder had she imagined the tension and starting to doubt herself. Ellen, she was certain, was just too young to sense the undercurrents that had undoubtedly been there. She resolved to quiz Josie once they were alone. The opportunity arose later that evening. 'Josie, was I imagining some tension at the party last night?'

'Probably not,' Josie, answered. 'There is a lot of politics going on around here at the moment. Don't worry about it.'

'I'm not worried, just wondering why I felt some hostility directed towards me and then I noticed some friends, like the Walshe's were not there.'

Josie looked pensive, even slightly embarrassed, but then continued. 'The thing is, Bridie, anyone, like yourself who was involved on the British side in the war, well, people, I suppose, are taking sides and not sure sometimes where loyalties lie. Just forget about it, things will settle.'

Bridie wandered outside musing over Josie's words and encountered Ellen sitting on a fence, apparently waiting for her. 'It is getting dark, Ellen, and cold. Are you sure you should be out here at this time?'

'I'm fine, Bridie. I thought we could have a little walk if you don't mind?'

Bridie fell into step beside Ellen as she chattered on, explaining she had completed school at fourteen as further education was not possible. It would necessitate going away as a boarder and that was not feasible financially for her parents. She now helped on the farm as girls were expected to learn household chores until they, in turn, married and had a family. Otherwise, it was the boat to England or America and that was a daunting vista for many an Irish girl, unless they had family or friends to whom they could go. Bridie explained how she had travelled to Dublin alone and, eventually, ended up in Liverpool. She confided that she had recently secured a place in a hospital in London to train as a fully qualified nurse, an ambition that grew and developed during her time in France.

'I was inspired, initially, by a wonderful woman called, Dr Kathleen Lynn.'

'Who is she?' enquired Ellen. 'Do I know her?'

'No, I don't really, either. She is a doctor I came across in Dublin who impressed me.' They rambled along in silence for a while, broken by Bridie, as she continued, 'My admiration for Dr Lynn encouraged me to fight for what I wanted. So, I battled against the odds until I was accepted, first as a VAD and now in the new hospital to fully train.'

Ellen listened with rapt attention as Bridie expounded on her firm belief that all women were as intelligent and equal to any man. Ellen gaped in awe as she listened to Bridie express an opinion, the polar opposite, of all she had been taught. The intriguing idea that girls should not settle for marriage too quickly but should follow their dreams, captivating her imagination. An excitement swelled through Ellen at such radical ideas. Also, the knowledge that if her path took her to London, Bridie promised a bed, ready and waiting for her.

Christmas morning dawned cold and frosty, and the entire family joined the traditional procession to the church for morning Mass. Across the mountainside, candles flickered in the dawn, as families made their way to the village in the half-light of early morning. The haunting lyrics of ancient Christmas carols resounded around the hillside, combined with the excited whispering of children. Bridie felt blessed to be part of such a magical tableau as they all, slowly, meandered down the boreen that led to the village church. She breathed in the cool dawn air, heavy with the scent of peat fires slowly burning and with the promise of new beginnings as daylight approached. A special morning, akin to those remembered from childhood, sprinkled with excitement that hailed a bright future, despite the constant political rumblings.

Josie and Donal and their six children, most now almost adult, led the way. Kathleen skipped in between Ellen and Sarah, rhythmically shaking their hands, swinging to and fro'. At the church gate, Bridie saw faces remembered from the past, particularly Annie Walsh, her childhood friend, now married with two children of her own.

'How are you, Annie, and your children? Was it Stephen McCarthy, who stole you in the end?'

'Aye, it was, he is over there now, with Danny.'

'Oh Danny, how is he doing?' enquired Bridie.

To her surprise, Annie took her aside and whispered, 'Like yourself, he is home for Christmas. Getting involved in politics now, so maybe, best not to talk too much to me. Happy Christmas, Bridie, and lovely to see you.' With that, Annie patted her shoulder and sauntered away, leaving a puzzled Bridie in her wake.

Gifts were never opened until they returned from Mass. The heightened anticipation and excitement meant the return journey was undertaken in half the time. Presents were never large, a new pencil for school or hand-knitted socks but all, nevertheless, appreciated. A highlight would be an orange or even some chocolate, if they were lucky. An unacknowledged awkwardness crept in as Bridie realised her, albeit small extravagances, were misplaced. She presented Josie with a silk scarf she would probably never wear and Donal with a tie, something he had only worn once before at his wedding. The girls, however, were delighted with their gifts, especially Ellen.

Bridie whispered, 'I have something special for you. Two books. The first is *Pride and Prejudice*. It is about a life you will never experience and that is what makes it fascinating. But it is also about a strong woman who refuses to be bartered for money and wishes to choose love for herself. Yet, she is confined by the codes of her class. You will find it interesting to read about another type of society. The second book is a small dictionary so that you can check out the words you don't understand.' Bridie smiled at Ellen and felt that same connection that suffused her when first she held her as a new-born.

Everyone appeared to sit down to dinner in good form. Brendan joined them but Joe was absent and although everyone forbore to say so, there was a general sigh of relief. Joe's temperament was volatile, especially when Liam was around. As usual, Christmas dinner was a stuffed goose with a variety of vegetables and potatoes, followed by traditional Christmas pudding and cake. There was also beer for the men and as the meal wore on, Liam, Josie's eldest son, enjoyed quite a few bottles.

Liam was a bit of an enigma. Strictly speaking, he was attractive, tall with dark hair and blue eyes, but he was introspective, his manner assessing. This intensity detracted from his appearance and made him seem aggressive and possibly, difficult. It was some years since Bridie had last seen Liam. It dawned on her, that despite being raised, practically as brother and sister, she never knew him very well or felt close to him. In all the correspondence from her sister Josie, there had never been a mention of a girlfriend and she wondered if anyone except Josie, understood him. Josie had explained that his focus was entirely on the current, political situation and he wished fervently he had travelled to Dublin and been part of the action when the Rising occurred. The subsequent execution of sixteen leaders and the imprisonment of many more haunted him daily. He abhorred the position of John Redmond and his followers that Irish men fight for Britain in return for Home Rule. Liam had been vocal in the area against the proposed conscription of Irishmen to fight on the Western Front and within his own county, had been a leading organiser of the general strike, on 23rd April. Now, a committed Sinn Féin follower, he refused to acknowledge many well-known neighbours who did not agree with his views. That antipathy was extended to Bridie's friends, the Walshe's, known Redmond supporters. The idea that Bridie had ministered to British soldiers festered within him. On Christmas Day, after a few beers, he could no longer hold back.

'You're a nurse?' he queried, from across the table.

'A VAD, a type of assistant nurse,' replied Bridie, conscious, that from the expression on his face that this was not an idle enquiry.

'And it is the British you nurse, is it? The soldiers who keep us oppressed and have occupied our land for countless centuries.' Liam took another long swallow.

Bridie responded quietly, 'I don't look at it that way.'

'So how do you look at it?' he swiftly retorted. 'I mean, our lads were wounded in 1916, and they could have done with some nursing. Instead, you look after those who executed our Freedom Fighters.'

Bridie was taken aback by his accusatory and belligerent tone but defended herself staunchly. 'I nursed wounded and injured men. I didn't take any side.' The scepticism in his bearing riled her to retort, angrily, 'And what did you do, Liam? Were you there in the GPO in 1916?'

'No, to my shame I wasn't,' he hissed and through clenched teeth, seethed, 'but at least I didn't betray my country by aiding her enemy.'

Lost for words, Bridie stood up and excused herself. Alone in the bedroom, she was annoyed for allowing him to agitate her. She felt it prudent to stay where she was so Christmas would not be spoiled for everyone. Lying down, the tension from the table began to ooze slowly away, and whether it was the long journey, or the silence of the night or to soothe the hurt she felt inside, she fell into a deep, dreamless sleep.

Chapter 6

No one uttered a word. Josie stood up abruptly, the piercing screech as her chair scraped across the flagstones breaking the stunned silence. Liam staggered to his feet glaring in turn, at each person gathered around the table. Grabbing his jacket from the back of his chair, he lurched a little unsteadily to the front door and went outside. Brendan, Liam's constant shadow, quickly followed. The two of them could be seen through the window leaning over a fence conversing. Brendan was as fair as Liam was dark but in the night light, this difference was not apparent. They had an easy companionship that soothed Liam's inner turmoil and tonight, Liam was especially glad of the company. He knew he had been rude and had blighted Christmas for everyone, but sometimes, he was consumed with a compulsion and agitation inside that could not be ignored. Try as he might, he could not understand how anyone could have believed the words of John Redmond and the promises of the English. Yet, Bridie, his aunt, had nursed enemy soldiers. His restlessness conveyed itself to Brendan and with that ease between good companions where words are superfluous, they turned simultaneously and sauntered down the lane. Liam was concerned about how often Brendan skipped school. He just wanted to help on the farm and regularly appeared before eight every other morning. He certainly pulled his weight, but Liam knew the time was coming when he would have to chat to his half-brother, Joe about it. However, it was not appropriate tonight. He waved Brendan goodbye at his front door and walked briskly up the hill, in an effort to calm his churning thoughts.

Back at the farmhouse, Josie, resignedly, began to clear the table and Ellen, Sarah, and Kathleen knew Christmas was now, to all intents and purposes, at an end. Together, the three girls retired to their bedroom each to deal with the abrupt end to the festivities in their own way. Kathleen, the youngest, unable to understand the complexities that underlay the ruination of her favourite day of the year, was sobbing and lay on the bed until sleep overcame her. Sarah was also crying, but a harsh opinion might suggest it was more for show. Within a few minutes, she was attending to her hair, her mouth curving approvingly at the image reflected in the mirror.

Ellen just lay on her bed and gazed at the ceiling. For a while, her mind meandered around the fine cracks in the plaster, too disappointed to focus on what had just occurred at the table. Reluctantly, she recognised, she could not ignore all the thoughts bombarding her brain and took them out one by one for examination.

She remembered the day Bridie arrived. She had skipped home from the village, looking forward to assisting with the preparations for the party the next night. She just knew it would be terrific and so different from Uncle Michael's wake the year before. That had been a strange night, a mixture of forced gaiety and sadness. It was the usual practice, when anyone was emigrating to America, that Mass was celebrated in the house before any food or drink was consumed.

That night, the house was packed with relatives, friends and neighbours, the swelling numbers spilling outside into the yard. The priest had barely finished Mass, and was just performing the final blessing, when Freddie, the fiddle player, began a tune, a signal the party was about to start. His son quickly produced his whistle, and while there were some who danced and others who sang, the sound of muffled sobbing accompanied the music. Tears came from all quarters, one setting another off, battling with the music, which responded by becoming louder and louder.

Tears came especially from Maggie, Michael's wife, rolling in a rivulet down her reddened cheeks. Michael was Donal's younger brother, and Maggie was convinced she would never see him again. She had two young children and although Michael promised to send for them once he was settled, Maggie wept as though he had died. She was still waiting to hear from Michael, so Ellen speculated that perhaps she had had good reason to doubt him.

Ellen had fervently hoped Bridie's return for Christmas would be nothing but joy. It was a long-awaited welcome home and a cause for celebration. Liam's outburst had just ruined the occasion and she dreaded that the renewed closeness she felt with Bridie would now dissipate.

The quiet of the room interrupted her reverie and she noticed the sobbing from both her sisters had ceased. Little Kathleen was asleep but Sarah, Ellen could see, was sitting up brushing her hair, admiring herself as usual. Sarah was fair with blue eyes, in total contrast to Ellen's dark, curly hair and eyes so full of expression, they flickered between blue and green, depending on her mood. Sarah was too aware of how pretty she was, surmised Ellen. One thing never changed, she mused, and that was the attention Sarah gave herself. Preening in front of the mirror, all the trauma at the table forgotten, Sarah glanced at Ellen.

'Cheer up, Ellen, it will all be forgotten tomorrow.'

'I doubt it,' was the terse reply.

Sarah was too young perhaps to understand the divisions that Liam had exacerbated within the family and among many old neighbours and friends. Ellen turned over to avoid further conversation. She knew Sarah said these things to goad her. Nothing seemed to affect Sarah too strongly but she readily perceived, Ellen, was the exact opposite. Sensitive and perceptive, Ellen dwelt on the meaning of words and inflections, worrying if anyone was upset, parsing what had been voiced. It was impossible for Ellen to sleep if sharp words had been spoken and fences needed to be mended before she lay down to rest at night. Very little perturbed Sarah. She shrugged her shoulders and sailed through life, openly admitting that she enjoyed intense pleasure from irritating Ellen.

Ellen sighed. She knew she could no longer postpone reflecting about

Christmas and what had occurred at the table. Liam was her brother and she presumed, she automatically should love him but there was no denying, he was dour at times and unforgiving. Liam could never excuse what he saw as a betrayal but why did he have to choose that moment to tackle Bridie?

Ellen had a reasonable knowledge of the Irish question, from Liam's perspective anyway, as the family was subjected to the tirades of all her brothers but especially Liam, most evenings. He would not countenance any viewpoint but that of the new emerging power, Sinn Fein. The notion that anyone could have legitimately believed that fighting for Britain in the war would lead to Irish independence, was not to be considered or condoned. He viewed all those fellow Irishmen or women who fought or assisted in that war as traitors or at best, misguided, hence his dislike of Bridie's actions and the assistance she gave to any man wearing a British uniform. Understanding the nuances and grasping the complexities of the Irish question, when she was only subjected to one side of the argument, only added to Ellen's confusion. She tried to muddle through all the issues bombarding her brain. She had seen Bridie speak to Annie Walsh on Christmas Day and knew that Liam probably had too. That may have been the catalyst that incensed him. Annie's brother Danny had just recently returned from fighting in France and, according to Liam, had the gall to now argue against violence. She knew Liam refused to acknowledge any of his neighbours who were Redmond supporters. Combined with the fact that Bridie had nursed British soldiers, Liam, after a few too many beers, was bound to flare up.

Bridie planned to leave a few days after Christmas as soon as transport was up and running again. Much to her disappointment, the tension that persisted over the following days underscored any possibility of rapprochement with Liam. The atmosphere in the house was stifling as they both took pains to avoid each other but in such a confined space, it was not always possible. The ensuing strain affected everyone, and even little Kathleen could sense the cool undercurrents. Josie was torn between love of her son and disappointment at how the reunion with her sister had transpired. In general, the family were conflicted between loyalty to Liam and an understanding of Bridie and her perspective. Donal, of course, as always, said very little. He cared for the farm during the day and wandered down to the village for his customary pint at night.

Donal's disengagement from the family tension made Ellen, for the very first time, wonder about her father and mother and the relationship they had. She felt her father should have at the very least attempted to intervene on Christmas Day. There was no effort made since to force Liam to ease the strain in the house. Why could her father not see the visible stress apparent on Josie's face? Instead, he acted as if nothing had occurred. Ellen loved her father, but she was a dreamer and wanted more from a man than he be gentle and kind, yet totally uninvolved. She wanted passion and excitement, and at times her father was genial and affable to a point of irritation. Ellen wondered how her mother coped with his apparent withdrawal from family demands and was puzzled as to whether they communicated at all. These thoughts swirled around in her head, and she understood two things. Her mother Josie needed support, as Liam was overwrought and agitated, and she was torn in two between her son and her sister. She also intended to take her time, like Bridie, and not settle for the first man who came along.

Liam was at his best and in communion with his world when he was alone in the morning, with mist rising from the stony brook shrouding both himself and the landscape in shadow. He was suffused by a sense of peace when leaning against a rock, melding into the mountain terrain, existing with no demands or torments to agitate his brain. He had earlier accompanied Brendan, his unlikely companion who had arrived as usual to help with milking, back down the lane to his father, Joe's, house. Afterwards, he struck out on his own to try and grapple with the array of conflicting emotions that were swirling around in his head since Christmas. He did not have much time for women, not since Eileen. That woman just could not wait until the time was right for him to commit and had married a farmer from another county. After she spurned him, he realised he was not overly disappointed and his mild irritation resulted in the main, from a dent to his pride. He decided to bide his time before he bothered with another woman again. Getting married was the expected path but if he was honest, his slowness to become engaged was possibly because, although fond of Eileen, he knew he did not love her. He liked peace and quiet and his own company and he had yet to meet a woman who innately understood that need. It seemed to Liam that all his irritations lately sprang from women, women like Bridie. He silently berated himself for speaking out of turn on Christmas Day, but the beer had loosened his tongue and he just could not help himself.

The evening before Bridie's departure, Josie went looking for Liam, finding him as he was preparing to herd the few cows into the barn. 'Leave that for a few moments,' she ordered. Then, taking him by the arm, she led him on down the lane to a rock overlooking the now, sluggish, and partly iced, river. As a child he used to sit on that rock eating an apple or, if he was lucky, a slice of apple pie, as Josie told him a story. Her choice of seat was therefore not random but a reminder of their bond. 'You know you were out of line, Liam, and you need to apologise to Bridie.'

'But, Mam.'

'No, do not interrupt, hear me out. Christmas was spoiled for everyone, but they will get over it. For Bridie and for me, it was more than Christmas, it was a reunion. We are sisters, but we haven't seen each other since 1913, and it was to be our special time.'

Josie paused as Liam sat quietly, unresponsive for a few seconds, his face a picture of defeat and sorrow. Inhaling a sharp breath of frosty air, he replied, 'Aye, I know, I know. I shouldn't have said what I said. I regret how things turned out, but I don't think I can apologise for saying what I believe.'

Josie stared unflinchingly at Liam, reminding him of their closeness as mother and son. 'You need to, for me, Liam,' replied Josie. 'I need my sister to feel she is welcome in my home, or else it is possible, I will never see her again.'

For some moments Liam was seemingly absorbed by the threatening clouds and darkening landscape, then taking Josie's hand he turned to her, noting the plea in her eyes. 'Aye, I will think on it, Mam, I promise, I will think on it.'

Josie patted his hand in gratitude. 'I will make the tea. Come in soon.' She walked slowly back to the house. She had a fierce love for Liam, her firstborn. People thought he was difficult, even hard, but she knew otherwise. He had strong beliefs that could not be swayed and was too outspoken for his own good, but he had a soft centre. She had seen it often with his young sisters and with herself. Even as a young boy he had known when she was weak from morning sickness or too heavy and awkward to carry water or turf. He was always at her side, easing her burden. His sorrow over Kathleen and the accident would never leave him and in part, that was the root of his prickly manner.

Liam went over to the barn the following morning and listened for Billy's cart to arrive to collect Bridie for the bus. He shuffled around inside, wanting to please his mother but knowing it was impossible for him to apologise to someone he felt betrayed the Irish cause, by assisting the enemy. When he heard the cart clatter over the stones, he sidled to the barn door. From his vantage point, he watched Bridie. Her departure was delayed while she hugged everyone in turn with promises to write and visit. That promise eased Liam's mind and his decision was made. As Bridie alighted onto the cart, Liam stepped out into the yard. The gulf was too great for an apology, but he caught her eye and gave her a brief nod, tipping his cap in salute. From the corner of his eye, Liam noticed that Josie had seen their interaction and she gave him a half-smile of gratitude. Satisfied he had mollified his mother, he set out on one of his long walks to shake off any irritating feelings of compromise. He had done what he could and hoped it was enough to satisfy Josie and ease Bridie's discomfort, should she wish to return.

Chapter 7

Bridie settled into her seat on the train and composed herself with her thoughts. The happy Christmas return had ended in disarray, and she needed some quiet time to decide where to go from here. Billy's cart had been anything but comfortable and it wasn't just the hard bench on which she had to sit. The odour from Billy's breath, combined with a heady waft from his body, could not be camouflaged by her faintly scented handkerchief, making what was a short journey, quite endless. Billy also had a heavy cold and his sleeve, miserably failing in its secondary job, was unable to prevent spray showering all around when he was overcome by a sneeze. The idea he should cover his mouth, an alien concept.

Bridie felt conflicted and disparate thoughts churned in her head. Liam's nod from the barn may have been an olive branch but possibly, she was deluding herself and misinterpreting his actions. Bridie was relieved in some respects that the busy house had prevented an opportunity for a private chat with Josie. Despite herself and her best intentions, she might have been tempted to discuss the relationship she had with Harry and that would surely have met with Josie's disapproval. There was enough tension with Liam without further complications. Surprised to be leaving Donegal so soon, she now contemplated whether to remain in Dublin or travel immediately to

London for the balance of her leave. Engrossed in her reverie, she was irritated at the commotion caused by another passenger attempting to store luggage and apparently, also invade the privacy of her seat. She looked up in exasperation as there were plenty of vacant seats on the train, only to be met with a friendly grin. Danny Walsh was tipping his hat as he sat beside her.

'My,' he grinned, 'Bridie. I thought I glimpsed you outside the church on Christmas Day. You're a sight for sore eyes.' Flashing an engaging smile, he sat down beside her, maybe a little too closely. Immediately hiding her reluctance, she smiled back. It was Danny Walsh after all, Annie's younger brother. 'Glad you recognised me, Bridie,' quipped Danny.

'Aye, and how could I forget you?' was the slightly sardonic response from Bridie, yet her smile stole the sting from her words.

Danny settled himself, evidently delighted to see Bridie on the train. He had always liked her, had a fancy to get to know her better but he sensed there was little interest from her direction. He was simply her friend's brother and at times, certainly a bit of a pest. It was many years since they had properly spoken to each other and despite perceiving a slight irritation on her part at being disturbed, Danny was not put off in any way. It had been an awkward Christmas with the horrors of the war still to the forefront of his mind and the family were exhausting as they attempted to pretend all was easy and jolly. The small, white-washed cottage had seemed so empty without his mother notwithstanding the best efforts of his brother and family. He had become visibly upset standing by her grave, the poignancy of his safe return a reminder of the arbitrary nature of life and death.

After the graveyard there followed the annual pilgrimage to the "Holy Well". His mother had been a firm believer in the curative powers of the "well," and always insisted the entire family undertake the short pilgrimage on St Stephen's Day. Annie, his sister, had wanted them to follow that tradition and it was on the return journey home that she told him Bridie had been in France, nursing. He now settled comfortably beside her. Danny was sure they would have an understanding in common of the difficulties settling back to normality.

The hours slipped by as an easy camaraderie developed between them. 'Annie told me you were in France, Danny,' said Bridie.

'Yes,' responded Danny, and a veil descended, as visions of bloodied and mangled bodies flooded his mind.

'I was there too,' murmured Bridie, patting his hand, immediately seeing some of the images now filling his mind's eye.

'Thank God we were both spared,' whispered Danny with a sigh of relief.

Seconds passed in mutual understanding before Donegal and their childhood and remembered antics of shared experiences, had them both laughing. The journey was usually long and wearisome, but together, the time flew by and the synergy between them astounded them both. Due to her abrupt departure, Bridie had no plans made. Danny recommended a small boarding house near Grafton Street and accompanied her to ensure she was comfortably settled. He bade her farewell with a promise to collect her at 6 o'clock the following evening and take her to dinner.

The next day, Bridie spent time renewing her knowledge of Dublin and preparing for her evening with Danny. That conditions had barely changed since 1913 did not surprise her but did disappoint. She returned to her lodgings slightly disheartened but as she prepared for her evening, that cloud of despondency began to lift. Her ten days leave were supposed to have been spent in Donegal but the more time she had spent speaking to Danny, this unexpected sojourn in the capital no longer seemed unattractive.

Danny was also pleased when Bridie said she would meet him the next day for dinner. He did not have extensive knowledge of Dublin and asked for advice from the landlady at his own lodgings as to where he should take her. *Wynn's Hotel* had been severely damaged as had the *Gresham Hotel* during the Easter Rising and anyway, he knew they both might be too expensive. He needed to avoid any embarrassment caused by a scarcity of money. His landlady suggested a small guest house in Glasnevin. 'I know the woman who runs it very well. It's quite genteel and she does a nice evening meal at a reasonable price.'

Danny walked over early in the morning to ensure the place was suitable and that there would be a table available for them at 7 o'clock. That evening, he dressed carefully in his one and only suit: a suit that had seen better days. Anxious to make an impression, he had splashed out on a new shirt earlier that morning and as he walked the short distance to collect Bridie, he hoped she would be favourably impressed. Eating out was a new experience for him although France had initiated him into the delights of a bottle of wine. Fervently, he hoped, if he could remember not to eat with his mouth open or talk when it was full, he might get through the evening without shame.

His plan now was to collect Bridie and together, they would travel by coach to Glasnevin. Bridie also dressed with extra care in preparation for meeting Danny that evening. She had one quite attractive dress, and although well-worn it was flattering, emphasising the changing colours in her eyes and the creaminess of her complexion.

Danny grinned shyly as he took her hand to help her into the carriage. They sat side by side, barely speaking or touching, restrained by convention that erected a barrier to their unspoken inclination to continue to hold hands. When they arrived at the small but elegant guesthouse, it was already brightly lit with an enticing scent of roast beef permeating the entrance hall.

Their table was positioned in a secluded corner, next to a window with a view of a well-tended garden. It was a busy dining room, occupied in the main, by aspirants to the steady, but growing Dublin middle class. 'Turned out quite a nice day, after all, Bridie,' said Danny.

'Yes, indeed. It seemed like it might rain, but the clouds soon cleared,' agreed Bridie, grinning, as the vagaries of Irish weather continued to dominate the conversation.

'We could probably do with a little rain, now,' suggested Danny, 'the crops need some water.' Her grin widened and as their eyes met, they simultaneously burst into laughter. Suddenly, Bridie felt herself relax for the first time since Christmas and Liam's outburst. Interest was now piqued by the occupants at other tables.

'Would you say he is a farmer, more used to a chunky mug?' she whispered, directing her gaze at an extremely large man whose chubby fingers were clumsily grasping a china teacup.

'I think so, looking at his boots,' murmured Danny and nodding in another direction, 'what about them? Guess their story.'

Bridie glanced at a table opposite to see an austere middle-aged woman, seated with a young couple. 'Mother and her daughter, with a young man the mother certainly does not approve of, and he knows it,' she replied.

The young man was grappling unsuccessfully with the cutlery, puzzling over which implement he should use. Surprisingly, the bright lights and bustling room did not prevent an intimate ambience surrounding Bridie and Danny. The attempt at delicate table manners, a glaring novelty for many guests, generated an intimacy between them as they wove outrageous life stories over roast beef and apple pie. To his astonishment, Danny did not feel intimidated; instead, he was totally comfortable, asking Bridie which spoon, knife, or fork he should use. As the evening wore on, they remarked on how they had not yet mentioned wars, or risings, rebellions, or elections. Afterwards, Bridie could only remember laughter as they speculated on the other diners and fascination when Danny began to speak of his dreams.

Inevitably, conversation drifted towards the future and the plans they both had. Over dinner, Danny told her how he was now fully demobbed from the British Army. In turn, Bridie explained that she was about to enrol in a London teaching hospital as she had been accepted to train to become a qualified nurse. This was both an exciting and nerve-wracking opportunity, but she was determined to give it a go. It had been challenging to achieve the placement, as there was a certain antipathy between the nursing profession and VADs, but she had been fortunate. When she returned to work in the hospital in Liverpool, she realised she knew one of the supervisors from her spell in France. The camaraderie that war generated was renewed, and through her influence and good auspices, the opportunity to train was offered. She would have to "live-in" the nurses' home for a minimum of two years, which was going to be difficult after having her own space, but she was determined to manage.

Danny related how when he first joined the British Army he was drifting and, on reflection, knew little about the ideals of John Redmond. 'My family were always ardent Parnell supporters and then, automatically, Redmond. I didn't question how or why; I just went along with them.' Twisting his glass thoughtfully, he continued, 'It took the horror of the war to make me begin the search for my own path. I suppose I also knew I had to leave Donegal at some point and, foolish as it now seems, the war looked like an opportunity and a way for Ireland to achieve Home Rule.'

The paradox, Bridie surmised, but didn't wish to interrupt Danny's flow by voicing her thoughts, was that although Redmond purported to pursue Irish Nationalism through peaceful means, he had encouraged Irish men to fight for Britain. Danny was not unaware of this, but his focus was on the wasteful and barbaric slaughter he had witnessed on the Somme. As such, his developing ideals had an instinctive aversion to violence. His intuition, although not yet finely honed, led him to believe more violence was inevitable in Ireland and he had already seen and experienced too much of it and the resultant horror it produced. Redmond or Sinn Fein no longer figured in his considerations. Danny's nebulous, political concepts had undergone a transformation as man after man, was killed or maimed on the orders of those sitting in safety. Young boys, crying at night for their mothers, fighting for a purpose they could not comprehend.

Danny expounded at length to Bridie on the tragedy of war although she knew those horrors all too well herself. First-hand knowledge had been garnered in the field hospital and she could recall all too clearly, the suffering and degradation of the men she had nursed. Danny paused, as if to give his next words more weight or maybe undecided, whether to give them voice. 'What I realised all too soon, however, was that I had volunteered like so many others to be fodder for a war machine. I really couldn't understand what I was fighting for, and I think, very few did. As news of the Rising came through, I wasn't sure where I belonged or which side I was on. James Connolly has been an inspiration and the more I read, the more I believe, that whether it be Redmond or Pearse or now Collins or De Valera, most people's lives will still be as miserable.'

They both concentrated on their food for a few minutes, before Danny paused once more and looked around the quiet dining room. 'Here we are in this small guest house having dinner and so many will never have that opportunity. You know, I never felt I was well off growing up in Donegal. There was constant work around the farm, and it felt like the wet and cold was never-ending, with mud everywhere. I sometimes think Donegal has as much mud as the Somme,' he said wryly, before continuing, 'yet there was never a night when I was hungry and, at the end of the day, there was a warm fire. There are so many layers around us, from those who have absolutely nothing, to those who have more than they can ever spend. In between, there are those like you and me who believe we struggle until we look below.' Danny grinned, eyes twinkling, as he continued, 'Do you know, I always thought you were well off, the gentry as it were?'

Bridie laughed, slightly baffled. 'Far from it but, maybe, because there was only myself and my sister Josie, I suppose, there was more to spare.'

'You had a proper farm, though,' smiled Danny. 'You had animals and space. All we had was a couple of acres and much of that was stony ground.' Sighing wistfully, he added, 'Our cottage was tiny and with nine children, life was hard. Sometimes, the smallest thing can be a flag of poverty, like not having enough plates for the family, so meals were eaten in turn or not having writing paper for homework. I cannot remember my mother ever having something pretty to call her own. There are only a few of us left in Donegal now, the rest scattered in Scotland, England, America, Canada even further afield.'

Danny focussed on his meal but not for long. His natural inclination to discuss made him comment, 'Belief in God gave both my mother and father and many like them the strength to carry on. *"Opium of the people"*, to quote Marx. What if there is no God, Bridie, and life is just endless hardship with no possibilities?'

Bridie looked at him intently, 'I don't know the answer to that, Danny. Belief in a God is an effort for me after the war but for many people it is a consolation and what keeps them going.'

For a while, they both concentrated on their food, but Danny, as always, had to keep the discussion going. 'I suppose war changes everyone's perspective. We all strive to attain more for our families and most of us feel we do not have enough, yet there are so many strands in society and so many who scramble for scraps. I despair when I think of those who had so little, they felt war offered a better choice and offered more opportunity than staying at home. To a certain extent, that figured in my reasoning too, but aye, I soon learned I was so much better off than I realised.'

Danny lifted his glass and studied the contents. The stem rolled between his fingers as he contemplated his next words. 'Bridie, I want you to know how important it is for me to be here with you this evening. You may not know it, well, perhaps you guessed, but for me, you were always special. Now, here I am in this lovely dining room, eating fine food, sitting with the one woman who filled my imagination and my dreams, and all I do is blather on about politics and social conditions. You must think me such a fool.'

Bridie felt herself blush, a glow that she was helpless to pause gathered momentum and suffused her cheeks with a red flush. 'Danny,' she stuttered. 'Stop. We are different people now, not the young innocents we were in Donegal. I love your ideas; I am fascinated by your insights, and I want to hear more. Please continue.'

A brief rush, of possible hope, perhaps a yearning, flickered across his face, replaced quickly by his usual insouciance. 'Well, if that is the case, let me continue. I hope you won't regret it.' His nonchalant tone belied his relief, camouflaging his nervousness, as he further expounded. 'Ye know war is really about class and those who have power retaining that power at all costs. There is no point in having self-determination if we keep the old class structure and systems in place and inevitably, just hand power to a new hierarchy. I firmly believe the Catholic Church is gaining too much influence and I fear a new dictatorship from that quarter. When I think of the recent election, eighty-five percent approximately, are Catholic, I cannot but worry that the predominance of Catholic thinking will seep into the way the country is run, isolating those of other faiths.' At this point, Danny was so lost in reflection and introspection, that Bridie just nodded in agreement. His words echoed many of the thoughts that swirled around in her own head, but he was much more articulate in their utterance. She had a fleeting wish Ellen could hear him. Danny interrupted her introspection as he reached forward, gently patted her hand and with a mocking smile said, 'Bridie, between us, we have to change our world. Time to go now before I ramble even more.'

Later that evening, as Bridie lay in bed, she pondered over Danny, his ideas, and his vision for the future. He was not the boy she remembered. Well, first, he was much thinner, his face no longer plump and wreathed in a silly grin. He was gaunt now with deep lines around his mouth and along his cheeks, a definite creeping grey along his hairline and certainly a lived-in face that had seen too much. She knew him well when they were both teenagers, but no semblance of that boy remained. She always suspected, knew he had a crush on her, but not only was he two years younger he seemed so empty then. Now, was a different story, and she looked forward to their next meeting in another three days.

After Danny left Bridie back at her hotel, he was restless, railing at himself for boring her with all his talk of politics and socialism. He went for a long walk, not yet ready to retire, smoking and ruminating. *She had seemed interested*, he argued with himself, *had interesting perspectives of her own.* But he wished he had toned it down a bit. Shrugging his shoulders, and with a purposeful shake of his head, he thought, *What the hell, that is who I am now. If we are to become more than friends, she must accept that. Anyway, she is returning shortly to London in order to complete her training so after this week, we will probably not meet again for a long time.* Danny admired the journey Bridie had undertaken from a domestic servant to now gaining a foothold in a profession. It reinforced his opinion that everyone could achieve and move beyond their born circumstances, if given opportunity. His own journey was only beginning. His first action was to source a publication that would be receptive to his ideas. He also wanted to become more involved in politics. He instinctively felt there was room for more than Sinn Fein on the political scene.

Their next evening was as serene and enjoyable as before without any lull in the conversation. Bridie and Danny meandered slowly along Sandymount Strand. Gulls screeched overhead, while the breeze was sharp, yet exhilarating. Danny spoke as fervently in his enthusiasm, forgetting his resolve to tone down his ideas. He further expounded on how society needed reform, striding at a quick pace across the sand. Bridie clutched her coat tightly for warmth, thankful it was a strong barrier against the now biting, wind. In turn, she clamped a hand on her head to secure her hat, while straining to hear Danny's words as they vainly competed with the cacophony above. As Danny spoke of a republic, the gulls shrieked of equal rights. The wind whistled of lost opportunity as Danny struggled to propound on changing structures that guaranteed security. He battled in vain against a sudden downpour and class and society were drowned in the torrent. Whether an egalitarian society was ever possible sank beneath the waves thundering in the bay. Danny's belief that class had become an awkward word, one no one likes to express, floated out to sea, his words sinking beneath turbulent spray. In vain, Bridie tried to reconcile this strong, intent, and perceptive individual with the frivolous, chubby youth, she had deliberately ignored before.

This was their last evening as Bridie was travelling the next day. Promises to write were made as Danny once more walked Bridie back to her hotel, but now he leant forward and brushed her mouth with his own. She was both surprised and pleased, and smiling, held him warmly. He arrived, as promised, early the next morning and assisted Bridie with her luggage. The day of her departure was bittersweet, and mournfully she gave him her hand before embarking. Without permission, he hugged her tightly and kissed her passionately on her lips, demanding that she write as soon as she was safely back home. Bridie dreamed she could still feel the softness of his lips on hers as she drifted off to sleep that night. In turn, Danny desperately tried to hold on to a faint scent, a muskiness so essentially Bridie, as he grappled with a sleep that was elusive. It was some time before they met again as both Bridie and Danny concentrated on their career paths, yet, through regular letters, they came to know each other's intimate thoughts and hopes.

Chapter 8

Christmas 1918 had faded from Liam's memory. Once his mother was no longer stressed, he did not need to dwell on the effects of his words on Bridie, or anyone else. So, adhering to a long-kept tradition, he walked down to the pub with a purposeful stride. Tonight, head bent against the wind, the current political situation was at the forefront of his mind. In January 1919, Sinn Féin established the First Dáil or parliament. Liam was in full agreement with their tactics but knew the British Government would feel compelled to resist the thrust for independence, with force, if necessary. Combined with the opposition in Ulster to any form of Home Rule, the stage was set for continuing conflict in the country. Liam felt his time had now come to stand up and be counted, and he was determined to play his part in gaining his country's independence, whatever the cost.

Although he was well known around the area, only an intrepid few approached him. Liam mostly kept to himself and showed little interest in any of the activities around the village. His focus was the current political situation and he only wished to converse with like-minded individuals but even those individuals found him awkward, and many avoided Liam when they could. At times, his brother Sheamus joined him, but rarely, Ciaran. All three were committed Republicans, but whereas Liam was never distracted from pursuit of the "cause", Sheamus had one eye always available for the local girls. No matter how intense his conversation with Liam, if he spied any female he fancied, he would instantly leave Liam and the pub. As for Ciaran, his only love was sports and he lived for each match. He was either playing a game or preparing for one, so he kept his drinking to a minimum. Liam now sat hunched in a corner musing over his pint. At intervals, his fingers tapped a rhythm on the table irritating those in earshot. He had a couple of issues on his mind, but Joe and Brendan were to the forefront.

Joe and Liam were not dissimilar in many ways. They were half-brothers with approximately eleven years between them. Joe had a chip on his shoulder that continued to grow. His mother had taken ill when he was two and passed away shortly afterwards. His father, Donal, was a labourer and despite the hardship of poverty and deprivation, Joe and Donal had lived contentedly in a small cottage close together in sorrow and later in companionship. Joe felt they had no need of anyone else and when Donal began to court Josie, Joe was at first agitated and then highly jealous when his father's intentions became clear. Josie was a bit of a catch coming as she did with her own farm, but all Joe could see was his father's affections diverted away from him. He was not the most attractive child with gingery hair, rather large ears and a ruddy complexion. With an added pout and distended lip, brought about by his belligerent attitude, he was not easy to love. His tantrums did not lessen as his father's courtship with Josie progressed, but they were to no avail, and Josie and Donal married the following spring. Josie tried her best and it seemed that after the first year some headway was made.

The farmhouse, although not much bigger than their old cottage, was warm and comfortable and Joe, at ten years of age, enjoyed helping on the land and caring for the few animals. He ignored Bridie, viewing her as a pest, but was comfortable with Josie and Bridie's father. Their father was now elderly and a little disabled but his kind and gentle manner soothed Joe's prickly nature. Joe developed a complacency, an acceptance, that the farm was now his home.

All was unsettled with the birth of a baby brother. From the start, Joe could not abide Liam. The attention he received and the dawning knowledge that he,

Joe, would now be overlooked, fuelled a jealousy that ultimately was lifelong. A canker ate at Joe and quarrelsome and temperamental, he reluctantly completed his chores. Donal and Josie walked on eggshells around him so as not to incense flare-ups that ended in arguments and rages. As Joe entered his early teens Sheamus arrived, followed closely by Ciaran. The realisation that the farm was handed down through Josie's family and it would go to her eldest son, Liam, in due course, cemented his isolation. He began to sleep in the old cottage and by the time he was sixteen, it had become his permanent home. It was musty and damp and lacked a lot of comforts, but he preferred to be alone. The farmhouse now contained his father Donal, Josie, their three boys and Bridie. Yet, despite the best efforts of Josie and Donal, Joe felt he no longer had a place in that family.

Joe was a lonely young man, but pride kept him isolated. His life took on the familiar pattern of many a Donegal man. He laboured on a variety of farms, rising early and working until darkness fell. Work was not always plentiful, but he also cultivated the small piece of land around his cottage and planted some vegetables for his own use. Once a week, he hitched his old jennet to the cart and traipsed from farm to farm collecting milk, eventually delivering the full cart to the dairy for processing. This was steady work, and by the time Joe turned nineteen, he was in a happier place. As such, his demeanour was more agreeable the evening he met Noreen at the local dairy, one fortuitous week. As he unloaded the cart she walked past, russet hair glistening in the winter sunshine. He paused to watch her as she bent to fill a bucket of water. Sensing his stare, she turned and caught his glance. Embarrassed, he moved swiftly away, convinced that such a beautiful creature would have no time for him but in that, he was wrong.

As the weeks passed, they saluted one another and eventually, he found the courage to speak and, to his surprise, an easy camaraderie developed. Noreen told him she was seventeen and came from a family of twelve and her mother had another on the way. Small talk gave way to longer conversations and Joe became impatient for each week to pass so that he could see her again. At night he dreamed of her, awake, he dreaded she would disappear from his life. Noreen, however, was not going anywhere. She liked this awkward, unassuming man, his gentleness and diffidence fascinated her, the opposite of the roughly hewn men in her own family.

When asked to go for a walk, she agreed with enthusiasm and within months, their burgeoning romance had blossomed into marriage. Noreen was thrilled with Joe's cottage. It was as small as her own home yet, despite its shortcomings, represented an idyll and a haven from the turmoil and claustrophobia of her family house. She added a few touches to the cottage, dressing the bed with fresh linen, a surreptitious present from Josie, and brightened windows with faded net curtains donated by her long-suffering mother. It was many years since Joe felt at such peace and he rose each day and went to bed each night in a place that had once seemed elusive. He had Noreen and a home and when a baby son, Brendan, was born a year later, he knew a turning point had been reached. He had his own family to love and work for and life had possibilities.

His contact with "Droimreagh" farm was minimal, but he now felt more able to keep in touch and reconnect particularly with his father, who was overjoyed to meet his grandson. Josie too was welcoming, extending a helping hand to Noreen. When Noreen announced she was expecting another baby, Joe was ecstatic. He felt a surge of ambition, a need to focus on a future where he could provide properly. He knew his abilities were limited but never one to shy away from hard work, he was determined to forge a path and do whatever was necessary to keep his family intact.

That cold November night when Noreen went into labour was scoured into his psyche. The pregnancy had been long and hard, but Josie had promised to be there to help when the time came. At four in the morning, Joe ran up the lane with fear gnawing at his heart. Noreen was in agony and feverish and Josie was urgently needed. Together, they worked ceaselessly through the night, but their help was to no avail. Three days later, Joe and Brendan stood at the side of the grave as Noreen and his baby daughter were lowered into the ground.

Whiskey provided some relief for Joe, but Brendan was lost. Joe tried his best but his will was defeated and Brendan was now a young boy without mother or father. As the days passed and his father became more and more morose, unable to move beyond his grief, Brendan developed the habit of walking daily up to "Droimreagh". He found solace with Liam, a loner like himself. Akin to his father, Brendan loved the farm and the animals, and Liam was glad of his help. Their companionship was easy but when Joe spied Brendan and Liam working and laughing together, his old envy returned, smouldering into a hatred that was fuelled by alcohol.

Now, as Liam mused over his pint, his dilemma was how to approach Joe. His concern was Brendan as he felt Joe was neglectful and should be more forceful about Brendan attending school. He wavered, undecided as to whether he should speak at all, conscious that his words could further incense Joe's antagonism. He believed that Joe had to know that Brendan came almost every day to the farm but the continual simmering rancour between them, meant his interference would not be welcomed and might only exacerbate the issue. Liam understood that Joe felt aggrieved about the farm, even if it was without just cause, and he was generally not receptive to any comments from Liam. However, Liam was concerned, and it was no favour to Brendan to have him grow up semi-literate.

He saw himself in Brendan, a lonely lad, not sure of his place, but comfortable in the hills and fields surrounding him. There was no doubt he was useful around the farm but with his own two brothers, Sheamus and Ciaran, there would never be a proper living for Brendan, and he needed to obtain some education for his future.

It had become customary for Joe to travel to Scotland in the autumn when the harvesting began and when that was completed, to obtain further work on various building sites. That way, he earned enough money to supplement his meagre earnings in Donegal. Liam hated the idea that this itinerant lifestyle might also become Brendan's but that was a strong possibility if he continued to skip school.

Liam's next issue was his father, Donal. He had become very infirm of late as his arthritis became ever more crippling and consequently, total control and management of the farm were almost entirely in Liam's hands. His father also seemed very vague at times, which was especially worrying. Sheamus had lately broached the idea of travelling to Scotland alongside Joe. Liam could understand the need in Sheamus to forge his future for ultimately, he would have to leave the farm, but right now Liam needed him to stay. There was too much work for just himself and Ciaran but moreover, he also despised the idea of any member of the family relying on the English Crown for support. How could they justify fighting for independence and at the same time have a reliance on the enemy for their livelihood?

Liam's third problem was Ellen, his sister, and her endless questions. Why was she unable to accept his viewpoint and instead, prattled on about women's rights? It was the influence of Bridie, without a doubt, and that very name unsettled him once more, adding to further irritation. She posted newspapers and magazines to Ellen that filled her head with foolishness and ideas best suited to Dublin and not, Donegal. Ellen continually agitated to go to Bridie in London and find work. So far, his parents had refused permission, but he knew it was just a matter of time.

As Liam assumed ever more charge of the family farm his opinion carried weight and he joined his voice to that of his parents, insisting that she stay. He still bore a grudge against Bridie and the idea of Ellen living with her was hard to stomach. It was Bridie who filled Ellen's head up with female nonsense. It was best she stayed home and married, like all sensible girls. That was the way of the world. Yet, Patsy O'Hara had glanced her way more than once and that had not gone unnoticed. The O'Hara's were not to his liking and not to be trusted. Sean, Patsy's brother, had, without doubt, been an ardent Redmond supporter, content to wait for Home Rule whenever the British saw fit to grant it. It was not to see Ireland remain under their yoke that the men of 1916 had given up their lives. He pondered over Patsy's interest and what it might mean. It was indeed a worry and best not encouraged.

Liam finished his pint and with a terse 'goodnight,' left the pub. *No time like the present*, he thought, as he knocked on Joe's door.

A gruff bark responded, 'What do you want?'

Liam was never one to baulk at anything, but Joe's brusque manner did not auger well. 'It's about Brendan,' he hollered through the still-closed door.

'What about him? What has he to do with you anyway?'

'Look, Joe,' replied Liam, 'Brendan keeps coming to the farm every morning and he is a great help, but he needs to be in school.'

'Well run him off if you don't want him around.'

'You know that's not the case, but he needs schooling. He will listen to you if you tell him he has to attend.'

The door creaked slowly open, and Joe stared at Liam, antipathy oozing from every pore. Shrugging, he responded with a pithy tone, 'Right, I will tell him. Now clear off. Don't know why he hangs around the likes of you anyway. Aye, sure he won't bother you too much longer, we are off to Scotland shortly.'

Suppressing his frustration, Liam continued his trek back up the laneway. Donal would need some assistance getting to bed and Liam was never sure when his brothers were around. Ciaran certainly had a match earlier on and Sheamus was always gone when there was a lull in the farm-work. Sarah and Ellen were lounging by the fire while Josie and Kathleen chatted away in the corner. He made himself some tea and carried a cup into his father. Daily, Donal seemed to become more disabled and worry once again beset Liam. Once Donal was settled, there was little else left to do that evening, so he slipped out by the back door, in no mood to listen to Ellen and her endless questions. He strode up the lane into the silent night, moonlight, his only companion.

Chapter 9

Ellen knew she irritated Liam with her constant questions, but she desperately needed to understand differing viewpoints. She still bore him a slight grudge because he had been the cause of Bridie leaving so abruptly. She felt entitled to badger him for answers, yet it was a hopeless exercise as he had only one stream of thought. She was maddened with his reluctance to listen to other opinions and how blinkered this closed attitude made him appear. The few days before that fateful Christmas had been so enlightening. Ellen had enjoyed every spare moment with Bridie, picking her brains, as she attempted to decipher the competing strands of thought that caused and continued to generate so much conflict in Ireland. The English stamp now heralded the arrival of the much-anticipated letter from London. Bridie wrote regularly, often enclosing newspapers and journals, material which Ellen avidly devoured. Whenever the post arrived, Ellen speedily undertook her chores and then retired to the barn where she could read undisturbed.

Bridie's letters were chatty but informative. They always began with anecdotes from the hospital, cheery references to the difficulties of living, once more, with a group of other women and descriptions of life in a big city like London. Bridie recounted how ignorant she had been when she left Donegal and although Bridie knew Ellen was still only sixteen, how important it was to understand the world around her and the one in which she lived. Josie and Bridie might be sisters, but their experiences were vastly different. Ellen was aware that Bridie's life journey had shaped her perspective in such a way, it now bore little resemblance to her mother's more insular understanding. As Bridie's letters grew in length and regularity, Josie wondered what on earth she had to say and from time to time queried the content. Ellen, with some reluctance, gave her mother Bridie's letters to read. Josie soon grew bored with what she regarded as 'Bridie's ramblings,' and lost interest as the months slipped by and the letters became less newsy and more instructive.

Bridie's Donegal timbre sang through her writing and Ellen was surrounded by her presence as she began the latest missive. *Ellen*, intoned Bridie, *Remember the Walshe's? Our families used to be quite close, and Annie was my best friend when we were growing up. Well, I met her brother Danny on the train when I was returning to Dublin after Christmas, and we have stayed in touch. Leaving Donegal broadened my perspective but from chatting to Danny, I am gaining deeper insight into how women are disadvantaged in so many ways. If much of what I write goes over your head, do not worry but it helps my understanding to express these ideas in my own words. I am, like yourself, still learning. In time, you will have questions of your own and these letters might provide some answers.*

Bridie's thoughts did not focus on the current, Nationalist conflict in Ireland, but centred instead on women and their place in the world. Ellen's mind drifted, and she could feel her eyelids starting to close as, Bridie's letter became more intense. Determinedly, shaking her head, she concentrated, as Bridie drew on Danny's theories to make her point.

He maintains, wrote Bridie, *that men have a power granted to them culturally and through the legal system. He believes the main disadvantage working men have is their class, which impedes their access to education and proper, secure employment. By virtue of being male, however, they are granted autonomy over their wives and children. The majority of us women are poor, working-class with little education, sometimes none, so we have no power at all.* This concept did ignite some interest in Ellen. Although she could not articulate her thoughts clearly, her whole upbringing had inculcated the belief that the natural order dictated women were subordinate.

Ellen's confusion was apparent from her reply. *Bridie, please explain to me what you mean. Women have always been cared for by their husbands and even the marriage vows say we must obey. After all, it is men who do the work and provide.*

Well, replied Bridie, *I know a lot of what I write is difficult to take in but think of it this way. Men indeed do a major portion of work outside the home but rearing and caring for a family is work also. Anyway, many women work at home and away from family as well. Imagine a job needs to be completed. A man undertakes it and is paid a certain amount. Why is it that if a woman can perform the same work to a level of equal value, she is paid less because she is female? Does this make sense to you? Anecdotally, it is said women rule the hearth but that is just a panacea, especially when many women do not have a hearth only an empty, sometimes cold, fireplace.*

Between letters, which arrived with a steady regularity every three weeks, Ellen, contemplated the implications of the ideas presented. Just when she felt she had reached a satisfactory understanding another letter posed more questions.

Despite her growing interest, and wish to expand her knowledge, Ellen sometimes just loved receiving a letter that held no more complicated concept than the latest London fashions. If the bulky shape of the post indicated that a newspaper was enclosed, she now often sighed at the thought of the work ahead. However, overall, Ellen knew that not only did Bridie mean well but that it was essential in the Ireland of the early twentieth century to be educated and informed. By contrast, Bridie noticed from Ellen's responses that she had not just an enquiring mind but a natural writing ability, that she believed she herself lacked. She appreciated Ellen's sometimes lyrical turn of phrase and vivid descriptions whereas her own capacity to articulate her thoughts was often inadequate. It was not that she could not understand the nuances, but she did sometimes find it difficult to express them eloquently.

Today's post was bulky, but the enclosed magazine fascinated Ellen. The description of the hats worn at Ascot and the artistic impressions of some of the outfits was awe-inspiring. After some time perusing the pages, she turned to read the letter. Her interest had been aroused in the lives of some of the women Bridie encountered in the hospital. She was hoping the letter contained some insight into how English as opposed to Irish women, managed the daily demands of family and work.

Hope you enjoy the magazine, Ellen, began Bridie. *It displays the gulf between how a minority of women live and how the majority struggle. My hospital caters to some of the poorest men, women and children and Ascot is as far removed from them as it is from you in Donegal. Danny believes...* wrote Bridie. At that point, Ellen put away the letter for another time, knowing that any sentence that began with "Danny believes" would not be an easy read. 'Not reading the letter today?' remarked Josie, startling Ellen's reverie.

'No, it is a bit heavy, so I will read it later. She seems to be very close to Danny Walsh, she is always quoting him.'

'Aye, and he was always a nice lad. Can I read it or is it full of her "ramblings"?'

'Here, Mammy, take it. You will enjoy the fashion bit, anyway.' Ellen wandered off to complete her chores and left Josie with the letter.

For once, Josie read it through, and a worried frown creased her forehead. She knew that Bridie had notions, but she did not want Ellen's head filled with ideas beyond what she could attain as a young, Donegal lass. Josie resolved to write to Bridie and ask her for some restraint. Her dearest wish was that Ellen would settle nearby at some point with a nice young man and give her grandchildren before she got too old herself.

That night, tucked up warmly in bed, Ellen, finished the letter. The opening line almost made her put it aside a second time, but she felt she owed it to Bridie, to continue. *Danny believes that radical political change is needed so poverty is alleviated, and women have full, equal rights. Women may have obtained the right to vote but we must be thirty before we can exercise it, whereas all men can vote from age twenty-one. What does that tell you about our worldview? Gender and class are the greatest barriers to advancement.* Ellen made an audible groan on reading this line, but she persevered. *Conversely, although power is denied to women, social class and education confer a status and that can transcend the power the law grants the working-class male. Middle-class and upper-class women are advantaged over working-class men because of education and economic comfort. Many of those women have been instrumental in promoting change. During the general strike in Dublin in 1913, I met women who were not held back by society's idea of what was appropriate for their gender. They rolled up their sleeves and helped those in need. Women who are trapped in poverty just struggle, often so ground down by daily life, that to battle for equality is just impossible.* Surprisingly, this struck a chord with Ellen, and she fell asleep formulating questions she would pose in her reply.

Ellen particularly appreciated when Bridie wrote about the social conditions, she encountered rather than political ideology, although she understood all were interconnected. Ellen replied, asking Bridie to explain more about the effects of poverty in both Dublin and London.

When I first arrived, in Dublin, she responded, *the deprivation astounded me. I never appreciated how lucky we were to live on a farm in Donegal because, despite the struggle, we still had fresh vegetables and milk. I never felt real hunger or cold. Yet, everywhere there was hardship, unseen, and hidden by a wild landscape and the isolation of our home. My eyes were opened in Dublin and what I saw was heart-rending. Women and children, barely clad, and grey from want of nutrition. Children too hungry to cry, with open sores on arms and legs, and mothers worn out trying to do their best to give comfort but needing comfort of their own. This same poverty was around me in Donegal, but I never noticed. So, look at your surroundings and try not to become too caught up in your own little life. Of course, Liverpool was no better and the more I understand, the more I realise how poverty festers everywhere. It is all around me now in London and patently obvious among many of the patients who frequent the hospital.*

The letters continued and Ellen's interest blossomed until she genuinely looked forward to pondering the ideas posed. Bridie constantly encouraged Ellen to read; hence all the newspapers and articles posted to her.

Ellen, I am reading so much myself now and I love getting your feedback and thoughts. I will send as much as I can to you as I know there is a dearth of material in Donegal and anyway, what is available is too expensive for you.

Ellen surprised herself with a genuine smile at the thought of the post to come, all groaning now left in the past. The letters and articles continued unabated, always instructive, but also necessitating contemplation, as they challenged the societal order dictated by Ellen's family, the Church, and the wider held belief of a woman's place. The continual references to Danny did not go unnoticed by Ellen and she made the mistake of enquiring about him one evening. 'Liam, you know our old neighbour Danny Walsh?'

'Aye, I used to, until he donned the British uniform. I have no use for his kind anymore,' responded Liam, and Ellen wisely said no more.

Mindful of the letter she had received from her sister Josie and anxious not to upset her further, Bridie's letters became more muted in tone. She gently suggested that Ellen read as much as possible and to remember that it was up to her and her generation to argue and fight for equality. *The law needs to change but so does the social context. Everyone needs equality of access and opportunity, regardless of gender. Unfortunately*, continued Bridie, forgetting her resolve to be more circumspect in her words, *many of us only feel we possess worth if we can look down on someone else. The only value many a downtrodden male can exercise is through his subjugation of women. I firmly believe that equality will always be a struggle if men feel they are losing their significance by granting women more recognition. This is especially true when men have minimal status in any other sphere.* Bridie's adherence to the Church of her youth had waned but she was loath to criticise it too forcefully, as it was still held in high esteem by all in Donegal. She just cautioned Ellen to form her own ideas and not be blindly bound by the rules and strictures of others and to question the Church rules as she searches for her path. *Many of their rules subordinate women and exonerate men, regardless of their actions. When you are older, and needless-to-say, with your parents' agreement, if you wish to come to England, you can have a home with me but for now, read as much as you can.*

Each night, Ellen mused long and hard on the perspective on life presented by Bridie. As witnessed at Christmas, even her attitude to the Irish question conflicted with Liam's. 'I didn't nurse British soldiers,' said Bridie. 'I nursed wounded men, men who were fighting a war because they had no choice. Yes, most were English, but there were Irish too, Scottish and French. What I have learnt is not to judge. There is never only one way forward, but it is always those without money and power who are forced to fight. If you are a woman, you battle even harder because if there are men with very little, there are women with even less.'

Some of the women that Bridie had spoken of were new to Ellen. She realised that throughout history there were always women who battled for equality. The celebration of Anna Haslam, as she cast her vote, on 14th December 1918, was well over by the time the news reached Donegal, but it was still exhilarating to read of the event. Here was someone who had fought for the rights of women all her life and finally, at almost ninety years of age, saw her work come to fruition. There had been division among the feminist factions fighting for civil and social rights and disagreement about the best methods to achieve their aims. Yet, when this elderly feminist went to cast her vote, all were united, and cheered with pride and joy as they presented her with a bouquet of flowers, a cascade of orange and green. This spectacle infused Ellen with a renewed purpose, and she vowed not to become just another farmer's wife submerged in his life but to learn to understand her own world and achieve her personal goals. Bridie may have left behind a naïve young girl in Donegal, but it was noticeable she was now writing to a young woman with burgeoning and ongoing questions and simmering with a determination to succeed and find answers.

Once Ellen took stock and gazed around, she wondered how she had blithely ignored her surroundings for so long. Tiny dwellings, some constructed of little more than mud, housed families of ten, twelve, or even more. Travelling families squatted in ditches. Journeymen, roaming from farm to farm working for food and scraps, sometimes just shelter for the night. The same level of bare subsistence that Bridie described in Dublin existed everywhere. It was just scattered in Donegal and not as compacted as the community in the city, therefore not always so visible. Although Josie was worried that some of Bridie's ideas would unsettle Ellen making her restless and anxious to leave, she did appreciate her growing sensitivity to those less fortunate. She realised she had neglected that aspect of her daughter's education, still viewing her as too young to see such hardship. She resolved to bring Ellen with her whenever she could, as unbeknownst to the younger members of her family, Josie was a regular visitor to the more poverty-stricken families around the area, dispensing what she could spare in the way of food and clothing.

Ellen accompanied Josie on her next trip but despaired at the little she could do. Josie explained that any spare food or old clothing was needed and welcomed. 'It isn't much, because none of us has a lot, but even a small amount helps. I must bring Sarah next time. It will do that little lady good to see how some people have to survive.'

Ellen felt a fleeting satisfaction at the thanks received whenever she was able to hand out some bread even if it was a little stale, but soon dismissed such a self-congratulatory and wasteful emotion. There was no pride in handing a canister of milk to a needy mother, often struggling with a baby in her arms and toddlers hanging on her skirts. Always close, a further bond was forged between Josie and Ellen, a depth of understanding that went beyond mother and daughter. Ellen began a journey in her own right with a dawning comprehension that women, although not equal in the eyes of the law or Church, were the glue that held families together. Women, she realised, were in many ways stronger than men. They often held a dual role, enduring hours of soulless work on farms or in the markets, while still managing to keep a home. The saddest sight was a family where the mother had passed away with the resultant helplessness housed in the fathers' stoop, soon to be reduced to despair.

Josie cautioned Ellen, 'You must keep your emotions apart, or you will be no use. You can only do what you can. Bridie's political ideals are required for change but in the meantime, we are needed.'

Josie's words struck an unusual chord within Ellen. It was apparent both sisters were socially aware but whereas Bridie was political, her mother was "hands-on". Ellen's fascination with the lives of women and how they managed, despite straitened and difficult circumstances was increasing and would blossom fully in time.

Ellen's sister, Sarah, had no interest in Ellen's developing ideas. Sarah, at fourteen, was still maturing but she enjoyed the interest of many of the young lads around. Her growing attractiveness paused more than one roving eye especially at Sunday Mass where, instead of bowing in piety, glances surreptitiously swept her way. She listened to Ellen, but the subtler ideas went over her head through lack of engagement.

Naturally, Kathleen had little interest in Ellen's newfound feminist ideas but that was to be expected at the tender age of ten. She was quite happy, living in her own world, tending her beloved garden. If the garden had no imperfections, Kathleen spent her days either playing or walking the dogs, perhaps helping her mother prepare meals. Strangely enough, Ellen found Ciaran the most receptive and the one with whom she could argue and discuss a variety of issues.

Ciaran had an easy manner and had time for all his sisters. He was a firm follower of the local GAA and after that, came Sinn Fein and politics. Class relations and women's equality were not issues he had ever considered but he was happy to indulge Ellen and counter her arguments if he could. He was surprised at the growing maturity of her questions and the analysis she brought to bear beyond her years. For him, Home Rule and Irish freedom were paramount, yet he listened and debated as Ellen attempted to discern and dissect her ideas in a clear manner, so she could come to an understanding of what she herself believed. Sometimes, as he sat quietly by the river, fishing rod finely balanced, he pondered over his chats with Ellen. Fishing was Ciaran's escape from the farm and politics but more and more, he pondered on Ellen's ideas and beliefs. To that end, Ciaran procured copies of the feminist newspaper, *The Irish Citizen* for her to read if only, he mused, to escape her questions and allow him to return to the joys of a possible salmon catch in peace. Most of the newspapers were old issues some dating back to 1912. Where he procured them was a mystery, but regardless, Ellen devoured them. Many of the issues affecting women were still unresolved despite the war and the achievement of the vote.

Hannah Sheehy Skeffington intrigued Ellen and, the more she read and investigated, she realised how valid Bridie's words were. Education may be the key to advancement for women but there was still a long way to go to achieve equality. An article on teachers' salary scales intrigued her. Female teachers and male teachers were equally educated but by virtue of their gender, women were paid less than men. An old issue from March 1913 highlighted a lecture, "Women's Place in the World", presented by the Rev. M. O'Kane. He believed he had a special insight into women and this knowledge came straight from God. His celestial connection enabled him to discern that a woman's place in the world was at home, in the kitchen. The more Ellen read and stretched her mind, the more she wanted to read and learn before she settled down to her expected role in Donegal, of the early 20th century.

1919 was a year of turmoil across the country and the arrest of Dr McGinley, in Donegal, incensed Liam. A large hostile crowd protested outside the courthouse and Liam was right in their midst. His presence did not go unnoticed by the authorities and although there were no repercussions, life within "Droimreagh", had a further added tension.

As Christmas 1919 passed into spring 1920, Ellen's desire to move to London increased as did pressure on her parents to give her permission. The turmoil within the country as Ireland attempted to free itself from British domination was known as "The War of Independence". It was a guerrilla war and reprisals on both sides were harsh and brutal. The imposition by Britain of a disorderly force, known as "The Black and Tans", who carried out brutal reprisals on civilians, heightened tensions still further. It created understandable anxiety within Josie and Donal and a reluctance to allow Ellen to travel to London. Bridie herself, suggested she postpone her trip until hostilities were concluded. Liam was adamant she should stay home for her own safety and reluctantly, Ellen knew she had no option but to concur.

As 1920 drifted along, the horror on both sides continued. Liam, Sheamus and Ciaran were often missing at night, their activities a closely guarded secret. On the 21st of November 1920, known as "Bloody Sunday", Republicans killed fourteen British operatives. Reprisal was swift and brutal. Members of the infamous and disorderly auxiliary division joined the Royal Irish Constabulary as they made their way to Croke Park, where a football match was underway. They opened fire and killed fourteen civilians, wounding sixty-five others.

The dawning of 1921, however, brought some hope that the war would soon be over, and it eventually ceased in July 1921. Seeds were sown, however, for further conflict as negotiations for a Treaty got underway.

Tension in the house and beyond made Ellen disengage from politics. Privately and hidden, especially from Sarah, Ellen started a journal recounting small anecdotes of life on the farm and fledgling ideas of what she wished for the future.

The summer brought warm and sunny weather and Ellen and Sarah felt they could move freely within their parish and enjoy meeting companions their own age, without fear. One love Ellen shared with her sister Sarah was dancing and she had noticed Patsy O'Hara was increasingly showing her some welcome attention.

The monthly church social was a "must-attend" for all the young people in the surrounding parishes. Ellen was now on the verge of turning nineteen and was basking in the increasing interest of not just Patsy, but many of the young men in the area. She was tall and slim with coils of long dark curly hair and frank bluish-green eyes. Ellen was confident in herself and, when she saw Patsy O'Hara make his way across the floor, she carefully composed her features to play it a little cool. She liked him because of the glint in his eye and because he made her laugh. He also never uttered a political word which was a welcome relief from Liam's one-way discussions, almost tantamount to lectures. She could sense his interest but had also heard from her friend, Mary, that Patsy had his eye on more than one girl. That was a slight annoyance, but possibly more a sting to her pride, when she was not ready yet to commit to a relationship. She still had dreams of joining Bridie and making something of herself, beyond marriage and Donegal. But it was fun to be admired by someone like Patsy and to whirl around the floor to the envy of many a girl, especially when her dream of London was currently still stymied.

Chapter 10

Patsy O'Hara was the youngest of two boys and the charmer in the family. His dress was fashionable for rural Donegal, as Patsy had a deep-seated dread, he might be mistaken for a farm boy. That prospect was something not to be realised. He did not possess conventional good looks but his curly hair with a ginger hue, combined with roguish eyes, was the passport that enabled him to achieve whatever he desired. *Until now anyway*, he thought.

The family had a small carpentry and furniture firm which provided a comfortable if not quite prosperous living, for them all. Patsy wanted to expand the business with his father and brother but so far, his ideas had little traction. Politics was always a burning topic at home and his father and brother were insistent that until the political situation was resolved, there would be no change. Politics held little interest for him, other than as a barrier, preventing the implementation of his plans for the development of the family firm. He had hoped once The War of Independence was over that some of his ideas might be considered but it now seemed more time was needed before his brother, Sean, was ready to engage.

Patsy studied Ellen McShane from across the room and liked what he saw. He had noticed her on and off over the past few months, perhaps even longer, but tonight, she looked especially attractive. He knew her brothers well, although he had no time for Liam who was in Patsy's opinion, too sour and morose. Sheamus was alright, much easier going and if he played his cards right, Sheamus could put a good word in for him with Ellen, even introduce him to the other sister, Sarah. She was possibly a bit too young, but another year or two and she would be a beauty.

He wandered over to Ellen and asked her to dance. Nodding agreement, Ellen politely joined Patsy on the floor, and it was this coolness that fascinated him. He could not resist a challenge and especially relished a challenge with a pretty woman. Contrary, to what he surmised, Ellen did like him but had no wish to be part of his fan club. Patsy liked to dance, feeling it was a necessary accomplishment for an aspiring gentleman, such as himself. Ellen was light in his arms as they gracefully whirled around, circuiting the floor. Politics and business were far from his thoughts as he held her lithe body and casually flirted, hoping to make some headway with her.

Patsy was aware that he was considered shallow, by some people anyway, and the idea was intriguing. *What was shallow?* he wondered. Was it a synonym for ambition and was ambition to be excoriated because it was not in agreement with a general social consensus? If so, then to a certain extent he could not dispute that doubtful opinion of himself. There was such a focus on the political situation that to be personally ambitious was not understood and considered a fault. He was full of ideas and knew if he had a chance to develop them, he could expand the business beyond Donegal.

His father's caution was acceptable to a point, because after all, his father was getting old and had seen a lot of political turmoil, but his older brother was a different matter. In many ways, Patsy was the antithesis of his brother. Sean was steady, contented with his lot, and wary of taking any risk until the current political upheaval had abated and peace assured. Whereas Patsy just knew that now was the right time to take a chance and move forward, Sean felt to remain steady and small, was more secure until the country settled. Patsy argued, unsuccessfully, that as Dublin emerged as a new capital city, there was bound to be a building boom and demand for furniture would escalate. This view was not an encouragement for Sean, quite the opposite. His response was more cautious, arguing that additional finance would be needed to purchase other machinery. Perhaps investment in new premises would be required and the extra employees would mean an escalating wage-roll. Patsy suspected his father had some reserves of capital but without Sean's input, there would be no access to the finance needed. His frustration was palpable. He knew if he had access to resources, he could strike out on his own and be assured of success. It was only his father and brother who were holding him back from pursuing his ambitions. Trying to persuade them seemed like a hopeless task so Patsy's thoughts were wandering in another direction, in a bid to advance his prospects.

He first noticed Teresa when he paid a trip to Killybegs and stopped into the local pub for a pint. Her father was the owner of what appeared to be the most prosperous public house in the bustling little town. Fishing was the main activity in Killybegs and, as such, it was always lively, with a constant demand for refreshment from thirsty men. More importantly, she was an only child and consequently, likely to inherit. Such was his confidence, he did not doubt if he displayed an interest, combined with his usual charm, she would reciprocate and who knew where that might lead. She was not as attractive physically as Ellen, being a little on the plump side with rather a long nose, but sometimes other attributes were more important. He had to admit she did have a friendly, sunny smile, and he could tell the lads appreciated her amply endowed figure as she bent over to wipe the table, before smoothly placing the always eagerly awaited pint.

Of late, Ellen had been uppermost in his thoughts but not for marriage. When an ambitious man married, he needed a wife with money. He knew Ellen was more of a romantic, but in time she would understand that there was no future without financial comfort. Eventually, she would learn that a husband with money was the key to her own survival. For now, if he were to court Teresa, his budding relationship with Ellen would have to cease. Patsy believed, however, there were endless possibilities in the future and to discount Ellen totally would be foolish. They might suit each other very well later on, when they were both settled and more comfortable. She might appreciate his head on a pillow some morning in the future and he knew he would enjoy seeing hers. So, shallow he may be to some, but he believed he was just ambitious, with depths yet to be plumbed.

Teresa enjoyed the attention Patsy was paying her, but she had buckets of common sense. She knew he desired more, and it was not her pretty face alone that interested him, it was very much what came with it. She was determined not to settle for just anyone. The man she married had to want her and not only her probable inheritance. As such, she made Patsy work hard to gain her affection but also, with the help of her father, she ensured the pub would always be hers and hers alone.

Patsy made the trip to Killybegs at least twice a week and to his surprise, he started to enjoy himself. Teresa had a keen sense of humour with a quirky turn of phrase, and he found himself almost looking forward to seeing her. A friendship, followed by a firm understanding, crept in, taking him by surprise. A fleeting thought that words and conversation can be more intimate than sex briefly crossed his mind, to be quickly dismissed as an idea not to be countenanced. He settled for the fact that she might not be the prettiest, but she had a brain and knew how the pub business was managed.

For her part, Teresa enjoyed the rogue in Patsy and the light, sparring, banter in which they indulged, was a welcome distraction from otherwise rather boring evenings. She knew he was ambitious and would provide a comfortable life and at almost twenty-six, she felt it was time to marry and have children. More importantly, Teresa believed she could manage him. Patsy thought he was making the right choice when he eventually popped the question, the notion he would not be totally in charge, was not one he ever entertained.

The necessity to cool his friendship with Ellen did not stop Patsy from still finding her attractive. On the off chance his plans with Teresa did not work out to his satisfaction, he continued to pay her some attention. As for Ellen, the fantasy that was Patsy continued to weave a spell around her as she blossomed into a beautiful, attractive, young woman. She knew she was not in love with him, but she enjoyed his attention, even if it was a little erratic. She remembered how she had shivered with delight as they danced and how, when he felt they were unobserved, his hand had caressed her back and strayed to the nape of her neck. Common sense told her he was not reliable. Lately, a few rumours had circulated that he was seeing a young woman called Teresa from the neighbouring town. Teresa's father was a well-known publican and Ellen had no doubt that status would attract Patsy. His ambivalence was more noticeable lately, as was her perception of his wandering eye.

Donal continued to become more infirm, and tragedy struck the entire family in September, when he collapsed from a suspected stroke and died within days. The family were united in grief and Liam became the rock that held them all together. He took control, organising the entire funeral arrangements and supporting Josie, aware her seeming detachment at the graveside was just a veneer, easily cracked. At night, he comforted Kathleen when she sobbed in her bed, too young to understand why her father was gone forever. It was only with Joe that his usual gruff demeanour was apparent but even that was tempered, as Joe had also lost his father.

Bridie was unable to return to Donegal for the funeral, but her letters brought them all some comfort. Patsy was unusually attentive, and Ellen began to wonder if the rumours about other girls, particularly Teresa, were accurate. As the family were bereaved, they could not socialise, but on Sundays, after Mass, Patsy made a point of talking to her, and she looked forward to those few moments all week. She was reluctant to question him about the gossip, not wanting to show too much interest. Still, curiosity overcame her and in as offhand a manner as possible, she enquired, 'Patsy, I hear you make regular trips to Killybegs and it's not for the fish.'

'Ellen, you know better than to listen to all the blather around here. Sure, you know I only have eyes for you.'

As time passed, however, rumours of an engagement began to circulate more frequently, to the point they could not be ignored. The definite news that Patsy was getting married stung, but only her pride. Ellen renewed her efforts to be allowed to visit Bridie in London. She had just turned nineteen and, worn down by grief and pestering, Josie agreed. Ellen could travel to London in the spring of 1922. The promise of London enabled Ellen to keep her head high amongst those peers who always delighted in another's misfortune.

Christmas 1921 was a sombre affair in Donegal. Donal's passing and

Bridie's commitments in London, meant two vital components were missing from what used to be a happy occasion. The new year was welcomed with relief, although the pending trip planned by Ellen in the spring was now a source of tension in "Droimreagh". Josie regretted her agreement to allow Ellen to join Bridie and seemed intent on forcing her to stay. At the same time, Josie appeared oblivious to other undercurrents in the house. Brendan was always a regular visitor, but Joe was now appearing more and more often, and the ensuing heated discussions with Liam, increased tension all round. It was undeniable that Joe felt through his father he was entitled to some share of the farm and was cheated out of a rightful inheritance.

Liam shook with anger as he roared, 'The will is clear. The farm was left to Josie and our father was just a caretaker.'

In response, Joe fumed, 'I'm entitled to something. I was the firstborn.'

Despite Joe's demands, the will was indeed clear and title to the farm, in the natural course of events, would cede to Josie's firstborn son, Liam. Liam was his usual belligerent self. In no uncertain terms, he told Joe where to go and this incensed matters further. Liam had no time for petty arguments, especially with a half-brother where relations had always been fraught. It was an irritation and distraction as trouble was now brewing with the signing of the Anglo-Irish Treaty. Liam knew what side he was on and planned on being well prepared to play his part. Yet the rancour harboured by Joe was not something that would easily be resolved.

Joe, always infused with a rancid whiff, one that continually seeped and lingered, left a trailing reminder that his rage was not to be readily dissipated. Brendan could sense the tension between his father and Liam, but either did not want to or could not understand what it was all about. He loved them both and wanted them to get along and his father's threats to ban him from the farm, or worse, to leave Donegal altogether, worried him and made him anxious. The small cottage on the edge of the village that Joe and Brendan called home, remained a cold, inhospitable place since Brendan's mother died. It was the warmth and comfort of the farm that drew Brendan there, almost daily, that, and his love of Liam and the animals. He dreaded that his father's acrimony would develop into an insistence that he stay away from "Droimreagh", altogether.

Ellen had remained in Donegal, unable to resist her mother's pleas to stay until August. Spring had been harsh with snow piled on the ground and, consequently, planting delayed. April had been hectic with Liam shouting orders and demanding everyone help in the fields. As usual, Brendan hovered around, and no one mentioned anymore that he should be in school. He was a tremendous asset and understood what Liam needed doing every day, until Joe would show up, demanding he leave.

'Don't be helping that lot. They stole my inheritance, and yours, aye, they did, but I'll get them yet.'

Throwing an apologetic look over his shoulder, Brendan desultorily followed his father back down to their cottage.

May was Ellen's favourite month, and Josie seemed brighter. They rambled the hills together, always stopping at Donal's grave. 'He was a good man, your father,' was Josie's usual comment. 'A quiet man, his family, the farm, and a pint, was enough for him. He used to wonder how he came to have a firebrand like Liam for a son, but you know he was proud of you all, aye he was.'

In early June, Josie, now more at ease herself, surprised Ellen with, 'Time we planned your trip to Bridie. I will write this evening. I would feel better if she met you in Dublin, safer like, for the crossing. Is that alright with you, Ellen? We will get some material for a few new things. Thanks for staying as long as you have, I know you were disappointed not to leave sooner but I needed you.' The two women hugged in the way that only women who have an unqualified love and are in communion with each other, can so do. 'Let us try for late August, before it gets too busy with the autumn crossings.'

Liam now held the reins within the household and that meant the purse strings. The request for some money to buy material for dresses was not an issue as Liam was more than willing to indulge his sisters. 'Both you and Sarah,' he began, 'and you too, Kathleen,' as he saw her look up with a frown, 'you all deserve a new dress after the effort you put in for the planting. Is it in Killybegs you buy this stuff?' There were eager nods, and Liam promised to have some money in a week. They planned to have the dresses ready for the next "crossroads dance" the first social occasion they could attend since the death of their father. Propriety demanded a lengthy mourning, which included absence from such events, and they had observed this religiously.

True to his word Liam handed over money the following Friday. The girls checked what patterns they already had and, that evening, they sorted what else might need to be purchased on their trip. The next day, Saturday, they hitched a ride on Billy's cart, smothering giggles into carefully positioned handkerchiefs whilst at the same time, managing to make pleasant conversation. Sarah was the most talented at dressmaking, so she took charge of the purchasing. Material in bright summery colours was chosen and cut from two bolts of cloth, enough for three dresses. In high good humour, they returned home, already planning to start cutting the first dress that evening.

As soon as they entered the farmhouse, they could sense trouble. Liam was glowering in the corner, Bridie's letter of reply to Josie, shaking in his hand. 'So, this is the reason you wanted a dress, Ellen? I thought it was preparation for the first dance after our father's death. Well, you can forget it, you are not going to London.' Liam stormed out with a slam of the door. The hushed silence that followed his departure marred any lingering enjoyment of the trip to Killybegs.

Ellen turned anguished eyes towards Josie. 'Don't,' Josie said, 'say nothing now. I will sort it for you with Liam, but we have to let him calm down.'

'What did Bridie say?' murmured Ellen.

'Well, you cannot go over until the end of September. She said she is looking forward to having you, but she arranged for a friend to stay with her for three weeks, from the end of August.'

'What friend?' enquired Ellen.

'She never mentioned any name. At least it gives us some time to work on Liam.'

In the meantime, Bridie, now a fully qualified nurse, had permission to leave the Nurses' Home and find accommodation of her own. She rented a series of inadequate rooms, moving regularly, before stumbling across an advert on the hospital notice board. Although it was a little more expensive than she had anticipated, she agreed to rent what was described as a small, two-bedroom cottage. It was near the hospital and offered her the privacy she always desired. The cottage consisted of one main downstairs room with a tiny, cupboard size, bedroom to the side and an outside lavatory. A creaky ladder led to an attic room, and this was where Bridie would sleep. Days off were now spent in the markets, hunting for bargains to furnish the cottage and make it home.

Danny continued to expound on his ideals and as the year waned, achieved some minimal success. Bridie followed his career with interest and, when she received news that he would be in London to speak to a possible publisher, she arranged leave so they could meet and spend time together.

After dinner, that first evening, she brought him back for tea. They spent the evening discussing his ideas and his deepening despair at what he considered the senseless violence on all sides. Soon his voice faltered as sleep began to take hold. Tired now herself, Bridie felt more discussion would be too exhausting. She placed her teacup on the saucer and leaning over, kissed Danny full on the lips. Danny appeared surprised at first, and then questioning? At a signal from Bridie, he responded instantly and rising, took her hand, gently steering her towards the bedroom.

Bridie's relationship with Harry had fulfilled a necessary need after the trauma of the war and had undoubtedly, given much-needed harbour and comfort. Her encounter now with Danny was passionate and tempestuous, without any boundaries, arousing an eroticism that she had not known she possessed. He was both loving and demanding and it was the early hours before they both fell into a satisfied, slumber. Danny stayed with her for the three days of his London trip, and, during that time, Bridie told him all about Harry.

'You don't have to explain anything to me, Bridie. War changed us, and we all made choices that in hindsight, we regret, or perhaps those choices made us strong, defined who we really are.' Before leaving, he promised her, 'I will be back in August, but you must come to Dublin soon, promise me. We have something special Bridie, you and I.'

Chapter 11

The signing of the Treaty, on 6th December 1921, heralded a ceasefire, but the agreement to allow six counties of Ulster to remain under the rule of the United Kingdom was the catalyst for further trouble. The new year heralded discord over the signing of the Treaty that was vicious and inflexible on both sides. One side saw betrayal, the other side compromise, and battle lines were drawn. By a narrow majority, the Irish Provisional Government supported the Treaty while Republicanism, under the stewardship of Eamon de Valera, opposed it. Conflict ensued and, by the end of June 1922, the bitter Irish Civil war was raging in earnest. Where once Irishmen and women fought alongside each other to defeat a common enemy, they now ranged on two differing sides, as disagreement over the Treaty split family, friends, and neighbours.

Patsy O'Hara railed against the continuing political upheaval, almost believing there was a conspiracy afoot, to prevent him from implementing his plans for the advancement of the family firm. Sean, his brother, would not countenance any change to the business until the Civil War was ended. Instead, he had taken temporary leave to train in Finner Military Camp, in preparation to play his part in protecting the new Ireland, firmly at one with Michael Collins and the signing of the Treaty. When not engaged in Free State activities, Sean was content to spend his evenings at home with his new wife and read the latest political developments.

Liam McShane was vehemently opposed to the Treaty, as were Sheamus and Ciaran. There was no doubt in Ellen's mind that they all undertook clandestine activities, but she had no firm details. The entire family were very much anti-Treaty and Liam expected all members to concur with this viewpoint. A contrary opinion was anathema and not to be considered. Ellen mentally thanked Bridie for her counsel over the years and for all her informative letters. She was still unsure of why or what she believed but her contact with Bridie had broadened her perspective. Bridie might have an opposing viewpoint, but she never blocked conversation and accepted there were many sides with all believing their positions were well-founded. The lectures each evening from Liam, without the possibility of debate, were exhausting. What made Liam believe right favoured him and everyone else was totally wrong was an enigma. Ellen could appreciate the viewpoint that having struggled for so long, that to only accept 26 counties was a betrayal. Equally, she could accept that gaining control of 26 counties and then focussing on achieving the final six, was also a valid stance. At least it was worthy of discussion, but Liam stifled all argument branding those who did not agree with him as traitors. Diplomacy, and the urge to persuade Liam to allow her to leave, bade Ellen keep silent. She fervently hoped she would soon be in London. Bridie was well travelled, and in Ellen's youthful opinion, sophisticated and worldly with a life full of excitement, adventure, and new ideas. She intended to be like her one day, if only, she was eventually able to leave home.

Despite Josie's best efforts to influence Liam, so far, her efforts were to no avail. There was no doubt that at one point Josie had hoped Ellen would stay and settle down. From time to time, she had enquired about Patsy ineffectually hiding her wish that marriage might be a possibility. Tactfully, Ellen had dampened her barely concealed yearning, gently outlining why he was not a man worthy of her consideration. She was personally relieved she realised how fickle he was before she committed her affections. Patsy would never be enough for Ellen if he did not respect her, and she was now more determined than ever to find her own path. Having persuaded her mother of this fact, Josie was now firmly on her side, despite some reservations about Bridie. Josie wholeheartedly loved Bridie but slightly disapproved of her suffragette sympathies, believing a woman's place was in the home and not on the picket line. One thing Ellen could not utter was the suspicion that Bridie no longer attended Mass on Sundays. This was too shocking an idea to voice within the house but gave Ellen an illicit thrill at something so daring. The very mention of such a possibility would be enough to block all chance of joining Bridie. It might even result in a visit from the elderly, but severe and autocratic, Fr Peter Clarke.

Having assuaged Josie's fears about Bridie's influence, Ellen had only to persuade Liam. A few of the figures that influenced Bridie were now well known to Ellen, but she kept her own counsel, afraid they might not be acceptable to Liam. Dr Kathleen Lynn for example, but others in the Republican movement had spurred Bridie to live her life outside the expected norm and achieve something for herself, but not all were now anti-Treaty. That stance alone would give Liam pause, possibly digging his heels in, and refusing to allow her travel.

Early October arrived with the predictable drop in temperature and no agreement from Liam. She had not anticipated he would be such a stumbling block or so immune to Josie's persuasion. Resignedly, Ellen accepted that she would be in Donegal for another Christmas, at least.

October sped by and November arrived dark and cold. On successive nights, Josie boiled a pot of potatoes that was hauled over and left in the barn. There was no mention of why but as if by osmosis, all the family knew the reason and took turns in assisting. Safe houses, providing refuge for those on the run, were a closely guarded secret and loose tongues, spread danger. If there were Free State forces in the area, an ebony cross was placed on the barn door as a warning for anti-Treaty Republicans to keep moving. Ellen, as part of the family, was expected to play her part and there was an automatic expectation she undertook any task requested without question, if it aided the anti-Treaty side. She submitted to the ritual, but her motivation was more to persuade Liam to grant permission for her trip to London. It was also to assist her mother who struggled with any heavy weights, so she volunteered regularly to heft the heavy iron pot over to the barn.

She now lugged the potatoes across the yard muttering under her breath. She hated the job, but it was a necessary tool for persuasion and, anyway, it was her turn. Besides, there was no bribing anyone else on this cold night to take her place, certainly not Sarah, and Kathleen was too young and unable to lift the heavy cauldron. The wind was raw, biting through her thin cardigan, while the searing heat from the handle of the pot scorched through well-worn gloves almost blistering her palms. Early frost crunched underfoot, glittering in competition with the stars. The charm and artistry of the night were lost on Ellen. She saw no beauty, she just wanted to be in the house by the fire with hot toast and tea, but that had to wait for a while. A small fire had to be set in the cavernous fireplace in the barn. Certain expertise was required as it had to be damped down as soon as possible otherwise, smoke would be a giveaway on a clear night, inviting enquiry from Free State forces. Heat was needed to dissipate the wintery chill and necessary strength, physical and emotional, was derived from the comforting taste of hot potatoes bathed in a little melting butter, all washed down by a jug of warm, freshly, strained milk. Ellen pondered for a moment about the men who might look for safety and linger in their barn and she hoped they appreciated the sustenance provided. Finally, she had to shake out the few blankets to be sure no mice had found a warm place to nest. Living on a farm she should have been well used to mice, but she still shuddered and jumped whenever they scurried nearby.

Preparations were almost finished with only one final task to be completed. Ellen checked the ebony cross was within reach of the barn door so it could be quickly accessed if needed. Chores concluded, she scuttled across to the house and pushed and bumped her way to a warm spot beside the roaring fire. This was only possible because two of her older brothers were not present. Their whereabouts and that of her third brother, Ciaran, were by common consent never questioned or discussed. This both intrigued and irritated Ellen. She assumed they were engaged in a covert operation on behalf of the Republican movement and her innate curiosity wanted more information. Her interest was piqued now by Ciaran, sitting across from her, noticing how strained he appeared to be. Thin, almost gaunt, his stillness seemed contrived and failed to hide a restless agitation. It would be a pointless exercise to ask questions, but Ellen determined to satisfy her inquisitiveness at the first opportunity.

The evening meal was now finished, and she sprawled comfortably in the chair. Dark brown, silky, tendrils of hair drifted unnoticed across her face as she gave herself up to the drowsiness induced by the fire. At ease now, the hypnotic effect of the dancing flames made her sleepy and so, at her mother's suggestion, she retired early to bed.

It may have been the unusual early night or the shuffle of footsteps from outside, but Ellen awoke in the early hours. Sarah and Kathleen were sound asleep in the bed beside her, both gently snoring. As the eldest girl, Ellen had the privilege of her own bed, but the beds were closely knit, side by side, in the small room. Anxious not to disturb them, she manoeuvred cautiously and crept stealthily towards the window to peer out into the gloom. The starry night illuminated her brother Ciaran, creeping gingerly across the yard to the barn. A small lantern, barely aglow, lit his way and he appeared to be carefully carrying a bucket or box of some sort. Interested, perhaps even nosy, but now, wide-awake, Ellen hastily threw on an old overcoat and sneaked outside. She entered the barn by the back door towards the end, furthest from the fireplace. It was pitch dark, and she had to pause for a few minutes to become accustomed to the gloom. Carefully, she made her way to a small loft that had, in years gone by, been the bedroom she shared with Sarah. The stairs always creaked on the third step, so she climbed up cautiously and avoided making any audible sound. Straw and sacking muffled all noise as she shuffled her way to peer over the edge.

A man lay in the semi-darkness on the blankets she had spread earlier that night. A quiver shuddered through his body at intervals and a moan, coupled with a sob, eerily broke the stillness of the night. Ciaran knelt beside him, his own trousers stained from the puddle of blood seeping from the injured man. Ellen could see Ciaran had a basin of water and was gently attempting to bathe the man's wounds. By contrast, in another corner, her other two brothers held a man at gunpoint. There was no shouting or cursing, but, even so, Ellen could sense their anger, and a fury, that radiated with a force that was almost physical. Possibly aware that sound would, at a minimum, disturb the family but also alert enemy forces that might be in the area, their faces betrayed what their voices could not utter. Furrowed and flushed red, they spewed vindictiveness and hate into the hushed silence of the barn. Then, surprisingly, Liam, possibly unable to contain himself despite the risk, stabbed accusingly at the shoulder of the hostage with his finger. It was difficult to hear, but Ellen caught the words.

'Betrayed your own... he is dead because of you, and Packie has been arrested, and may as well be dead too. If we find out ... is injured... another death on your conscience.'

Regardless of the gun pointed at his head, the response was defiant. 'The more dead, the better... I'm more of a Republican than you'll ever be, McShane, it's you lot are the traitors. There won't be peace until yer all gone, and we will defeat ye all, aye, you'll see.'

Ellen clutched her overcoat with one hand while biting on the other, lest she betrayed her presence. The gun held by Sheamus was still levelled at the man's head but now she saw her oldest brother, Liam, move behind the captured man.

'For God's sake, what are you doin', man?' was the frightened roar, bravado now replaced by panic. 'Liam, for Jasus' sake, I'm married with a child on the way, we're neighbours, after all, oh my God, Liam.'

Light from the embers in the fire flashed off the steel, visible now, in Liam's hand. The incongruity of a quick sign of the cross while almost in tandem, coolly slitting the man's throat, escaped Ellen. Her gasp of shock, rendered so audibly to her own ears she thought the noise would register with all three brothers. Yet no one moved, although Ciaran did glance in the direction of the loft. How she managed to creep back down the stairs and stumble back to her bedroom, she cannot recall, blinded as she was by an unstoppable river of tears cascading down her face. With effort, she managed to avoid being physically sick as the face of the man now undoubtedly dead, flashed relentlessly across her mind. He was a neighbour, a friend, someone with whom her brothers had played football in the not-too-distant past. It was Sean O'Hara, Patsy's brother.

The night was endless with no possibility of sleep. Ellen shivered uncontrollably as she recalled the entire incident, frame by frame, unable to block the images from her tortured brain. She was so pale the following morning, Josie sent her back to bed but to no avail, as sleep was still elusive. Ellen tossed and turned, unable to shake the vision of her three brothers, active and complicit, in ending the life of Sean O'Hara. Jumbled thoughts churned around inside her head and she eventually rose, late that afternoon, quite sure her knowledge would be visible on her face. Yet, Ellen saw nothing untoward in any of her brothers' demeanour and barely a glance came her way. Hesitantly, she went over to the barn, but it was as always, and with a sense of relief she began to wonder had she dreamed the whole affair. How could they have cleaned up so much blood, disposed of one body and attended to another injured man? All seemed as before, tidier, in fact. As the evening progressed, all three brothers went about their chores on the farm and chivvied Ellen to do the same. She thought Ciaran looked enquiringly at her from time to time, but she could not be sure, and anyway, to discuss the horror she had witnessed was not a possibility.

The next day, the weather was a little warmer and with the change, came the rain. The showers were light at first but by midday, became heavy and continuous with the resultant rising tides and swollen rivers. The rain fell in torrents for the following three days and in turn, roads were flooded with many impassable. When word was received that Sean O'Hara was missing, Ellen's faint hope that she had imagined the night in the barn was shattered. The search proved fruitless at first, hampered for several days by the weather.

It was a full week before Sean was found, semi-submerged in a stream Despite the toll from jagged rocks and incessant rain, it was impossible for Patsy to accept the official verdict of the authorities when they ruled the death accidental.

'Must have slipped in the rain, too much porter perhaps,' mumbled the local sergeant, but his voice trailed away, on encountering Patsy's look of withering disdain.

Sean had inexplicably gone out that evening without mentioning where he was going. It was generally known that anti-Treaty forces were in the vicinity and trouble was brewing. Patsy understood little of Sean's activities and made a point of remaining ignorant. Despite that, he knew Sean was active on the pro-Treaty side believing the best deal had been obtained from the British. His vision of a new Ireland needed commitment and Sean had argued that the best way to move ahead was to accept the offer on the table. A mixture of politics and perhaps the subtle threat of more unrest was the path for securing the remaining counties.

Patsy was slightly concerned when Sean failed to return by nightfall. It was not like him to disappear on the rare occasion he was home from Finner Camp to see his wife. When Nellie woke Patsy at 3am, his senses were instantly heightened. Yet the hours ticked by as he waited, unsure what to do, nervous of intruding and perhaps hampering some clandestine operation. Tension and the sleepless night, combined with the patter from the steady downpour, lulled him eventually into a stupor. Patsy remembered how he had lounged on a chair, snoozing on and off, counting the minutes, unable to move, and finally settling into a troubled doze. The official alarm was raised later that morning when there was still no word from Sean or news of his whereabouts. Everyone rallied to help, but the search was hampered by high winds with flooding on low ground.

By the time Sean's body was found, Patsy's mother was utterly distraught, and his father's face was grey with fatigue and distress. A doctor was called for Sean's wife who was expecting their first child and had become quite hysterical. Sergeant O'Dwyer commiserated at Sean's tragic accident but only the foolish believed the judgement was impartial. The fair-minded were even-handed, the biased openly sceptical, and the perpetrators relieved. Patsy fumed and protested claiming the verdict ridiculous and a travesty. It was immediately apparent to those who cared that the death was not accidental. No rock could have slit the man's throat, but the official verdict was, "Death by Misadventure". Allegiances were known in the area, and no one was fooled by the findings.

As was usual, the wake was held in the house and Patsy took control, his parents too shattered by the loss of their son. Patsy's father was stunned and kept insisting it could not be true, visibly ageing twenty years in two days.

Patsy's mother never uttered a word but sat quietly, absorbing how her world had disintegrated. With his new wife, Teresa, Patsy greeted relatives and neighbours and made no comment on those he felt were suspect.

'There will be time enough for that,' vowed Patsy to Teresa. 'Payment will be made in due course.' All Patsy knew was that the McShane's were somehow responsible for his brother's death. Gerry, Sean's constant companion, had told him that all three brothers were seen out that night with a group of "irregulars". Of necessity, Gerry had kept out of sight, but not before he had seen them all in a heated discussion and at their very centre, was the unmistakable face of Liam McShane.

Where Sean had gone was a mystery and Gerry could not enlighten him. 'Suffice to say, Patsy, he was going about business for Ireland.'

Until the funeral was over, Patsy decided to keep his own counsel and not dwell on what Gerry had to say or what he learned from other sources. Revenge would be cold and planned well.

Ellen was agitated and dragged herself around on leaden legs. She did not attend the wake, unable to face the family in such an intimate setting, but like all the villagers and local farm families, it was obligatory to attend the funeral. She took a seat beside Sarah at the rear of the church. She was numb since the incident in the barn, trauma causing her to move on automatic and robotically perform her duties. Ciaran had queried how she was feeling, and the suspicion surfaced once more that he had glimpsed her in the loft. Nothing was said, however.

The church soon filled, with the entire parish in attendance, including factions from both sides. The hypocrisy but most of all the futility, stirred Ellen. Some of those offering condolences would know the circumstances of Sean's death and agreed with its necessity. Others were just ignoring for the moment the demand for retribution that would inevitably erupt, once Sean was buried.

Patsy led Nellie, Sean's widow, down the aisle and his parents followed behind. Teresa, Patsy's new bride, followed next. Sorrow shrouded the family, emanating in waves around the church. Ellen shrank in her seat as Patsy's eyes caught hers for one moment with a question, before turning back to his mother to guide her to her place. Shame washed over Ellen even though she had taken no part in the horror in the barn. She could not break her silence, and as such, that action made her an accomplice.

The ensuing Mass was a solemn affair that did nothing to disguise the tensions within what was once a tightly knitted community, now fractured, seemingly beyond repair. Ellen slowly approached the altar to shake the family's hands, as was the custom. She was in a line just ahead of her brothers. She first shook the hand of Sean's young pregnant wife, so distressed she had lost all composure. Sean's mother clasped her in a warm embrace. It frightened her with such intensity, the urge to break her silence became almost overwhelming but common sense forced her to hold her tongue. Sean's father was next, a man now visibly broken, and Ellen was unsure if he knew what was even happening. Finally, she reached Patsy who coolly enfolded her, his face devoid of expression, and then swiftly turned to the person next to her. Feeling almost dismissed, she once again took her seat and from her vantage point watched as first Liam, then Sheamus, and finally, Ciaran, were warmly encircled within the arms of Sean O'Hara's mother. Ellen wondered at their thoughts as they calmly offered their condolences. Were they regretful, remorseful? Was their cause so righteous that any action was justified in its name?

Liam was first to reach Patsy. Patsy sat beside his mother, head bowed, but he looked up and stared solemnly at Liam for a few seconds. As Liam stretched out his hand in condolence, Patsy pointedly kept his own by his side, just steadily holding Liam's gaze. Liam, flushing, let his hand drop slowly and then, steadily, turned away. The heat of Patsy's glare assaulted his retreating back, before Patsy swung eyes bright with contempt, towards Sheamus and Ciaran. They, however, did not attempt to shake Patsy's hand but nodded, and passed on. Ellen thought that their actions were very telling and did nothing but confirm guilt in Patsy's mind.

Their secret remained locked like a stone inside Ellen's breast and there was no way to relieve its pressure, but she felt sure their actions in the barn were well known. If she had been able to read her brothers' thoughts, she would not have been surprised at the way their minds worked. As Ciaran took his seat, he was relieved that he did not have to shake Patsy's hand. Although he did not wield the knife, he had been an integral part of the events in the barn, and he felt extreme shame and remorse. Sheamus just wished the funeral to be over and, with the passage of time, the death of Sean O'Hara would become just another tragedy of war. Liam had the ability to separate his sorrow at the death of a neighbour and the necessity to express condolences to the family, from the crucial actions that were unavoidable, but essential, to win the Civil War. Such a dichotomy enabled him to move on without regret.

The funeral Mass was finally over and the long walk to the graveyard began, with the coffin carried high on the shoulders of family members. Close friends and neighbours followed, all encased in a sombre shroud. A solemn procession, a black line snaking around the hills with faint sobbing competing with the mournful tune from a piper, echoing over the mountains.

Ellen contemplated the tragedy that had befallen the O'Hara family at the hands of her own as she joined the slow march to the cemetery. As they reached the gates, eight uniformed Free State soldiers relieved the burden from the family. Draped in the Tricolour, the coffin was proudly borne, shoulder high, as they slow- marched to Sean's final resting place. As the coffin was lowered down, in keeping with military tradition, the haunting sound of the "Last Post" resounded around the still graveyard. Crows scattered from the trees, their raucous caw reverberating in Ellen's, now throbbing, head. At the direction of their captain, the soldiers fired a volley of gunshot, a final mark of respect for a true Irishman.

The sorrow in the O'Hara family would linger for generations, as parents grieved the loss of their son, a wife now without a husband and with a child to be born without a father. For Patsy, the loss of a brother and soulmate would alter the direction of his own life and put plans on hold, until Sean's death was avenged. How had Ireland come to this state that, together, they had successfully fought a common enemy and now looked on each other in bitter hatred? Eyes locked across the graveside with blatant hostility, foretelling more sorrow to come.

Chapter 12

The events in the barn could not be easily erased from Ellen's mind and intruded on her sleep and every waking thought. So much so, that although Liam had still not agreed to her trip to London, she desisted pressing him for the moment. When surprisingly, he broached her plans himself, they reached a mutual agreement. She agreed to stay until spring 1923 and Liam smiled in acquiescence, promising to help when the time came. It meant spending another Christmas in Donegal which ensured Josie was happy, but Ellen worried Bridie would be disappointed and alone over the holiday. She need not have been concerned.

Bridie had plans of her own. Danny had finally received confirmation that an article of his would be included in the January issue of *The Socialist Stand*. He was to travel to London to talk to the publishers and spend Christmas with Bridie. That time together became one of the happiest Bridie could remember. A red candle twinkled in the window as they both spent hours by a blazing fire, reading, discussing anything and everything, and playing endless cards. Wrapped in their own cocoon, at intervals, they kissed long and sensuously, stirring passions that could only be assuaged in the bedroom upstairs.

By contrast, Christmas in Donegal was tranquil if a little muted, the absence of Donal very evident in all their thoughts. The peace helped Ellen to come to terms, in a small way, with her inner turmoil, at least on the surface. She still dreaded going out in case she met any of the O'Hara's and this restricted Sarah. At seventeen, Josie and Liam felt she should not socialise alone. Sarah, never slow to show her annoyance, demanded that once she turned eighteen the following April, she be given full freedom. Privately, Ellen was relieved she would miss the battles ahead between Sarah and Liam.

Spring arrived and with it, an exceptionally hard frost. To accommodate an expected late potato planting, the Parish Priest announced the St. Patrick's Day social was to be held two weeks earlier than usual, on Sat 3rd March. The church social on St. Patrick's Day was one of the highlights of the year and there were mixed feelings when the change was announced, albeit with some sighs of relief that at least it had not been cancelled altogether. Dances were usually outdoor events at the crossroads but twice a year, the Parish Priest allowed a social to take place in the Parish Hall, which was in effect, little more than a barn.

The reflection in her mirror made Sarah smile as she prepared for the evening. She had chosen the dress well. Of course, it was initially her mother's and worn subsequently by Ellen, but if Sarah had one talent, it was needlework. Now she pouted, pursing her lips in discontent as her thoughts turned to Ellen. Ellen had taken some persuading to agree to accompany her to the dance and her agreement to attend was still tenuous. She had been acting very strangely lately, but Sarah was too caught up in her own world to enquire. She just supposed it was anxiety about her pending trip to London and dismissed Ellen from further consideration.

Finally, they left the farmhouse together at 7 o'clock to walk to the village. There was a noticeable sting in the air that caught their breath as they sauntered down the lane. Their boots crushed grass, already stiff from frost, with the sound crackling loudly in the still night. Sarah always insisted they pause when they reached the curve in the road as, from that vantage point, the view across the bay was breath-taking. On a clear frosty night such as this, it was magnificent. Stars twinkled in a velvety sky, while an almost full moon cast a luminescent glow over the water. Sarah threw her arms wide and never felt more alive and ready to embrace whatever came her way. Ellen stood morosely at her side, wishing she were at home in bed asleep, with images of the barn banished forever to the background.

The lengthy-time Sarah had taken to prepare added to Ellen's irritation, but Sarah knew how important it was to look good and she needed to impress, Tomás. Sarah's hair was fair, and her glossy tresses flowed down her back, almost reaching her waistline. Her eyes were a deep blue and with her sensual smile, she was as captivating as only a seventeen-year-old can be. Life was in her grasp, and on the cusp of womanhood, it glittered and glowed with promise. She continued to delay a little as she walked into the growing darkness compelled, as always, to savour the essence of the beauty of her surroundings.

The slight delay also allowed her to relish the start of what she knew, would be a wonderful night. Sarah was in love with life and sparkled and embraced the twilight as she waltzed down the lane. Her hair shone, her newly sequined dress glistened, and her boots kept the mud from her feet. She hobbled along now to catch up with Ellen who carried a small lantern, the only light to guide their way. They were both in Wellington boots, carrying their dancing shoes, but Sarah was hampered in her stride. Her boots were Ellen's cast-offs and a little on the large side.

Eventually, they arrived at the church hall and greetings flowed from all quarters. As they neared the front door, Ellen was disturbed to see Patsy standing in the churchyard with a group of his friends. It was not considered acceptable for him to be there so soon after his brother's death. The added optics of a newly married man without his bride, who was most likely at home alone in Killybegs, and tongues were bound to start wagging. Hoping he had not seen her, she ducked into the doorway.

Sarah quickly swapped her Wellingtons for her dance shoes, but Ellen was slower to change, drawn instead towards the heat emanating from the fireplace at the far end of the hall. The warmth from the blazing fire made toes tingle and cheeks glow after the cold walk.

The social was a genteel affair overseen by local matrons affiliated to the church. Dancing was carefully scrutinised and anything resembling, "close proximity", was immediately halted. Oil lamps and candles were strategically placed in shadowy corners to prevent couples from sneaking an illicit few moments. The glow from the lights cast a magical aura, emphasising to Ellen how disconnected she felt and how she longed to be back home.

The matrons observed Sarah and the instant attention she garnered from the local boys. By tacit agreement, it was decided she was too pretty by far and could be an *'occasion of sin.'* She would be observed carefully to ensure she didn't misbehave and lead any young lad astray.

The girls' entrance had indeed been eagerly awaited by many of the local boys. Their eyes always peeled as Sarah, in particular, had not gone unnoticed. She was only seventeen but when she entered a room, all the lads turned towards her, moths to a flame. An allure tantalised, from the swish of her hair and the swing of her hips to the mesmeric quality in the curve of her smile. Young and inexperienced, Sarah enjoyed the attention, but she was innocent and oblivious of the strength of desire. The charm she exuded gave rise to whispering from some and the generation of spite, from others. Some of the local girls groaned because the competition from Sarah meant the night would inevitably end, for a few, without at least one dance to avoid humiliation.

Sarah was blissfully unaware of any jealousy but not unaware of her appeal. Except for the absence of Tomás and the unwelcome attentions of Kevin, she happily whirled away the first hour. Johnny had been the first across the room, whisking Sarah onto the dance floor before she could protest. As she spun around, she scanned the entrance for Tomás. He was always late, so she was not overly worried that he had not yet appeared. She longed to see him and to feel once more that tingle of excitement as he grasped her hand. When he whispered in her ear, there was an instinctual desire to turn her head and feel his lips on hers. The need to inhale his scent was barely understood, as she battled the urge to become closer to him.

For now, she danced gaily with Johnny and then Brian under glistening lights that emphasised the watchful scrutiny of some of the local matriarchs. Kevin, of course, also observed. His hungry eyes followed Sarah's every move. Sensitive to his stare and uncomfortable with the naked longing in his gaze, she attempted to move out of his view, but his eyes penetrated, following her every step. Kevin was extremely tall, with a thin, pinched face, which was not particularly attractive. The problem, however, was not his appearance, but his inability to disguise his craving. It was that palpable longing that made her uncomfortable. His necessity to always stand too close to her, so close, his breath brushed her neck, made her inwardly withdraw. He was nineteen and totally infatuated since he first noticed Sarah, two years previously. Despite his best intentions, he continually followed her. He could sense she had little time for him and shrank whenever he drew too near, but he was unable to help himself. He saw how she blossomed whenever Tomás Kelly was around, and a surge of hatred rushed through him. He consoled himself with the thought that the relationship would never last. He knew what Tomás' father was like, and he wouldn't stand for Tomás marrying until he was much older. When he did, it would have to be someone willing to work, not a butterfly, like Sarah.

Ellen was sorry she had agreed to attend the church social, but Sarah's pestering was so intense, it was easier to give in. Exacerbated by the sight of Patsy, images of that dreadful night were insidious, sneaking into her consciousness, hampering any possibility of enjoyment. She developed such a headache with the effort to pretend all was well, that the desire to escape early and return home to bed, was overwhelming. It was approximately 10.30 when Ellen finally approached Sarah and said she needed to leave.

Sarah thought Ellen sounded more irritated than unwell, when she snapped, 'I am going home now, had enough, are you coming with me?'

Sarah hesitated. She wanted to stay but hated the trek back without Ellen. The clamour of offers from Johnny and Brian to see her safely home, and the tentative offer from Kevin, was not what made Sarah agree to remain. It was that sudden rush of excitement as she felt Tomás' hand slide into her own. 'I will stay, Ellen, I am sure someone will walk me up the lane to the house.'

Nods of agreement followed, and Ellen turned and walked away. Sarah succumbed, without any hesitation, to the flush of heat inside her as Tomás brushed her lips with his own. Even the tap on her back from Mrs Reilly and her sharp rebuke did nothing to dent her happiness. 'Behave yourself, young Sarah McShane or I will have words with your mother and brother.'

When Ellen left the hall, she passed close to Patsy chatting to a couple of lads. Patsy, as custom dictated, did not attend the social inside but he was dapper as always, with a dark suit and red tie, totally unsuitable so soon after Sean's death. She felt uncomfortable as she walked past especially, as he turned studiously away, deliberately ignoring her. However, the headache was such that his actions only impacted for a moment, and after a slight pause, she just hurried on her way, breaking into a run once she saw the farmhouse lights beckon.

The house was quiet, so no awkward questions had to be answered. Kathleen had taken to sleeping with Josie, so Ellen now only shared a bedroom with Sarah. Relief that Bridie was arriving the following month to accompany her to London surged through her, and gratefully she sank into bed and sleep within seconds of her head touching the pillow.

Inevitably, midnight arrived and the conclusion of the social. Tomás said he would wait outside while Sarah went to retrieve her woollen shawl and boots. When she re-joined him a short while later, he was engrossed in conversation with Kevin, but seconds later, both Johnny and Brian appeared. 'So, who is the lucky one walking the beautiful Sarah home?' piped a voice from behind and a startled Sarah turned to see Patsy O'Hara grinning at her.

Instantly, there was a clamour of voices. 'I can, it is on my way so, no bother,' said Johnny.

'Tomás?' enquired Sarah and knew, by his expression, that he would not be the one.

Tomás felt uncomfortable. His one desire was to walk Sarah home, but his father kept him working late and checked the time of his return, and he was unable to face his wrath, day after day. Tomás pecked her cheek and wandered over to Patsy.

Sarah walked up the lane, Johnny and Brian on either side jostling for the best position, Kevin trailing behind. Deliberately, Kevin shoved aside a gnawing sense of exclusion knowing it was enough, for now, to be close to Sarah. All three lads carried a light of some sort to show the way.

'I thought that was your girl?' intoned Patsy to Tomás, as they watched the four fade into the distance. 'Looking like that, if she were mine, I wouldn't let her walk home with anyone else.'

Tomás looked away and, frowning, replied, 'I'm off then,' and headed in the opposite direction.

Patsy, after some contemplation, also sauntered away.

First one, and then another of Sarah's companions, drifted off home. As always, she needed to stop at the rise on the hill, and tonight she was so exhilarated, she threw caution to the wind and did just that. She knew she probably sounded a bit daft, rhapsodising about the stars, but the social had been so exciting with Tomás that she was not ready to reach home and bed just yet. She hugged her shawl tightly around herself for warmth and turned to gesture and comment on the surrounding beauty, to her companion. The ensuing kiss was unexpected, and she succumbed for a second, before sense reasserted itself. Awkwardly, she tried to pull away, almost afraid to offend, but was suddenly clutched far too tightly. Sarah pushed back but was now engulfed in a stranglehold from which she could not escape. Terror consumed her and she felt unable to breathe. She struggled, but the arms were too strong and insistent and as she was forced to the ground, she hit her head painfully against a rock. Although stunned, she attempted to rise, only to crash once more to the sodden earth, as her attacker, forcefully and adeptly, easily overcame her efforts. The ache in her head was intense, but nothing like the agony shooting through her as suddenly he thrust himself violently inside her. She quietened then, accepting his advances without demur, too shocked and stunned to move. The violation was harrowing and humiliating, and Sarah just wished it to end as quickly as possible. She drew into herself, disassociating from what was occurring and as his agonising thrusts continued, she stared at the stars and floated to a distant world. Momentarily, the waves of hot searing torment abated.

It took Ellen only a few seconds to realise what had happened to Sarah. Jumping from her bed, she bade her be quiet, and quickly and efficiently she tended to her physical wounds and rinsed out her bloodied clothes. She gave her a cup brim-full of whiskey stolen from the kitchen cupboard, with the fervent hope no one would notice. Sarah sat unmoving on the bed, hugging her bruised body, hair still entangled with twigs, while blood continued to seep slowly from numerous cuts.

'Oh, Ellen, I have sinned,' she chokingly sobbed. 'What will I do?'

'Ssshh,' whispered Ellen, and as best she could, soothed her into a restless murmuring. It was imperative their mother have no inkling as to what had occurred. Also, her brothers, because if they found out there would surely be blood spilt. 'Our secret,' she whispered to Sarah. 'Only you and I will ever know. Tell me who did this to you.'

Sarah hesitated, repeating, 'It was my fault. I stopped and he must have thought I wanted him. I said no but he must have thought I didn't mean it,' she rambled. 'All my fault, not any of the lads,' she mumbled, until exhaustion and restless sleep claimed her battered body.

Ellen kept watch all night as Sarah tossed and turned. Guilt consumed her and she berated herself for not staying to walk home with Sarah. Seeing Patsy had reignited memories of his brother Sean and the manner of his death, and with those events continually playing on her mind, all her decisions were affected. Instead of receding as the social got underway, the scene in the barn became more vivid with each passing hour and she had needed to get away.

Ellen watched Sarah, asleep in seconds from shock and alcohol but it was a restless slumber disturbed by moans and defensive, reflex reactions. Ellen was unsure how to help but she knew the knowledge would be too much for their mother to bear. She hoped there would be no repercussions and over time, they could all move on. She was unable to fathom who would attack Sarah. They knew every boy around and none seemed capable of such a vicious act. She had indicated that Johnny, Brian, and Kevin had walked her home. Sarah knew them from childhood and Ellen instantly disregarded them unable to countenance, for one moment, that any one of them could be the perpetrators. Tomás was there of course, but not only did he live in the other direction, he also was never able to stay late. Ellen knew Tomás had a fancy for Sarah, and she liked him in return, but she could not imagine him capable of such viciousness. Disappointed as she was in Patsy, Ellen still could not believe he would have bothered Sarah either.

It was soon evident to all who knew Sarah well that something was amiss. For three days Sarah took to her bed refusing to eat and to speak. It was only her mother threatening the doctor that made her attempt to return to a semblance of normality. Aimlessly, she undertook her chores, refusing to go out beyond the farmgate and barely nibbling at food. The damage to her spirit was striking. Josie knew something was wrong as did all Sarah's brothers, but Josie was unable to answer the questions they posed.

Josie, in turn, looked to Ellen for answers, but Ellen merely shrugged her shoulders and prevaricated. 'I don't know for certain, Mammy, but I think a boy, probably Tomás, upset her. In her rush to get home, she slipped and fell.' She hated to lie to her mother but felt she had no choice. Her excuse was weak, and the family watched, puzzled and anxious, not knowing how to react to a vivacious young girl who seemed to be deadened inside. Daily, Ellen saw her bow and pray where before there had been a carelessness about any form of devotion. When she felt she was unobserved, Ellen saw Sarah slip away to the outer reaches of the farm and enter the ruins of an old church. Head bowed, she witnessed Sarah mutter to herself and grapple with a scrupulousness that could only bode ill. Here was a young girl who needed regular persuasion to attend the nightly recital of evening prayers and now, spent hours, on her knees.

Sarah knew Ellen covertly observed her actions sensing the bewilderment inside her. Desperately she tried to grapple and come to some semblance of peace, but confusion reigned within, and she hoped the turmoil would be eased by prayer. She tried to rationalise what had happened. She had trotted quite happily up the laneway, enjoying the cool of the frosty night after the heat of the social. An inner compulsion made her stop at the crest of the hill to view the beauty of the landscape, bathed in the serenity of the starlit sky. A delaying tactic really, she just did not want the night to end. She froze momentarily when she felt an arm slide around her waist but then automatically turned around. In hindsight, she realised that was her mistake, that he thought it was encouragement and she wanted him to kiss her. She shuddered as she recalled how she had tried to pull away, but his grip tightened, his breath hot on her neck and loud in her ear. Even as she attempted to cry out and shout 'no,' his hands were grappling with her.

As the days passed, she hoped that the scars would heal and prayed the nightmare would recede. Sarah was unable to utter his name, although she knew him well. It was less real if she did not give him voice. She believed that protecting him was essential because, of course, she was at fault. If she uttered his name, everyone would know she had led him on and made him sin. Sarah vowed to obtain forgiveness and once more and for the third time that day, knelt in prayer.

Living on a farm had taught both Ellen and Sarah the rudiments of biology. Morning sickness was a condition Ellen recalled with clarity when Josie was expecting Kathleen. By the second week of April, Ellen reluctantly acknowledged to herself that Sarah was possibly pregnant. The advent of queasiness in the morning was a flag that could not be ignored, the only comfort being Sarah was not physically sick, so suspicion was not aroused. Ellen knew she had to find a remedy and that meant talking to Bridie. Sarah placed her entire being in Ellen's hands and was willing to do whatever Ellen asked. Yet, Ellen remained fearful, that unable to endure the weight of her secret, Sarah, would tell their mother what had occurred. Her nights were disturbed as she relived what happened, but Ellen calmed her, promising all would pass. Always strong, Ellen was still overwhelmed by the enormity of issues to be sorted. Firstly, their mother could never learn what had occurred. It was a death knell for a woman's future if she lost her virginity before marriage. The humiliation in their small village would be too much for Josie to bear. The trauma of Donal's death had receded but the shame of a "spoiled" daughter, would set her back. Secondly, she had to persuade both her mother and Liam to allow Sarah to accompany her to London. Undoubtedly, a formidable and daunting task, perhaps unnecessary, in the unlikely event her suspicion was unfounded. Thirdly, she had to emphasise to Sarah the necessity to continue to stay silent and let Bridie help her.

Ever since that night, Sarah felt locked inside herself with a wall blocking her connection with the world. She felt grubby, convinced she had somehow led the lad on and forced him to transgress. The belief, inculcated by the Church, was that control lay with the woman and it was the woman who tempted the man and caused him to commit sin. Sarah was strangled by a Church's teaching that subordinated women and exonerated men. Ellen could only guess at what went through Sarah's mind, but the ravaged face gave an indication of her inner turmoil.

Ellen, like Sarah, had been taught the Church's tenets that women were always to blame for the temptations of men. Unlike Sarah, reading newspapers and journals posted by Bridie, or purchased by Ciaran, had opened her mind. However, she still was bound by specific codes of the day that impinged on her ability to cope. She rejected, wholeheartedly, the Church's teaching that Sarah was at fault. Yet in later years, Ellen sobbed softly to Bridie and expressed sadness at her handling of the situation. 'How my actions must have exacerbated her shame. Aiding her to hide what had happened implied she did wrong. It was a reflex, to protect our mother and to prevent our brothers from seeking revenge. I thought I was helping but I just made her feel more humiliated. I should have comforted her, told her to hold her head high.' Tears of regret, of guilt, but mostly of palpable anger at a Church and society that condemned a raped girl, excusing all men, streamed down her cheeks.

When Ellen spoke to her mother, Josie, and requested that Sarah be allowed to join her on her trip to London, the readiness with which Josie agreed took her aback. Perhaps Josie was too worn out to care anymore or had guessed the situation and felt unable to handle it. The lack of opposition from Liam was stranger still, but Ellen made no attempt to question his motives for fear he would withdraw his permission, and therefore the financial help they needed to travel. Either way, agreement was granted, and Ellen wrote immediately to Bridie.

While Sarah occupied all Ellen's resources, her own troubled mind had not calmed. It had merely quietened until the time was appropriate for Ellen to, once more, examine how she felt about the events she witnessed in the barn and the death of Sean O'Hara.

Chapter 13

B ridie read the news with dismay. She was happy to have Ellen come to stay and, in anticipation of her arrival, had arranged her little home to accommodate her. Sarah was just turning eighteen and not such comfortable company as Ellen. The fact that Josie was letting her go so quickly, considering the hard-won battle to allow Ellen to leave Donegal, filled her with some disquiet and provided food for thought. The small house would be cramped with the three of them, but more importantly, to obtain a good position for Ellen would be difficult enough to acquire, never mind one for Sarah. The antagonism towards the Irish was extreme in the current climate and although Bridie rarely felt the brunt of anti-Irish feeling in the hospital, she was not unaware of its existence.

Obtaining time off had not been easy and necessitated juggling some schedules in work but she managed to procure a week of annual leave towards the end of April and into May. She had already written to Danny, advising him she would arrive in Dublin on Saturday, April 27th and stay for three days, before travelling on to Donegal to collect Ellen. She hastily scribbled another letter alerting him to the change in plan, and that Sarah was now to join them in London. Danny knew Bridie had not seen her sister, Josie, in some time, and was looking forward to her niece Ellen, returning to London with her. The new missive, indicating another niece was to join the troupe, implied that Bridie had some misgivings about the change of plan.

Danny met Bridie off the boat in Dun Laoghaire and, as usual, it was a typical Irish day, dull and wet. Nothing, however, could dampen his spirits. That did not apply to the rest of him and when Bridie finally disembarked, he was thoroughly soaked. Water dripped from his hair as he bent to kiss her lips but when he moved away, she drew him back. Ecstatic, he kissed her more passionately than public manners allowed. An elderly woman with a vicious umbrella assaulted his legs, and laughing, Danny grabbed Bridie by the hand, and together they hurried out onto the busy street.

'What happened there?' said Bridie

'Never mind,' grinned Danny, 'you don't want to know.'

This visit would present little opportunity to be properly together, so the passionate kiss had to suffice for the moment. Despite the limitations on time, they still enjoyed three days of companionship and their friendship and mutual attraction continued to blossom. Bridie felt she could confide in Danny about anything, and he would not be judgmental or disappointed. In turn, she listened attentively to his frustrations and aspirations and hoped he would achieve some of his ambitions. For now, they were both content to be with each other and unfulfilled desire, heightened the emotions of their attachment.

That first evening they had so much to talk about, and Danny knew no one was as receptive or understood him, the way she did. Bridie felt the same connection. Perhaps it was their similar childhood experiences or the shared tragedy of war heightening their perception and generating an appreciation of the other's viewpoint, without necessary agreement. Their letters had continued steadily since last they met, expanding in length and depth, as both expressed thoughts and hopes for the future. Their yearnings and wishes were not dissimilar, and the more they were together, the more they instinctively knew that each could depend on the other and their lives would forever be entwined. He now listened intently, as Bridie explained why she was travelling to Donegal. She mused over the reasons, unable to fathom why Sarah was to accompany Ellen and voiced her worries to Danny. He suggested she should request that Sarah stay behind until Ellen was sorted with employment. That would give her some space, figuratively and physically. Bridie agreed, provided her one unspoken suspicion was not a reality.

The three blissful days in Dublin sped by and Danny knew the time was right to voice his one unspoken desire. 'Marry me,' he urged on their final evening. 'Come to Dublin and be my wife. Work here, I would never ask you to leave what you love but just be with me.'

Bridie looked up solemnly and smiled. 'I was wondering if you would ever ask. The answer is, yes, yes, but first, I must sort out my two nieces. Just be patient a little while longer.'

'I am not going anywhere. You can never get rid of me,' was his smiling response.

After waving Bridie goodbye at the train station, Danny walked towards Liberty Hall. He was usually uneasy after they spent time together but today was different. He no longer worried that he rambled too much, spouting unformed thoughts and flawed ideology, afraid she would become bored. Not once had he sensed any lack of interest or saw her expression glaze over. Today he walked purposefully, happy now that she had agreed to become his wife. He continued, quite oblivious to the stares from passers-by amused at his wide grin and jaunty gait.

Danny continued to have some minimal success with his writing with a few minor articles published in British journals. He had been asked to address a conference in Dublin, and his theme was how the new, emerging Ireland, could heal once the vicious Civil War ended and what type of Republic would ensue. He hoped his presentation would be received well but Danny knew he had to be careful. His passion for a subject and the earnestness of his ideas were so intense, that he often lost some of his listeners.

As the Civil War continued unabated, Danny despaired at the vicious way his country was being torn apart. He was apprehensive about how society would develop once the war ended and could already foresee how power and control were being ceded to the Church. He readily accepted that Catholicism had been a rallying call for nationalism. Still, it seemed to him that Nationalists were exchanging the power of the Crown for the power of the mitre. The aspirations of the Proclamation and James Connolly were being ignored. The equality of men and women and the acceptance of the equality of difference was being discarded in favour of a new domination, where women were deemed, second class. There was no discussion of equal pay and women were once again relegated to the home despite the prominent role many had played in the Rising, on an equal footing, with their male counterparts.

Marching along, he rehearsed in his head what he intended to say. Education was key, and he intended to promote that idea at the conference. Although free education was available up to twelve years of age, for many children that was haphazard at best. The need to earn money, even if it was from begging, superseded the necessity to go to school. Danny fervently believed that the social conditions that obviated the need for children to work had to be implemented. Unions had a responsibility to advance that ideal and that education in schools, such as it was, needed to be taken out of the hands of the clergy. In his opinion, the clergy indoctrinated a class hierarchy and power structure which retained the poor at the bottom, through a belief that others were their betters and reward was to be achieved in the afterlife. The retention of class advantage was preserved by preventing those most in need of education, from advancing. This avenue of thought was rejected by some of the more conservative union members as Catholicism was the backbone of their lives and clerical pronouncements directed their thought processes. Danny had faced criticism when he suggested that even within healthcare the Church was meddling, insisting on a Catholic ethos overseeing medical practice. Danny would have been far more outspoken had he any inkling of the practices in operation in Church controlled homes for women with children conceived out of wedlock, but he was of his time. As such, he had no knowledge of the cruelty that resided behind closed doors, secrets to be unravelled by future generations.

It was not surprising that no journal in Ireland was willing to publish an article that criticised the Church and so Danny was increasingly despondent of ever having much of an influence in the political sphere. The union was at least open, in some small regard, to his ideas but he despaired at times of it ever embracing a bigger picture. A penny rise here and there was nothing but a sop to the unions. The ideological change he craved was as elusive as ever. A full revolution of the workplace was needed where job security trumped favouritism, and where both men and women could earn a living wage. All organisations consist of different strands, and the union was no different. On the surface it appeared there was a united goal. Yet the union was not homogenous having within itself, factions of its own. It had not gone unnoticed among some of the union hierarchy that whenever Danny Walsh addressed a gathering, afterwards, there was a notable uptake in union membership. He could be called upon to rally workers for strike action but if he appeared too strident, the union would have no compunction dispensing with his services. It would be easy to cite irreconcilable differences and ideology not in keeping with the union's own. In other words, Danny was expendable.

Danny was not oblivious to that sentiment, but being useful if only for a while, assured him of employment for the time being. In turn, that allowed him the freedom to focus on his writing. Although not a vain man, he recognised an ability within himself to stir passions and infuse emotions, whether through his oratory or the written article. There were others in the union who, although professing a need to unify and strike for workers' rights, were also in thrall to the Church and did not want to offend. Many of those felt inadequate when debating with employers or clergy and were of little use to those who needed them most. The members Danny most despised were the career union officials, who utilised the union as the vehicle for their own personal advancement and monetary gain. However, for the present, he had a job and for that, he was thankful.

Billy collected Bridie from the bus, smelling as ripe as ever. He had put on some weight, so a gap in his shirt now allowed a sneaky peek at some flabby white belly, decorated with a few wayward grey hairs. Despite having a freshly scented handkerchief, Billy's aroma was not to be stifled, and Bridie was delighted to reach the farm before she began to retch.

As she alighted from the cart, it only took one look at Sarah for Bridie to guess why she was planning a trip to London. Whether Josie knew was the question now uppermost in Bridie's mind, but Josie was her usual welcoming self with no discernible underlying stress. Yet how could she have failed to notice Sarah's changed appearance? She was no longer the lively, vital girl with shining eyes and hair. Her skin was dry and pasty with an unhealthy grey sheen. She seemed unable to lift her head, instead, her focus was perpetually on the ground, which was not just unbecoming but indicated heartfelt emotional anguish. Assuming her intuition was correct, Bridie did not believe that bringing Sarah to London was the solution to the problem. Single mothers were no more welcome in London than in Dublin, or Donegal. Ellen also appeared troubled, jumpy, and edgy, and had similarly lost a lot of weight. Perhaps it was worry over Sarah, but inexplicably, Bridie felt there was more to it.

That evening was supposedly spent relaxing over a meal but there was an unacknowledged strain, and the conversation was stilted. Liam, at least, gave her a few nods, and if that were to be the sum-total of cordial conversation well, Bridie could live with that. The heat of the fire and tiredness from her journey made Bridie's eyes flutter and, against her will, attempt to close. Summoning her last shred of strength, she rose and retired early to bed, only to find sleep elusive as she pondered for a solution to Sarah's dilemma. Fervently, but with little faith, she hoped her suspicions were groundless.

Sleep eventually overcame Bridie's churning thoughts only to be disrupted by a gentle tap-tap on her bedroom door. To her astonishment, Liam was outside with a lantern beseeching her to follow him. The moon lit their way as they crossed the yard to the barn. Inside, lay a dishevelled and scruffy figure, bleeding profusely from his thigh. His face was flushed, and he shivered in spasms, clearly in the throes of a fever.

'Can you help him?' muttered Liam. 'He was shot, about an hour ago, by a Free-Stater.'

'I am no doctor,' replied Bridie, 'but I will do what I can.'

'That is all I am asking of you, and he is one of ours,' retorted Liam.

'That is not important to me,' was her curt response. 'I don't care who he belongs to; a wounded man is a wounded man. Now press here until I get back, as he is losing a lot of blood. I need to collect a few items to help him.' After scrubbing her hands, Bridie promptly returned with towels, hot water, and a sharp knife. She probed the wound gently, as images of the war and similar situations flashed through her mind. The tenderness of her touch could not eliminate excruciating pain but there was no indication from the prone figure, bar gritted teeth and a clenched fist. 'I think the bullet is still in his leg. Sterilise that knife on the fire before I try to remove it. I have nothing to give him for pain so you will have to hold him.'

Liam nodded, but the young man grunted, 'I will be fine, just do what you have to.'

There was not a murmur as Bridie, best as she was able, extracted the bullet and drew the sides of the wound together. The sweat gathered on her brow, dripping steadily onto her hands, as she sewed the wound with the most robust cotton thread from a reel found in Sarah's sewing box. She bound him with strips of cloth and warned him not to move unless it was essential. They had worked through the night and dawn was breaking when Bridie quietly trod her way back to her bedroom. It was then she heard the rattle of Billy's cart. Her warning not to move him was being ignored so she prayed Billy would deliver the man safely to his home with, the vain hope, that Billy would not be the source of further infection.

Bridie walked up the laneway the following morning, mulling over the conversation with Josie over breakfast, unable to make sense of it. 'Josie, is Sarah, alright? She seems unwell to me.'

Josie looked up at Bridie and then immediately dropped her gaze. 'Sarah? Ah, she is a bit distracted lately, but she is often like that. She will be fine once she is away from here.'

'But why, Josie? Why are you letting her go to London when she is not yet quite eighteen?'

Josie turned away, so Bridie could not see her expression. 'Ah, Bridie, let her go with you. Is that too much to ask, there is nothing for her here? You, above all, should know that. Now, I have to go out.' Josie turned on her heel and left a bemused Bridie.

No opportunity arose for another discussion as Josie, probably by design, ensured she was never alone with Bridie for the rest of the short visit.

Two days later, Bridie, and her two nieces, were driven to the train station. Before leaving, Liam had quickly thrust a crudely wrapped package into

Bridie's hand. 'Something for the journey,' he grunted, and moved his arm in a semblance of a wave "goodbye".

Smiling, Bridie shocked everyone, including herself, by giving him a quick hug. He turned away, muttering incoherently, as a slow, red flush, visibly crept up the nape of his neck. Once they were all comfortably seated on the train, Bridie opened the parcel. Inside was a box of *Urney's* chocolates. Ellen, and even Sarah, became animated.

'Oh, my heavens,' giggled Ellen, 'they are lovely chocolates.'

'They look good,' responded Bridie, 'but I haven't seen them before.'

'They come from a small factory, not long opened, just across in Tyrone.'

All three took a sweet, and savoured the lusciousness for a few seconds, but then Bridie wasted no time in getting to the nub of the problem. 'When are you due, Sarah?'

Both Ellen and Sarah gulped in shock. 'How did you guess?'

'I am a nurse,' replied Bridie. 'Sometimes, you get a sense.'

Sarah's eyes now welled up with tears and it was down to Ellen to speak of their plan. 'I am sorry if we have upset you, Bridie, but we didn't know what to do or who else to turn to. Mam doesn't realise or, at least, I don't think she does. We thought if we could get to London, maybe you could deliver Sarah's baby, and I could work and help her look after it.'

Their naivety astounded Bridie. 'Tell me first about the father.'

Sarah continued to sob. Ellen glanced appealingly at Bridie, before continuing in a flat, emotionless voice, 'Sarah was raped, Bridie, and she hasn't told me who was responsible. She won't speak of it.'

Bridie lay back on the seat and closed her eyes. 'Let me have some time to think what is best, girls.'

The train meandered slowly towards Dublin, but no easy answer sprang to mind. Bridie mentally accepted and rejected, all possible solutions as impractical. She had planned that Danny would meet them from the train, escort them to their lodgings, and afterwards treat them all to a relaxing tea. The following morning, all three were then due to travel back to London. As soon as they alighted from the train and Danny saw Bridie, he instantly sensed her distress, and guided all three women to a nearby teashop so they could speak quietly. This unobtrusive teashop was still an experience for the two girls so, for a few moments, they forgot their predicament and looked curiously around, while waiting to be served.

Bridie filled Danny in on the situation. After ruminating for a few moments, he stated that in his opinion there was only one thing to be done. 'There is a solution, Bridie, and it is not great, but it is the only option because you cannot have the responsibility of Sarah in her condition, as well as caring for Ellen. Anyway, what will you do when the baby arrives? So, there are homes that can help. For all that I have problems with the Church, in instances like this, they do provide a safety net. Let me take you all to the place where you are staying. I will make enquiries and be back early in the morning.'

Capable Bridie, sighed, glad to be able to lean on another's strength and nodded her agreement. She knew there would be arguments from the girls, but she could handle that.

Danny was not so much shocked at what had happened to Sarah, as despairing. He pondered as he strode speedily along. *What kind of society do we have, that a young girl could be raped, and the fault considered hers alone?* For a fleeting moment, he felt ashamed of his sex, but common sense prevailed. There were always violent men who perpetrated such acts, and it would, invariably, be thus. Yet, it was men who devised society's rules and the codes to which society adhered and until women had more power, there was little possibility of change. Unfortunately, the Church did not help with its attitude towards women, yet he knew it was to them he had to go for assistance. Sarah hanging her head in shame made him so angry, but the situation now had to be handled in the best way possible.

To his ultimate distaste, he made enquiries in the local parish. The prurient interest of the priest nauseated him, but Danny needed help, so held his tongue. He was finally directed to Inchicore and his destination was the aptly named, *"Convent of St. Francis, Refuge for Women and Orphanage for Children".* A rather austere and grim nun bade him enter and he was instructed to wait for Sr Reginald. The wait seemed interminable but was only about ten minutes. Sr Reginald proceeded to take copious notes while he explained the predicament.

From time to time, she looked enquiringly at Danny. 'Is there no possibility of marriage?'

'None,' replied Danny. 'We do not know who the father is.'

'Ahem,' was the curt response and, with raised eyebrows, 'hmmm,' again.

Danny felt he was being judged and found wanting and suspected the nun presumed he was the father. Finally, it was agreed that Sarah should be brought to the convent the following day. A donation towards her upkeep was suggested and, although he had few savings, he promised to provide what he could, as soon as possible. True to his word, Danny returned to the women's lodgings early the next morning. All three women looked tired, and Ellen was emotional and tearful. Sarah was quiet, fatalistic, and accepting.

'It's as though she thinks it was all her fault and she has sinned,' whispered Bridie. 'She keeps praying and agrees to whatever I suggest. Ellen is the one who is unable to accept that this is the only solution.'

Danny took her hand. 'I have a taxi outside. Let us all go to the convent and see if we can sort things out.'

The journey to the convent took only fifteen minutes. A dark, imposing building confronted them but then, all convents seemed to look like that. Sr Jude led them into a waiting room to wait for Sr Reginald, the imperious nun Danny had encountered the previous day. The swish of rosary beads announced her arrival and she glided, as though on oiled wheels, over to the desk. Tall and regal, formidable in her dark robes, she bowed slightly to Danny and slowly assessed the three women. 'Which one is Sarah?'

'Mmmee,' stuttered Sarah, with head bowed.

'I might have guessed,' assessed the nun, then responded with a frown, 'well now, you will stay here until after the birth. You will work in our laundry to cover your keep. After the baby is born, decisions can be made. Adoption is the usual course of action.'

Not expecting any answer, Sr Reginald stood in dismissal, but from a lonely corner in Sarah's mind, she whispered, 'I want to keep my baby.'

Sr Reginald turned her head and nodding in Sarah's direction, said, 'We will see when the time comes. Now, good day to you all. Sr Jude will see you out. You, come with me.'

Ellen and Bridie hugged Sarah, promising to write and return for her when she had delivered the baby. 'We will have a permanent solution worked out,' promised Ellen, with a final clasp of Sarah's hand.

'Come along,' said an irritated voice and grabbing Sarah by the elbow with unnecessary roughness, Sr Reginald all but pushed Sarah through the door.

Ellen, Bridie and Danny were abruptly ushered outside by Sr Jude, the haste and forceful locking of the door, preventing further queries.

Sarah followed Sr Reginald without uttering a sound. She accepted her allocated place in the dormitory and listened, impassively, to the set of instructions. This was her penance, and she was ready for it to commence so that she could atone for her sins.

Sarah was unprepared for the stifling heat and the raw, humid, atmosphere of the laundry. Eyes streamed, sore and reddened from salty sweat. Her back and legs ached from the long hours on her feet, and the steady trickle of perspiration that flowed from under her arms and down her back was a perpetual irritation. The continual use of bleach, to ensure garments were pristine white, an accolade for which the nuns were renowned, assaulted her hands, swelling and cracking the skin. Despite this, there was a certain camaraderie among the women that lightened the day. Yet, it was a unity wrought by the knowledge that an inescapable sadness was ahead, for every one of them. Some of the women had been there for years with no knowledge of where their babies had gone. They worked automatically and accepted their lot, despair in the stoop of their shoulders, that even penetrated Sarah's shell. Others had been sentenced by the courts and arrived with full intent to leave as soon as possible until their belligerence disappeared, all too soon replaced by a fatalism. No one questioned the power of the nuns to decide their fate and that a battle was ahead if they wanted to leave, especially with their child.

Sarah glided through each day, performing her duties, rarely speaking, acquiescing to all requests, her demeanour belying that, inside, a determination was steadily growing. Come what may she was going to keep her child. She would complete whatever tasks or functions were required by the nuns. She would not complain or cause a fuss. She would repeatedly pray for forgiveness, but she would leave when the time came and leave with her baby.

Chapter 14

The journey to London was long and arduous. An exhausted Ellen gasped a sigh of relief when they reached the little house that Bridie called home. Ellen was enthralled when she saw the cottage. Despite being small with threadbare furniture, it was warm and cosy once the fire was underway, and Bridie's little touches added colour and atmosphere. Ellen was to sleep in the tiny downstairs side room. There was only space for a small box bed, but it was enough.

If it were not for the trauma of Sarah, Ellen would have been bubbling with excitement. Bridie recognised that Ellen was changed from the carefree but curious girl of the past. She assumed her sister occupied Ellen's thoughts but resolved to probe deeper once the opportunity arose. From Ellen's perspective, although she could not obliterate the horror of the barn from her mind, it was sufficiently buried to enable her to function and focus on Sarah. She intended always to keep the secret of the barn to herself and let time lessen its impact.

Gradually, as the first week passed, the magic of London took hold. Ellen wandered the streets exploring and stumbled across the Tower of London one day and Buckingham Palace, another. She prepared lunches of bread and milk as the warm sultry days invited leisurely afternoons in Hyde Park, enjoying the serenity and the manicured beauty.

By contrast, the London traffic was also a fascination. There was traffic in Dublin, but nothing prepared her for the tooting of horns and the cacophony that assaulted her on the streets of London.

By week two, the urgency to find employment took hold. Liam had financed their journey with a little extra to tide them over, but it was only enough for a couple of weeks. It was imperative to find some employment before too long. Danny had also promised money to the convent for Sarah's upkeep and Ellen felt honour bound to repay that as quickly as possible. Signs that stated, "No Irish Need Apply", meant securing a job was more difficult than anticipated. In fairness, the signs were not numerous, but the sentiment was indisputable, even when it was not so blatantly stated. Whether ongoing rancour affected Ellen's prospects, or whether it was her accent or lack of education, her hopes to obtain work in a shop were in vain.

The news that the Irish Civil War was over, and hostilities had ceased gave Ellen only a short break from her worries. She was relieved that her brothers had apparently come through the war unscathed, but Donegal, and what was happening on the ground seemed a distant memory.

The Civil War in Donegal had a different dynamic in comparison to most other counties in Ireland, because of its proximity to the disputed border. The execution or murder, depending on one's viewpoint, in March 1923 of four anti-Treaty rebels by pro-Treaty forces, further ignited enmity that was already inflamed. Known as the "Drumboe Martyrs", four men were taken into the woods early in the morning and summarily shot. Sheamus and Ciaran were incensed but Liam's anger was controlled and calculating, demanding retribution, and his anti-Treaty activities increased threefold. As such, Liam came to the attention of the authorities as details of reprisals, undertaken by anti-Treaty forces, leaked within the locality. Tensions were very high with bitterness between family, friends and neighbours creating a toxic atmosphere.

Meanwhile, Patsy had his own axe to grind, and he wondered if the current hostilities might play to his advantage. There was now a child on the way, and he was learning the ropes in the pub, serving behind the bar on an odd night. Teresa, his wife, did present a challenge. She knew her own mind and, although Patsy did enjoy the odd verbal spat, he wished she had more appeal physically. Now the marriage was consummated he felt he was entitled to be generous with his favours elsewhere, should he feel the need, but surprisingly, he had other priorities. Although his schemes for expansion of the family firm had not entirely gone to plan, he was no longer concerned. Convinced Sean was murdered, his energies were now focussed on another direction. Until that issue was resolved, the business could wait. At some point in the future, he would again consider how to grow the firm, but his father had aged so much since the death of Sean, that Patsy did not want to trouble him further. His mother, too, had not fully recovered and he felt a responsibility to take care of them both. Other schemes now took precedence and plans for vengeance consumed him daily. His hatred of Liam McShane had transformed from red-hot anger into a cold, calculated thirst for revenge.

Patsy's preoccupation with Liam McShane was such he had almost become adept at sensing Liam's presence. Walking briskly from his parents' house, he spied a figure in the distance and instantly knew it was his nemesis. There was a satisfaction in having his brother's blackthorn stick to hand and he automatically gripped it tighter. Sean had fashioned it himself, preferring the ancient method where the wood was lathered with butter and then placed up the chimney to cure. This particular type of stick was known as a "loaded stick," because one end was weighted heavier than the norm. It was well blackened and gnarled, invincible in Patsy's hand, as only a fool would expect to get the better of Liam McShane without a weapon. Against his better judgement and unsure of his reasons, Patsy followed Liam, who was so engrossed in his thoughts he was oblivious to the fact he had acquired a shadow. He was taking his evening hike over the mountains, a ritual he savoured whenever possible, arriving circuitously back at his farm.

Curiosity overcame common sense, and Patsy hunkered down behind a rock, ignoring the sharp edge piercing his thigh, his compulsion making him inquisitive. Despite the growing darkness, any activity might be noticed down below so it was imperative movement be kept to a minimum. Although crouched low, the yard was visible from his vantage point and Patsy could see Sheamus relieve Josie of a cooking pot which he then carried into the barn. The significance of the pot, probably of potatoes, was not immediately apparent. Noticeably, Sheamus also carried a bale of straw. Shortly afterwards, a spiral of smoke emanating from the barn chimney, signalled a fire had been lit. Sheamus now emerged from the barn and stooped down to lift a rock beside the door, before replacing it as before. This action intrigued Patsy, and a vague idea of what might be happening began to form. He resolved to return later that night, when all should be asleep, to investigate. His interest was piqued further when Joe, Liam's half-brother, noticeably inebriated, rounded the corner. The animosity between Joe and Liam and the reasons why, were well known. He railed at Liam with increasing regularity, jealous that his father had died and left nothing to his eldest son. Now, taking care where he placed his footing, Patsy ventured closer, keeping to the shadows, in an attempt to hear what was said.

Joe started yelling for Liam before he reached the farm gate, obviously, the worse for wear having spent the afternoon in the pub. 'Would ye ever feck off, Joe,' roared Liam, blocking Joe's path, so that he couldn't encroach further into the yard.

Patsy watched with glee as Joe took a swing at Liam, but Joe was so unsteady, he fell flat on his face. Liam used his foot to roll him gently over, but Patsy was too far away to hear what was said. Joe stumbled shakily to his feet and spat at Liam who turned his back and marched away, slamming the gate in his wake. The animosity might prove a useful tool in the future, so Patsy vowed to check from time to time, to see how matters developed. Joe might yet be an ally, his antipathy towards Liam, possibly advantageous.

His thoughts started to drift now to Ellen. She appealed to him physically in a way that Teresa never could. More importantly, what he had overlooked was how useful she might have been to him. He regretted at times the speed with which he had dropped her, believing he could have wheedled or cajoled her to reveal some information about Liam. News on the grapevine indicated that she was in London but at some point, she would return, and who knew what might be rekindled? He took a moment to remember how beautiful she was and how holding her, touching her, and smelling her scent, had given him a type of thrill that was missing when he was with Teresa.

Once dinner was over, Kathleen slipped outside. She always felt at peace in the quiet of the evening before dusk began to fall and silence shrouded the landscape. Kathleen was a pretty girl with candid, green eyes and flowing silky hair. She still limped slightly, but, overall, her gait had improved as she grew. Although still only thirteen, it was hoped that, eventually, any difficulty with her walking would be barely noticeable. It never bothered her at all, although she knew Liam still winced when he saw her struggle or appear tired. She had a cheerful, sunny disposition, insulated from the world, finding happiness and solace within her family. She bent over her garden, anxious to remove some insidious weeds before they became too entangled to easily extract. It was early May with a lengthening stretch in the evenings. Her ministrations had enabled the family to enjoy a variety of vegetables and more importantly in Kathleen's mind, an abundance of flowers.

The previous two years had been traumatic for Kathleen and sometimes she found it difficult to process all that had happened. After the death of Donal, her father, the home seemed to fall apart. Her mother, understandably, found it difficult as she came to terms with her grief. Last Christmas had been a quiet affair, the dynamic altered because of Ellen's pending departure and the unresolved issue between Liam and Joe. Brendan had joined them for a while, but the tension generated by his father continued unabated, and he returned home earlier than usual. The antagonism Joe created upset Kathleen and, when she could, she avoided the almost daily confrontations. She furiously brushed away a threatened tear and studiously bent her head, an attempt to ignore Liam shouting ferociously after Joe and noisily slamming the gate.

'Fuck off, and don't come back here again.'

Joe's equally vicious response was, 'I'll get you back, you wait and see.'

Kathleen continued pulling weeds, as Liam stormed past, his brow furrowed, lips thin and tight. Joe's fury was not spent, and Kathleen surreptitiously watched him as he stood unsteadily in the laneway, staring after Liam, spitting on the ground, hostility and rage, a vibrant, tactile force, emanating from every fibre of his body. Bending over the flower bed once more, hoping Joe could not see her, Kathleen sensed the heat from his rage, searing her back. She longed for the peaceful days when all the family were home, at ease with each other, relaxed by the fire.

Both of her sisters had left for England with Bridie about five days earlier, leaving a void that was difficult to fill. Ellen had been her comfort when her imagination ran riot. On windy nights, when she heard the howl of the banshee or when the grass rustled with the running feet of a fairy or a roguish leprechaun, Ellen's bed and outstretched arms, were her sanctuary. When she heard that Sarah was to leave with Ellen, she was inconsolable for days, sobbing nightly, unable to accept the breakup of her family. Easter Sunday had been especially depressing, a quite dismal affair. Sarah had refused to take part, spending the whole day in her room. She was the one who always boiled the eggs and organised the paints. She loved the old tradition of "cludog", where the family traipsed to the edge of the farm. After the tramp down the boreen and up into the hills, Sarah would arrange the hard-boiled eggs in a circle and organise the painting competition. Each year she had taken pains to teach Kathleen how to mix and recreate the magnificence of the rainbow. None of that had happened this year. The arrival of Bridie on the first of May to accompany her sisters to London, had intensified Kathleen's despondency still further.

Kathleen had been pleased to see Sheamus take the pot of potatoes off her mother, glad he was there to help tonight. Quite often, none of the lads were around, and although she was far from helpless, heavy lifting was not something she was able to do. Her job, on "potato nights", as she named them, was to look after the two dogs and keep them calm. A little extra food and a bed by the fire mollified their protective nature, dulling senses usually alert to a stranger in the yard.

She bent over to tackle a final bit of weeding before it was too dark to see anything. Some creeping thistles had found root in the far reaches of the flower bed. The plant crept through the soil, well protected by prickly leaves, and needed uprooting before it ran riot. Kathleen checked there was no one around, before bunching her skirt up around her knees to tackle the weed. That way, the skirt would not get so dirty. She only possessed one other and it was needed for Sundays.

Once finished, she stretched and gazed around the yard. Dusk always created a shadow on the rocks to the rear of the barn. The shapes made her fanciful, her fantasies conjuring wild animals or banshees, sometimes a handsome prince. Her romantic musings made her think of Ellen and wondered if she had stayed, would she now be married to Patsy O'Hara. Her imagination wove a story that he was pining for Ellen but in her heart, she knew it was only wishful thinking. Ellen was not returning any time soon and it certainly would not be for Patsy O'Hara. Even Kathleen had heard he had married a publican's daughter from Killybegs and there was now a child on the way. Thoughts and hopes of Ellen and Sarah moving home, married nearby with babies of their own, was a recurring wish and dream.

A cool breeze was generating a chill, but she was reluctant to go inside until she was sure Liam was calm and the house was peaceful. She delayed, and just as she felt she had no choice but to seek some heat, she was relieved to see all three of her brothers leave the house and stride purposefully down the lane. Kathleen saw to the dogs and the next hour was pleasurably passed playing cards by the fire with her mother.

'Time for bed, Kathleen,' hinted Josie, but her words trailed away, interrupted by a muffled tapping on the door.

Josie peered cautiously outside and hurried instructions were issued before the visitor hastily retreated. Kathleen watched from the window as her mother, by the light of a lantern, made her way across the yard. She bent down to the rock adjacent to the barn door and retrieved the ebony cross that lay underneath for just this type of emergency. Carefully she placed the cross upon the door, the signal for those on the run to keep moving as, tonight, the McShane's house, was not safe. Josie returned and said nothing but Kathleen, always perceptive, assumed there must be pro-Treaty forces in the area. It would not be their first visit to the farm and each time the disharmony created took several hours to abate and filled Kathleen with a sense of dread. As Josie caught Kathleen's worried eye, she disguised her concern and gestured with a smile "I think it's your deal, Kitty", using the 'pet' name she bestowed on her youngest born, thoughts of bed now forgotten. Silently Josie offered a prayer, beseeching Mary, the mother of Jesus, to guard her boys this night.

Earlier, Patsy had repaired to the village and the pub as it was too far to travel back to Killybegs. He entered the bar and once his eyes became accustomed to the semi-dark interior, he spied Joe in the corner, nursing another pint. A few hours and a few pints later, Joe rose and left the pub, staggering in the direction of the laneway that led to his own but also, the McShane farmhouse. Patsy followed, interested to see if Joe would cause another scene. Clouds covered the night sky obliterating any light, but this presented no problem for Patsy, used as he was, to Donegal lanes and byways. Despite being the worse for wear, Joe, not hindered by a slight sway, walked effortlessly enough, passing his cottage and continuing to the farmyard.

Patsy made his way back to his original spot, to what he now considered to be his rock, from where he could overlook the farm with ease and settled down to wait and watch. A breeze teased the thin curtain on the farmhouse window, its fluttering dance illuminating the yard in snatches, seeking out the shadows where frost shimmered and sparkled in sudden flashes. The moon edged slowly, tantalisingly, from behind the clouds, playing hide-and-seek, but sufficiently joining the mystical dance to provide enough, if scant light, for Patsy to watch the scene below.

Joe moved around the yard for a while and then unlocked the barn door and went inside, ignoring the creaking noise that echoed loudly in the stillness. All remained quiet. Patsy was too absorbed by Joe's actions to feel the cold or notice the creeping frost now appearing in patches on the grass. Still, he could not ignore the stiffness now penetrating his limbs and just as he was about to move, Joe reappeared. He stood at the door, seemingly in deep contemplation, holding an item that was indistinguishable to Patsy at such a distance. Patsy was unable to decipher what he was up to, but he was apparently in no hurry as he took his time, before he finally disappeared into the darkness of the night.

It was now Patsy's turn to enter the farmyard and he stealthily crossed to the barn, pausing at intervals to listen for any sounds, anxious not to make any of his own. Despite his furtiveness, the door groaned but no one stirred and more importantly, no dogs barked. Inside, he saw a full pot of potatoes simmering on a low fire that had been hastily but insufficiently banked, and so remained glowing. A cracked plate with some butter and salt was placed on the hearth. A rough blanket had been thrown over a bed of straw, perhaps ready for an occupant later that night. There was no doubt now in Patsy's mind that one of the "irregulars" intended to seek sanctuary, on the McShane's' farm. He closed the barn door gently and studied the adjacent rock. Thoughtfully he scrutinised the ebony cross hanging on the barn door. It was crude, made from bog oak, frosty speckles glittering silver in the moonlight, its purpose obscure. Patsy pondered for some more minutes, considering the reason for the cross, finally nodding to himself. He returned to his rock, deep in thought, as an idea began to form.

In the shadows, a lone figure sidled across the yard slithering close to the wall, barely perceptible under the dark night sky. The figure jumped as a fox scuttled close by, almost startling him into making a sound. The cross was hastily removed from the barndoor which was simultaneously opened, just a crack, but wide enough to allow entry. The old fireplace dominated the barn, beckoning, and he strode purposefully across, a hiding place already taking root. He knew that such a worn hearth, previously utilised for many years, was bound to have quite a few loose bricks, the mortar dried and flaking. Spying the thin blanket thrown on the makeshift straw bed, he wrapped it around his hand and arm, a vain if ineffective barrier from the diminished but still smouldering fire. A loose brick, one of many, was quickly sourced, and the cross slid inside with ease, disappearing from view. The dangerous night's work done, he hastily retreated into the darkness, pausing to draw welcome breath from behind a hedge, before slinking away.

Further down the lane, the cloudy night granting some protection, another shape stirred. Creeping cautiously, hidden in the obscurity of the ditch, he reached the farmyard. Moving swiftly, he entered the barn, seeking the promised safety. He lay down and closed his eyes, oblivious to the sound of the vehicle pausing some distance away, to enable Free-state soldiers to sneak unheard up the laneway.

Chapter 15

The shouts and scuffling from the yard in the early morning hours first woke Kathleen, followed by Josie. Liam and Ciaran were nowhere to be seen but Sheamus came rushing around the side of the farmhouse to check on the commotion, almost colliding with Josie in his haste. She turned when she saw him, urging Kathleen, 'Go inside and close the door.'

Kathleen did as she was bid but left the door open just enough to see and hear what was transpiring. Her mother was huddled outside, tightly clutching her old coat, visibly distressed, Sheamus by her side. State forces were hauling a struggling man from the barn. His arms were secured tightly behind his back as he was roughly held upright by two soldiers. An armoured car rumbled slowly into the yard. With excessive force, the man was beaten and shoved into the back of the vehicle and bound further. Sheamus stepped forward, shouting, 'Get off him,' but he faltered, sprawling backwards as the force from a rifle butt sent him careering to the ground.

'Hiding traitors are ye?'

'Feeding them too,' said another, glowering down at a spread-eagled Sheamus, preventing him with his boot from attempting to stand. 'Think we should take you with us an all.'

Sheamus glared at his attacker, the details of his angry face forever ingrained in his memory, even as he postulated, 'Never saw him before, ye have no reason to arrest him, he is just an oul tinker.' His response was antagonistic but prone on the ground it was without threat and to no avail.

'Aye, sure, and the pot of potatoes was for the pigs,' jeered the soldier brandishing the rifle once more.

'Aye, that's right,' muttered Sheamus. 'Pig swill is all was in there. We have an oul sow over there.' Both men held their gaze, one threatening and one defiant, even in defeat. Josie made a move towards Sheamus, before he roared, 'Get back in the house, Ma,' and Josie slowly backed away, moving haltingly, until she was inside the farmhouse where she clutched Kathleen.

A mocking taunt followed, 'You get up and into the house with ye, too.' Sheamus stood and followed Josie, his back and shoulders breathing defiance. 'We'll be here tomorrow for yer boys,' scoffed one of the soldiers to Josie as she slammed the door.

Josie and Sheamus now looked at one another unable to comprehend what had happened. The ebony cross should have signalled that the man needed to keep moving. Josie glanced over at the barn door. It was still dark, but the door seemed curiously bare from the distance with no visible cross to be seen. From her bedroom window, Kathleen watched as the man was driven away, battered and bruised. Josie attended to Sheamus as he was bleeding profusely from a wound over his eye that was rapidly swelling and turning blue. Once the blood was staunched, Josie and Sheamus sipped tea until Liam returned, followed closely by Ciaran.

Liam stared at the open wound that revealed a new parting in Sheamus' hair. 'The bastard,' roared Liam. 'Did you get a good look at him?'

'I won't forget his face too easily,' replied Sheamus.

'Well, in due course we'll be paying that boyo a visit, that's for sure, but for now, we have to sort what happened here.' Turning to Josie, Liam did his best to contain his frustration. 'Did you not put the cross on the door?' he demanded, his face turning a violent crimson from his attempts to control, his anger.

'Of course, I did,' replied Josie smartly. 'As soon as Mick knocked and told me, I did it immediately.'

'Where is it then?' demanded Liam.

'I don't know,' cried Josie. 'I looked, but I cannot find it. It is still too dark to see anything now, anyway.'

'And you, Sheamus, where were you?' barked Liam, turning towards Sheamus.

'Oh, calm down, Liam, I came back once I heard there were searches going on in the area. I checked the door, and the cross was hanging there, just as Ma said.'

'What time was that?' queried Ciaran.

'About half-past one,' responded Sheamus, 'and then I slipped out for a smoke and whatever. I never heard anyone in the yard.'

'What does "whatever" mean?' interrupted Liam, with ominous, quietness. 'It is almost 4 o'clock now. How long were you gone before the soldiers came?'

'Jaysus, Liam, I was just down the road with young Sally. I left her abruptly earlier on when I heard about the searches, just wanted to say a proper goodnight,' was the belligerent response.

'Are you telling me you came back here, knowing the farm might be searched and still left your Ma and Kathleen alone? Just for a young one, Sheamus, is that right? And while you were gone, someone moved that cross. And you, Ciaran, where were you? You both knew you had to be back early tonight.'

'I fell asleep in Paddy's place, after the match,' was the sheepish response.

'See,' accused Sheamus, fiery eyes glaring, first at Liam and then Ciaran, 'yer roarin' at me but at least I was nearby.'

The tension in the kitchen was unmistakable as all three brothers and Josie faced each other across the table. It was only Kathleen, peering anxiously into the kitchen, that made Josie announce, 'I am going to bed now. I suggest you all do the same, and we can talk again in the morning.'

The next morning, the yard was thoroughly searched in the event the cross had fallen off the door and been kicked into a distant corner. It seemed it had simply vanished, and the only conclusion was that it had deliberately been removed. Kathleen was seriously affected by the whole episode. She had seen her mother place the cross on the door and the hook was so secure, it was impossible to imagine it could have fallen off. The ebony cross had disappeared, and the finger of suspicion lingered because no culprit could be found. The continual tension between her brothers upset her and even her garden could not assuage her stress. Josie looked on in sadness as her three sons argued, from shame, responsibility, and remorse. She was convinced a neighbour who sympathised with the pro-Treaty side had removed the cross. Although that was a possible scenario, the question of how and who, remained. Recrimination and argument were the daily fare and Josie despaired as her family ripped itself apart.

Ceaselessly, the arguments pounded in Liam's head with no resolution and no one admitting culpability. Liam was like a dog with a bone and could not let the subject rest. He turned once more to Sheamus but also directed his questions, to Ciaran. 'Did either of ye mention to anyone, even by mistake, that we are a safe house?'

'Don't be daft, Liam,' said Ciaran, and in an aside, 'anyway, everyone around here knows we are.'

'Do they now?' countered Liam. 'If so, it was a good night to come calling, with our mam and baby sister all alone. You both knew I would be very late, yet, Ciaran, you fall asleep and, Sheamus, you go off to that fancy one.' Liam's fists clenched and unclenched with barely concealed disgust. His fury was such that he stormed off, slamming the door in his wake, heading towards the mountains, hoping the calming effects of his beloved landscape would bring him some ease. Sheamus, his very stance combative and aggressive, stared after him, contemplatively.

Josie could hold her tongue no longer and tackled Liam on his return. 'Mam, I'm only asking the same questions that they'll have to answer when the investigation gets underway, and there's a big difference here, I am their brother, we're family. Ye know I don't mean to suggest either would betray us, but they have to be ready to explain their actions.'

'Liam, you better make amends before it's too late. I don't want to see my family broken up any more than it currently is,' declared Josie.

'I am just trying to convey the seriousness of the situation. I am the

Quartermaster General, of the South Donegal IRA, a position your own uncle Mikey held for many years and his father before him. A position of respect. If one of ours was not safe on my own farm, under my watch, do you know what that does to the morale of the whole movement? But hush your worrying, I'll talk to Sheamus and Ciaran later, I'll sort it.'

The investigation was not long getting underway, and answers required. Josie and even little Kathleen were questioned but no one seriously considered either was at fault. 'What went on here, Liam? A good lad arrested, and we can all guess what will happen to him.'

'We're as puzzled as you, Jimmy, me mother put that cross on the door, she swears it, and Sheamus checked it later on.'

'Aye, and I believe her, and Sheamus. But someone removed it.'

'Aye, that's right, Jimmy, and when I find out who's behind the treachery, it'll be a sorry day for him, or her, whoever it might be,' responded Liam.

Ciaran and Sheamus were subjected to an intense cross-examination, but overall, no one believed a McShane, staunch Republicans and Nationalists for generations, would betray the "cause". Yet, the pall of suspicion could not be dissipated. There was no direct accusation, just insinuations and pointed fingers. Gossip, that maybe they were not to be trusted precipitated some heads to turn, silence to deepen, so until the culprit was apprehended, and the treachery exposed and dealt with, confidence was shaken.

Rumours began circulating that the lad from the barn had been imprisoned and was to be shot, but it was difficult to ascertain the full truth. The uneasy truce between Liam, Sheamus and Ciaran was short-lived, and anger flared once more when the fate of the volunteer became known. They all felt a sense of responsibility when it was confirmed he had indeed been executed the day after his capture but not before he suffered torture at the hands of the Irish Free State Army.

Liam gave no detail as to where he had been, beyond saying he was helping with some campaign planning. He felt let down by his brothers who knew a volunteer was expected at the farm that night. His shame, that such a thing could happen on his farm tormented him and he knew there would always be a cloud hanging over all of them. Sheamus bore the brunt of Liam's ire as he had returned to the farm only to leave again, but Ciaran did not escape unscathed. He claimed to have gone out with the football team to celebrate a win and afterwards had fallen asleep in Paddy's house. When he awoke, he had trekked home, arriving after the whole episode was over. Ciaran agreed that to fall asleep on such a night was stupid and unforgivable, but apologies did not stop Liam's continual, verbal assaults. Sheamus felt aggrieved, as he had returned as requested, rejecting the insinuation that he was somehow at fault. Sally lived just a short distance away and he was back as soon as he heard the commotion.

Liam could not let things go. Again, and again, he went over the events of that night, retracing each possibility, but continuously going around in circles. The suspicion that either Patsy O'Hara or possibly his half-brother Joe was somehow involved continually niggled. Yet, who would be daring enough to trespass knowing what the consequences would be if caught? He considered Joe, as he had been skulking around, not just that day, but most days. Joe knew what went on in the barn, but Liam felt that even Joe would not sink that low. Yet, the bitterness and promise of revenge that spewed from him on an almost daily basis could not be ignored. As for Patsy O'Hara, wasn't his wife expecting a child? Her father, Cormac, had a strong arm, and anyway, weren't Cormac's politics in tune with Liam's own? Liam believed he would ensure Patsy toed the line if he wanted the benefits of the pub. Yet, Patsy had been seen at his parents' farm that day, so the possibility had to be considered.

With the ceasing of the Civil War a few weeks later, there was no further need to boil extra potatoes, but memories were long, and bitterness permeated every household. On the surface there was peace, but households were still divided. There was no forgiveness, and each side was still consumed with hatred. The ending of the war was even more poignant, occurring as it did a few weeks after the ebony cross disappeared and the execution of the lad found in the barn. The agreed ceasefire between both sides of the conflict, combined with the passage of time, saw all three brothers drift in disparate directions. In late November, Sheamus announced he was moving to Scotland. Joe and Brendan had travelled to Glasgow the previous week and had a place to stay with room for Sheamus. Sheamus had no argument with Joe and never got involved with the dispute between him and Liam. It was a comforting thought to have a friendly face when he arrived in the city and he was glad to leave Donegal, believing there was no long-term future there for him. The recent events, with lingering hostility, had confirmed that the time was well past to move on and build his own life. For the first time he had also managed to save some cash and that would help to make the transition to life in Scotland that bit easier. Ciaran kept his thoughts to himself as he quietly began to make plans for his own future. Liam had no intention of going anywhere. He stayed on and held his head high, as harsh, and aggressive as always. He continued farming and going to the pub and it would be a brave man who challenged him even when, unusually for him, he began to have a little more than a couple of pints each night.

Chapter 16

After five weeks in London, Ellen had no option but to look for employment as a domestic servant. She was offered a position as a scullery maid in a house that was within walking distance of the cottage. Although she gratefully accepted the employment, she intended to continue to look elsewhere. Scullery maids were the lowest ranking servant, and their duties were physically demanding.

It was mid-June, and the mornings were generally bright and clear, but it was still difficult to rise at dawn each day. The house was a fifteen-minute walk, so Ellen needed to be up and dressed before 5.30am to be on time at 6 o'clock, each morning. Clearing ashes from the kitchen range and the numerous fireplaces downstairs was her first duty. She then had to set water on to heat, before filling and hauling steaming jugs upstairs, which were placed on the small tables outside each of five bedrooms. If the occupant rose late, the water had to be replaced. By the time these tasks were completed cook had arrived and help was required to set the breakfast table and begin preparation of the food for the day. Once a member of the family appeared downstairs, Ellen had to immediately go up to the bedroom to collect the chamber pot. The house did have one indoor closet, but this was not used by women during the night. As might be expected, this was Ellen's least favourite chore. All pots had to be scoured daily, and as the lowest member of staff, it was her job alone. Afterwards, hands bright red from scrubbing with disinfectant, Ellen chopped vegetables and prepared meat for the day's menu.

The sumptuous daily cuisine astonished her, used as she was to simpler foods unless of course there was a special occasion. The variety of poultry and meat, accompanied by such a range of vegetables and sweets for a small family, was a revelation and generated a sinful waste in Ellen's opinion. However, the rigorous attention to detail demanded by the cook meant Ellen learnt skills which were to stand her in good stead in later years. Standing on the cold kitchen floor dicing and whisking, her mind always drifted to home and the difference in diet. Donegal fare had consisted of porridge in the morning with home-made brown or soda bread. There was never a shortage of scones, dripping with thick yellow butter and jam from the fruit growing wild on the hedgerows. Dinner was always midday and invariably a potato and vegetable stew, seasoned with a piece of mutton or, more usually, rabbit. If Ciaran had been lucky while out fishing, his broad smile lit up the room when he returned home with a salmon or several mackerel, relishing the smiles and shouts of glee as he swung the fish onto the table to be prepared. Choice meat and poultry were kept for special occasions, such as Christmas and Easter.

As was the custom, the scullery maid did not eat with the other kitchen staff. Ellen was relegated to watch over the ovens whilst the others had their meals and then ate alone. Her final task of the day, at 7.30 in the evening, was the washing of the kitchen floor, after which, she was free to trudge home. The first few weeks generated a tiredness, so overwhelming, she was barely able to converse with Bridie when she returned home, let alone have a cup of tea. Almost as soon as she came in the door, she tumbled into bed, waving a hand to indicate the promise of a chat the following day.

Although the hours were long, with an early start and late finish, Ellen never uttered a word in protest. By mid-July, her body had adjusted, and she had settled into the daily routine. She had also made friends with Susie, a parlour maid, and together they walked part of the way home each evening. Susie was bright and lively with a comic turn of phrase and Ellen had a sense of contentment as they chattered along the way. It was only thoughts of Sarah and how she was managing, that marred that contentment. Those thoughts intruded with unsettling regularity, while the events in the barn receded, buried ever deeper in her subconscious.

Susie asked Ellen to her family home as they were holding a get-together to celebrate her parents' wedding anniversary. Ellen was nervous, fussing over what to wear, mindful of her limited wardrobe but innately knowing her nervousness sprang from the anti–Irish sentiment that appeared to permeate everywhere she went. She need not have worried, receiving a warm welcome from all of Susie's family. Their house was tiny, even by Donegal standards, and the entire group of ten happily squashed inside.

Tony, Susie's brother, was particularly attentive. He had a barrow and sold fruit and vegetables down at the markets. He made a point of sitting beside Ellen the entire evening, engaging her in chat. Similar, to his sister, he had a quirky turn of phrase, sometimes she could barely understand him, and often he was flummoxed by her accent. This made them both giggle, generating a comfortable camaraderie in just a few hours. Perhaps, given a chance, the seeds of a relationship might have flourished but Sarah's problems meant the need to work and provide was a priority. Also, inspired by Bridie, the wish and the drive to make something of herself in her own right, made Ellen hesitate to take the friendship further.

Bridie was disappointed that the best position Ellen had been able to obtain was a scullery maid. She had hoped something better would have cropped up by now, but she was mindful of how her yellow, flowered jug, was slowly emptying of cash. There was an urgent necessity for Ellen to keep working and provide some additional income. She also knew but forbore to mention it, that although lyrical, Ellen's Donegal tone was difficult for many Londoners to understand and so mitigated against any position that required interaction with the public. So, for the moment, this job would have to do. The pay was very little for the hardship of the labour but even the few pennies helped pay bills and added to the savings for the next Dublin trip.

Josie, of course, and the family in Donegal, assumed both girls were settled in London. The necessity to write home regularly was an added strain on Ellen. The letters she received in return indicated how much they were missed, especially by Kathleen. The subterfuge of pretending all was well and that Sarah was just her usual flighty self and perhaps too busy to write was a stressful pressure, on top of the long working day.

By mutual consent, neither Bridie nor Ellen mentioned Sarah too often but thoughts of her were uppermost in both their minds. It was also disquieting that Sarah had not replied to any of their letters. Kathleen had written how she hoped her sisters would be home for Christmas and Ellen had difficulty framing a reply. In the end, she blamed it on the expense, saying it prohibited travel, but hoped they would all be home at Easter. As Christmas 1923, drew near, so also, did the expected birth.

'What do you think, Bridie?' enquired Ellen. 'Should we persuade Sarah to have the baby adopted? I know it is not what she will want. She seemed so determined to keep the child. It was the only spark of interest she showed in all the proceedings at the convent. Yet even my short time here, has shown how difficult it would be to keep a baby without a husband.'

'Ellen, I just don't know. I think that might be best but let us wait and see how Sarah is. Do you think your mother guessed Sarah's plight? Would it be possible to go home to Josie?'

Ellen shrugged, 'No, probably not. I think she knew Sarah was out of sorts, but not that she was expecting. Sarah was always demanding. I think she was allowed to leave for peace's sake. And you know, Donegal can be a very cruel place for an unmarried girl. I don't think Sarah can go back.'

As always, the conversation fizzled out with no solution, both seeking solace in the belief that Sarah was currently in a safe place. All their rearing had conditioned them to accept that nuns were inherently kind and godly and would care for Sarah, and her child.

Bridie had provided Ellen with oil to soothe her roughened hands. As the months rolled on, Sarah's hands, with no balm to erase, even slightly, the effects of the laundry, became increasingly inflamed, swollen, and stiff. At night, she had difficulty opening the buttons on her dress and the morning was even worse. The carbolic soap and the bleach stung when in contact with what were now, open cuts. Sarah welcomed the pain in silence, convinced the more penance she undertook, the better prepared she would be to take care of her baby. She had an innate belief in confession, penance, and forgiveness. She profoundly believed she had been at fault, tempting her attacker. She had been the *'occasion of sin'* and needed to make reparation. She also knew she had caused trouble for Ellen, Bridie, and her friend Danny. She wondered about her mother. *Has Mam guessed my sin and wanted me gone? Do my brothers know I am a fallen woman?*

Sarah tormented herself, believing she deserved punishment. Her irrationality stunted her ability to process logically what had occurred. Instead, she sank to her knees as often as she was able and prayed for forgiveness, an action that found approval from the nuns. Their blessing, further inculcated within her tortured mind the now unshakable belief that atonement was required.

Christmas approached and Sarah had a new worry. Her instincts told her the baby was overdue and her terror increased as each day passed by, with less and less noticeable movement. Her body was heavy and ungainly, and she found it difficult to stand for hours at a time. The days became endless, hours of misery and distress, with backache and dizziness from the steam in the laundry. Bouts of nausea permeated the day and garnered irritation, rather than sympathy, from the nun in charge. Christmas Day saw a reprieve from work although the fare was no better than usual.

That Christmas night, Sarah went into labour. Nothing had ever prepared her for the agony of childbirth. She called for Josie and Ellen as she endured the endless hours, mostly, alone. At times she thought she might die. Young Sr Oliver's gentle smile and her soft caress when, occasionally, she mopped her brow, her only solace. Sr Oliver was replaced by Sr Margaret, a "Bride of Christ", cold and severe in her disapproval. Sarah struggled, almost unaided, to bring her child into the world, Sr Margaret providing minimal assistance during delivery. The loneliness of that pilgrimage was soothed and eased when, in her exhaustion, she finally held her son. Sweat dripped from her weary body as she kissed his head and named him Stephen, in honour of the day. A steely determination swept over Sarah. She was not going to let her child down the way she had others in her life. She had endured her penance and she would now dedicate her life to Stephen.

Bridie walked to work one late December evening, still pondering over her discussion with Ellen and the correct action to take regarding, Sarah. The emergency room was crowded, as per usual, and within minutes she was tending to fractured limbs and swabbing deep, wounds. Her soft Donegal tones dispensed comfort to frightened children and worried mothers, in equal measure. The shouts from a drunken ex-soldier, who had fallen from an over-indulgent celebration of Christmas upset the small, frightened little girl, whom Bridie was attempting to comfort. 'Please be quiet, there are children here, and you are scaring them.'

The soldier rounded on Bridie once he heard her accent. 'Bloody Irish, go back to your own country. Yeh wanted shut of us. If you can't manage on yer own, don't come here takin' our jobs.' His belligerent hostility took everyone aback in the emergency room. His rant, a continual stream of abuse to all who came near. Bridie attempted to calm him, so his wound could be dressed, and he could be sent on his way, but he swung at her, knocking her to the ground. Another nurse rushed to help Bridie as the porters took hold of the drunken patient. Bridie was upset and shaken with a swollen cheek that, by the next day, would surely sport a colourful bruise. She was not capable of completing her shift and the kindly porter hailed a carriage to bring her home. Ellen made her sweet tea and listened sympathetically, as Bridie, now tearful with shock, stuttered about Danny and home. It was never more apparent to Ellen the debt owed to Bridie, how she had put her own life on hold to help them. Ellen quietly promised herself that neither she nor her sister would hold Bridie's life back much further than they already had. Yet, they still needed her help until Sarah was sorted.

After much discussion, a plan was hatched and agreed upon between them. As money was tight, once they were sure the baby was born, Bridie would travel alone back to Dublin. There she would meet Danny, and together, they would go to the convent. Whether Sarah would accompany Bridie back to London, with or without her baby, was still unclear, but decisions would have to be made once Sarah's child was safely delivered. There was still no letter from her which was a continual worry.

Chapter 17

Bridie undertook the gruelling and laborious journey to Dublin, in January 1924. She first travelled to Liverpool by train, but the few hours spent waiting to board the boat, were spent in the rain. Her boots soaked through and squelched like a sponge. Her skirt slapped rhythmically and uncomfortably against her legs. She clutched her thin coat tightly in a bid to keep out the breeze, as she stoically endured the onerous boat trip. Her eyes briefly lit up when she spotted Danny on the dockside, but she was too tired and cold to kiss him with any enthusiasm. Yet, when he clasped her firmly and stroked her cheek she felt an inner peace, and knew she was home.

'Don't go back,' he whispered, 'I need you so.'

It took all of Bridie's control not to agree on the spot. 'Soon, Danny, it will be soon, you know we first must sort Sarah,' was the weary response.

The rain had not stayed in Liverpool and Danny was just as wet as Bridie. Together, they squelched their way to a small hotel in Kilmainham, not too far from the convent, and where Danny had booked a room. As Mr and Mrs Walsh, they renewed their love for each other, spending the next hour languorously exploring each other's body. Tentatively, Danny's lips savoured Bridie's soft skin. Together, they aroused and caressed with a sensual and erotic abandonment that had been suppressed for too long. Afterwards, they went to a nearby café for some food, and over the meal, discussed the best way forward for Sarah.

Bridie decided it might be best, after all, to make the first approach to the convent on her own. It was January 28th, so despite receiving no word from Sarah, the baby must now be a few weeks old. The fact that no news had been forthcoming niggled at the back of Bridie's mind, and she was anxious to get to the convent to ascertain all was well. It took some considerable time with repeated, heavy knocking on the solid oak door, to receive any response. A shadowed face peered enquiringly through a slight aperture and Bridie requested entry to see her niece, Sarah.

'There is no one by that name here,' and an attempt was made to fully close the door.

Bridie held her ground and refused to leave shoving with more force than she had intended, so the nun had to stagger back to maintain her balance. 'Oh, I am sorry, I didn't mean to push so hard, but I must speak to the nun in charge. Her name is Sr Reginald,' demanded Bridie.

Whether it was her peremptory tone or the mention of the nun's name, the desired effect was achieved. Yet, it was with apparent great reluctance that the door was opened further, to allow entry. Quite a pretty face, encased in the large wimple and veil of the order, was spoiled by a sour, unwelcoming demeanour. She nevertheless motioned Bridie to sit on a hard bench in the hallway. 'I don't think she is available today, but I will see. Wait here.'

The time dragged slowly, and one and then two hours passed, before Sr Reginald obliged her with her presence. 'May I ask why you are here?' she enquired.

'To see my niece, Sarah McShane and her baby,' responded Bridie.

'She is no longer with us,' was the curt reply. 'The baby was, unfortunately, still-born, and she left shortly afterwards. So please leave now as you are disturbing the smooth running of our home.' The autocratic instruction was also a dismissal, and Sr Reginald turned on her heel and departed.

Bridie was left feeling stunned and inadequate with a hundred, unanswered questions. *Where has Sarah gone? Her rare and only letter, received last July, gave no indication that she intended leaving.* The letter, in fact, was almost a quest for reassurance that Bridie or Ellen would return and assist her once the baby was born. The door was being held open by quite a pleasant-faced nun, a flicker of compassion, quickly suppressed, briefly flitted across her features, whilst a nod of her head indicated Bridie should now leave. There was nothing further that Bridie could do for the moment, so she returned to the hotel and Danny.

Danny was incensed at the treatment meted out to Bridie and the disregard for Sarah, who must be bereaved at the loss of her baby. 'If she left, they have to know where she went. We are going back tomorrow.'

'The nuns have no reason to lie, Danny, so she must be gone, but yes, they should be able to tell us where she went. I mean, surely they wouldn't let her leave after giving birth, with nowhere to go?'

Danny was beginning to reassess his opinion of nuns but said nothing more. Tomorrow they would insist on answers. They rose early the next morning, anxious to resolve the mystery and, if necessary, start hunting for Sarah. They both dressed formally to present the best impression possible. Again, they had to knock for some considerable time before the door was reluctantly opened by the same young nun from the previous day. They were immediately rebuffed and refused entry. Danny's insistence, or perhaps because he was a male and spoke with authority, overcame the nun's reluctance, and despite her apparent unwillingness, they gained entrance to the hallway. An instruction was given that they would have to wait for some time for Sr Reginald, as she was busy with convent business. Exhaustion set in as the minutes and then hours, ticked by.

'They just want us to leave,' reposted Danny, 'but we are not going anywhere, even if we have to stay here all night. We need answers.'

And as they waited the light faded and the bench became harder and buttocks became so numb, the discomfort was barely noticeable. Just as Bridie began to believe they might indeed have to stay all night, a rustle down the hallway alerted them to another presence. As though conjured by a magician, an apparition, in the guise of Sr Reginald appeared.

'I told you yesterday, she left after the birth and unfortunate death of the baby. Stillbirth, not an unusual occurrence,' she snapped peremptorily. 'I have nothing further to say, so you are wasting everyone's precious time lingering in this hallway.'

Danny studied her for a moment. There was no way she was going to intimidate him. He had met too many people in the past few years who believed they could obtain their own way through an insinuation of superiority, in tone and action. Slowly, he stood up, and suggested they retire to her office to discuss what happened. 'That is tragic news, Sister. I am sure such a charitable institution has details of where Sarah is now staying. Let us all go to your office and obtain the address, so we don't clutter up the hallway any longer.'

Sr Reginald was nonplussed but only for a few seconds. 'Leave, please. I don't keep details of those types of women.' The sharp words were interrupted by the noise of a door opening and a group of young girls entered, preparing to polish the parquet floor. They each had a cloth and an allotted corner to begin their work. There was no mistaking that among them was Sarah, gaunt, grey, and skeletal, but still Sarah.

Bridie immediately jumped up and hugged her. 'Sarah, oh my goodness, Sarah.' Sarah looked blankly at Bridie. 'Sarah, it's Bridie, your Aunt Bridie.' For some seconds, Sarah stared, then appeared to crumple and fall, and it took all Bridie's strength to hold her upright.

Danny glared accusingly at Sr Reginald, as she responded, 'Oh, you meant her, my apologies, I was thinking of someone else.' Sr Reginald swung around, the only sign that she was discomfited displayed by the quick knotting of her rosary beads through her fingers.

She marched swiftly towards the door, but Danny stalled her with a question. 'What about Sarah's baby?'

A quick intake of breath was followed by, 'I told you, he died,' and with that sharp rejoinder, Sr Reginald disappeared through the doorway.

The young nun, who had held the door for Bridie the previous day, appeared startled by the revelation and smothered a gasp with a bout of coughing. The urgency to remove Sarah as quickly as possible forbade any further questioning. In hindsight, both Bridie and Danny regretted not taking time to query her, on the off chance, some light might have been shed on baby Stephen.

Danny and Bridie brought Sarah back to their hotel, but in view of the state she was in, it was thought best that Danny return to his lodgings and leave Sarah to share the room with Bridie. Bridie was hopeful that the hotel surroundings would stir some interest. Yet, Sarah remained passive and just agreed with whatever Bridie suggested. Her only wish, to Bridie's consternation, was to kneel and pray for an hour before bedtime. It soon became apparent that Sarah could not be left alone especially as she continued to insist her baby had not died.

'I nursed him for three weeks. He was fine. He just disappeared one day,' she whispered. 'I went up to feed him and he was gone. Some of the women said it would happen, but I never believed them. I wrote to you and Ellen. I told you about him. He didn't die.' Tears rolled down Sarah's cheeks, before the ever-present need to pray, resurfaced. 'I need to pray for him, I need to pray,' and Sarah dropped to her knees to enter a twilight world that no one could penetrate, for at least an hour.

Neither Bridie nor Danny knew whom to believe. Sarah was sure her baby was not only born alive, but she had fed him herself. 'But, Danny, would the nuns blatantly lie and to what purpose? I know they were a bit unpleasant, but to lie like that...' Bridie's voice trailed away as she looked for answers from Danny.

'I don't know, Bridie. I don't know what to think anymore. Sarah said she wrote to you, but you never received letters. If he is still alive, then where is he?' The discussion went around in circles with no result until the day of departure for London, dawned once more.

They were both aware that Sarah's issues were preventing the commencement of their lives together as planned. 'Bridie, you have to speak to Ellen and tell her you are returning to Dublin, as soon as possible, to marry me. Resign from the hospital, you will get work here.'

Bridie concurred but knew the road ahead was going to be difficult. 'I will speak to her, I have already, to a certain extent.' Bridie insisted, however, that she had to bring Sarah to London while she discussed the future with Ellen. 'I just feel so responsible for them both but particularly Sarah. I think Ellen will agree to return. London has not turned out as she expected.'

Danny assisted them, as usual, to board the boat and kissed Bridie gently on the lips, in farewell. It was so sensual and loving that Bridie's resolve to return to London with Sarah was weakened and she was tempted to stay. She clung to him, lingering, but the insidious blast from the foghorn intruded and common sense prevailed. Bridie shepherded Sarah aboard for the lonely journey back to London.

The first night that Ellen ever spent alone was when Bridie returned to Dublin to check on Sarah. It was also the first night when the events of the barn began to surface once more. She guessed it was the focus on home and Donegal, and the events that led to Sarah's predicament, not least, why she herself left the social early. Whatever the reason, she found herself rising in the early hours, jerked awake by the spurting of blood, and haunted by Liam's contorted features. Passers-by might have frowned at the extravagance of gas lights at 3 am, but when Ellen awoke, panting, she needed light to calm her churning thoughts. Grabbing a warm, woollen blanket, she huddled in a chair by the dying embers of the fire. Restful sleep was now elusive, but the dawn was still a distance away. She questioned had she lived her life until now as a shadow, someone without substance, a canvas for others to write upon. She had been absorbed by Bridie and her ideas. She had nurtured Sarah as best she was able through her trauma, but she had never spent time on herself. She was now on her own with no distractions and vivid images of Liam wielding the knife could no longer be banished from her mind. She denied sleep for as long as possible each night hoping exhaustion would induce an intense, dreamless, slumber. Instead, she staggered to work each morning in a state of utter fatigue.

Ellen considered her relationships with her three brothers and how they varied from one to the other. Liam never altered in his ideas, strong and straight, challenging, but always honest in his dealings. Sheamus liked an easy life, never intruding, and always seemed indifferent to his sisters. In many ways, he was the most difficult to understand or know. Despite his confident appearance, his easy chat with the local girls, he was quiet and introverted to a fault, his inner thoughts privately held. Ellen never felt close to Sheamus or had the comfortable relationship she experienced with Ciaran. Ciaran touched her heart in a unique way and had always been there to listen to her. She still wondered if he had seen her in the barn and if he regretted his part in Sean's death. Despite her differing relationships with her brothers, all three, were her family. To have watched them take a life, especially of someone she knew, could not be sanitised any longer. Ellen had known Sean, met his wife, and been fond of his brother, Patsy. To rationalise and accept that the taking of the life of one Irishman by another Irishman, in the name of freedom, was justified, was too difficult a concept to comprehend. For that act to have been perpetrated by her brothers was still a more bewildering puzzle, hence her disturbed sleep. Now she was alone with time to think she could not deny her own confusion and how distraught she was at witnessing what had occurred.

The first time she put pen to paper was at 4.30 in the morning, huddled in a chair, with rain beating against the windowpane. All she scribbled were her brothers' names but the following night she attempted to describe them. Each successive, early morning sojourn, while Bridie was in Dublin, she began to write the moment her sleep was disturbed. In a roundabout way, she chronicled the night in the barn and what she had seen and the more she spilled onto the page, the less troubled became her sleep. The spectres that haunted her dreams faded into the mist and eventually disappeared, as they gained form in her notebook. When Bridie returned with Sarah, Ellen was more at ease within herself and in a better position to aid her extremely distraught sister.

Bridie and Sarah arrived, exhausted and dishevelled, and thankful that Ellen had a hot meal, ready and waiting. Ellen was visibly shocked at the state Sarah was in, and the strain on Bridie's face, told of an arduous journey from Dublin. There was also no sign of any child, but innate wisdom bade Ellen hold off on her questions until she was alone with Bridie. Once the meal was over, Sarah retired for the night. Ellen thought she was tired and ready for sleep, but before long, the drone of repetitive praying could be heard, and Ellen looked questioningly at Bridie. Bridie was too tired to give a detailed account of all that had occurred in Dublin but knew Ellen deserved at least a brief outline of what had transpired. Ellen's anguish, when she heard of the baby's death reached new depths when she learnt that Sarah could not accept that the little boy had died. She had hoped Sarah would be more at ease with herself, but it was clearly, not so.

Although unspoken that night, it was paramount that plans for the future needed to be urgently formulated, and that a long chat was essential as soon as they had a quiet hour together. Bridie now rose and said goodnight. The little cottage would be cramped with the three of them, and with Sarah in the tiny bedroom, Ellen settled for sleep on the elderly couch. She lay listening to Sarah's steady breathing through the thin walls and rather large gap in the ill-fitting door, worrying about the once vivacious sister, who was now a vague imitation of the girl she used to know. The relief that Ellen experienced when she first saw them both arrive safely home had dissipated. Bridie had relayed a little of the difficulties encountered on the journey. 'Ellen, Sarah was docile to the point of helplessness. I had to ensure she ate, force her to help me carry cases and I was so exhausted with the muttered prayers, embarrassed, at times. I was never so glad to reach the cottage. We must accept there is a major problem with Sarah, so decisions on what is best, must be made as soon as possible. Sarah is going to need constant monitoring and attention for the foreseeable future.'

By now, Ellen had been over ten months in London, a time spent in a monotonous drudgery that she had not experienced before. Although a farmer's daughter from Donegal, she had never encountered that sensation of inferiority, which was almost a daily occurrence. When Bridie first mooted the idea that they all return to Dublin, Ellen agreed promptly. She had to concede that Sarah needed help and they might find that assistance easier to obtain on familiar ground. Obtaining employment would once again present difficulties but she firmly believed no position could be any worse than the one she already had. Her hopes for London had certainly not materialised in the way she had envisioned so with no qualms whatsoever, she once more put her faith in Bridie. All three would return home as soon as money and required notice allowed. Together, Ellen and Bridie organised a budget and they decided that with a certain amount of thrift they should be able to afford to leave, by mid-

or-late, May 1924. Preparations for their departure would take a few months as there was a fair amount of organisation required. They had to give notice to their employers and landlord and pack their belongings. Buying the tickets for the boat used up a large portion of their financial resources, but once plans for the move were set in motion, Bridie wrote to Danny, and he set about arranging lodgings. They also set a wedding date, for October 14th.

Christmas in Donegal had been a strained affair. Liam and Ciaran barely spoke while Josie pottered about, attempting to ease the tension, and preserve a semblance of normality for Kathleen. The atmosphere in the house was stifling and, quietly, Ciaran began preparations for a future move of his own. Silent regret over his many undertakings for the "cause", preyed on his mind. He understood Sheamus' desire to leave and start afresh and felt it was time for him to do likewise and leave Donegal. The strain of the past few months had taken its toll on them all and he fervently hoped that time apart, would heal any rift in the family. Ciaran delayed announcing his plans until Easter 1924, when he was satisfied, he had enough savings to purchase his passage and see him through the first month in America.

His mother's sadness when he announced his plans upset him, but he comforted himself with the knowledge that Liam, and especially Kathleen, would still be around. For his part, although he would miss Josie and Kathleen, Liam's contrariness was beginning to grate on his nerves as was his questioning over the accumulation of enough money to emigrate to the States. Liam's motives were nothing other than his need to control and direct the family, but he was irritating in the extreme. Ciaran had money because he rarely drank and that was that. When he learned that his sisters and Bridie were now ensconced in Dublin and that Bridie's wedding was set for October, he wrote to Ellen and asked could he stay with them for a few days, before the ship sailed. It was customary to have a "wake" prior to emigration to America, but in the circumstances, Ciaran felt it best if he just went quietly. However, he would be in Dublin in time for Bridie's wedding and to say goodbye to Ellen, Sarah, and Bridie.

Chapter 18

It was just tenacity and pure luck that enabled Danny to sort lodgings on South Circular Road. However, there was no doubt it would be a cramped space once the three women were installed. Danny's bedsit was not too far away but until Bridie and he were married, everyone would have to make do. As always, he met Bridie, and now Ellen and Sarah, on the docks. For a change, the sun was shining. Happiness exuded from both Bridie and Danny as the realisation dawned that, at last, they were now about to embark on their life together. He helped with their luggage and saw the three women settled in their lodgings, guaranteeing, it was only a temporary arrangement. Obtaining work was now the most pressing requirement so the following morning, Bridie, dressed in her best, walked the relatively short distance to St Ultan's Hospital, leaving Ellen to unpack and take care of Sarah.

St Ultan's was a pioneering institution in the Ireland of the early, 20th century. Two women, Dr Kathleen Lynn, and Madeline Ffrench-Mullen were the driving force and instrumental in its establishment. It was a hospital with a mainly female staff and offered a pathway for many female doctors to gain experience and advance their careers. Poverty and its effects, and the general health of women and their babies was the primary concern. There was an upsurge in venereal disease at the end of the First World War and St. Ultan's catered for these women and their babies, in addition to tending to Dublin's poor. The hospital also became centrally involved in the treatment of patients suffering from the raging flu' epidemic. Dr Kathleen Lynn envisioned not just a hospital but an education centre, where women learnt how to care for both themselves and their children. There was an emphasis on breastfeeding, fresh air, and cleanliness. Lectures to educate mothers and the promotion of child-centred education, advocated by Dr Maria Montessori, was provided, and seen as a method to help eliminate poverty. Harry Clarke, Jack B Yeats, Sean O'Casey and other leading artists and writers of the day, assisted in fundraising and the promotion of a multi-denominational ethos. Many activities were in Gaelic thus linking the hospital, subtly, to the advancement of Irish Nationalism.

However, it was a sunny July morning, when Bridie slowly climbed the steps to St Ultan's Hospital. She was anxious at cold calling in search of a position. She knew her knowledge of both paediatrics and midwifery was limited but hoped her general nursing skills would offer sufficient expertise, if indeed, there were any vacancies. There was a welcoming aura as soon as she entered the reception area and she felt relieved when asked to sit and wait. Ankles crossed, she sat primly for about fifteen minutes before a middle-aged woman, with a gentle voice and soft eyes, asked her to step into an office. Once preliminaries were over, and details of her experience had been offered and vouched, tea was provided with a request to wait another while. The door opened to admit Dr Kathleen Lynn. Bridie, of course, remembered her clearly but was pleasantly surprised when Kathleen herself, recalled the incident in Liberty Hall. They chatted awhile, and Bridie told Kathleen of her journey into nursing and how she was hoping for a position in the hospital.

Nurses were always in demand, so Bridie was employed immediately and walked back to the lodgings on air. She was to start the following morning. Ellen had a similar experience to that in London. She spent the first few weeks in Dublin, fruitlessly searching for employment but without a reference other than as scullery maid, positions were impossible to come by. When Bridie returned one evening and announced a kitchen maid was needed in the hospital, Ellen decided to apply. For the first time, her experience in London stood her in good stead and she joined the busy kitchen team the next week.

The food in the hospital was plain and wholesome, but although the kitchen was well staffed, much of the administrative work fell to the principal cook, Mrs Dooney. Market lists were required daily and in-depth record-keeping of the costs of all purchases was vital to the smooth and economic management of the kitchen. The problem in the kitchen was literacy. The staff had little education and, as such, were reluctant to take on the administrative work. Ellen slowly took over the maintenance of the books with grateful thanks from Mrs Dooney, who could now attend fully to the cooking. Consequently, Ellen had to liaise with the main office and to her delight, began to assist more and more within the office, gradually leaving her kitchen duties behind.

Ellen discovered she had an affinity for order and over time adjusted the filing system so, even the most haphazard could locate what was needed. The esteem from work that was useful, enjoyable, and productive, gave her a confidence that showed in her face, her walk, and her overall demeanour. A large portion of Ellen's duties required the typing of hospital records. As she was not accomplished in the art, typing was undertaken slowly and laboriously, yet gave a certain satisfaction once completed. She gradually improved her speed and efficiency with the assistance of a book from the library and a dedicated hour each evening, once her duties in the hospital were completed. Her work also required contact with patients arriving or in the process of being discharged. A camaraderie developed, not least because Ellen had trouble understanding the Dublin accent and her, "culchie" accent, was incomprehensible to many of the women. She laughed and chatted with the mothers, admiring their latest baby, as they related stories of love and hardship, fun and hunger.

At night, when she had time alone, Ellen once more took up her pen and, slowly, began to document life in the tenements. What she would do with the stories she had no idea but the more tales she heard, the more the compulsion to write, blossomed within her. She took to carrying a notebook and pen, jotting down words, or amusing anecdotes if they struck her as especially interesting or entertaining, lest she forget the details by the time she returned home. She was not ready yet to allow anyone to read her scribblings but for the first time since leaving Donegal, she felt at ease, purposeful and fulfilled.

Bridie's sympathy for Sarah was starting to wear a little thin. For a while, an affinity had developed between Bridie and Ellen that wavered between compassion for Sarah's grief and sorrow and, indulgence, spiced with humour, at the constant supplication. Bridie appreciated her trauma over losing her baby, but the continual praying was exhausting and an irritation, especially after a demanding day in the hospital. There she saw women with dreadful diseases and a houseful of children left alone. Women, whose only source of income was the street with all its dangers from infection and violence. Bridie's growing lack of patience and compassion was not intended to diminish the ordeal Sarah had endured but she believed Sarah lacked perspective and needed to learn to cope.

For some time now, the two women juggled their lives so, whenever possible, Sarah was never left alone. This was only feasible because they both worked in the same hospital. St. Ultan's Hospital possessed an unusual empathy and understanding of Sarah's problems, and as such, facilitated them both to stagger their working hours. Yet, Bridie questioned whether this was a help to Sarah or whether they were just preventing her from moving on.

The First World War had despatched Bridie's adherence to formal religion. Ellen's time in London had stunted her devotion and her loyalty to the weekly rituals of Mass and Communion, rituals that had structured and dictated the blueprint of her childhood. Yet, for peace and not to cause Sarah further distress, they both reluctantly took to accompanying her on a Sunday to the local church. Bridie was now of the opinion they had pandered and indulged Sarah long enough. How to support Sarah to go forward was the conundrum and it was Ellen who had the first idea which she broached to Bridie.

Despite the seeming passivity in Sarah, she was not insensitive to the difficulty and worry she was causing to those around her. The problem was an inability to motivate herself to relinquish the past, afraid if she did, that the memory of little Stephen's warm body snuggled tight to her breast, would fade. Reared as she was in a devout family, she thought continual intercession with Mary, the mother of Jesus, might enable her, at some point, to find a pathway that would lead her to her son. She could sense she was a growing irritation, particularly to Bridie, and was alert to the debt she owed both women, but to let go of her memories was to diminish her baby boy. She had embraced the experience in the convent home as a type of penance for her sins, refusing to acknowledge she was not the one at fault. The endless, exhausting hours in the heat of the laundry were a catharsis and when Stephen was born, she had felt reborn herself. Her sin of seduction had demanded she pay a heavy price, but she had endured, and was not afraid of the long road ahead now that she had her little boy. Sarah nursed him with the rich milk overflowing from her breasts and the surge of happiness that glowed inside, eliminated all the anguish of the previous nine months. The rules would only allow her into the nursery at certain hours, but she had written to Ellen, and expected she would arrive very shortly to collect them both.

The Friday morning when Sarah went to the nursery for the first feed of the day would forever be seared in her memory. The empty cot, the surge of panic as she frantically scanned the room, the gentle hand on her shoulder and the sympathy in the eyes of the young nursery nun, foretold a story, that the peremptory words, 'I will deal with this,' confirmed. The young nun was summarily dismissed, 'You may attend to your duties, Sister.' The older nun turned to Sarah and stated in a voice, devoid of warmth, 'I am sorry to inform you that your baby has passed-away. It is most likely for the best. God has his own mysterious plans and works in wondrous ways.' Shock rooted Sarah, as her mind refused to process what she had just heard, and a keening sound emanated softly from her lips. 'Come, come, enough of that. You may take half an hour from your duties and pray in the chapel for his beautiful soul. He is with God and opening the nursery door, Sarah was ushered swiftly away.

That night, her breasts ached as they grew heavy with milk and leaked whenever she whispered his name, despair at his loss, unendurable. Yet the real agony began when the milk started to dry up, and she realised her ability to give Stephen life and sustenance was draining away, as was her hope of seeing him again. Sarah once more entered a twilight world. The only way forward was more prayer and penance, for she knew in her heart Stephen had not died, that the nuns had lied, but if she prayed hard enough and long enough, maybe she could find a way to trace him.

The fact that both Bridie and Ellen had secured employment with relative ease in an era where work, particularly for women, was not easy to obtain, enabled them to relax financially to a minor extent. Unwittingly, this gave Sarah a breathing space, as there was little pressure exerted on her to find employment herself. As plans for the wedding were set in motion, Ellen suggested to Sarah that she design and sew Bridie's wedding dress. Sarah was taken aback at the sudden interest that flickered and then surged, within her. Yet, she was hesitant to agree.

'I don't know, Ellen. It's a long time since I did any sewing.'

'Oh, Sarah, you were blessed with that talent, and you should not waste it. You have to move on, and think how good Bridie has been to you, to both of us.' Ellen paused, not wishing to be too forceful as the spark of interest animating Sarah had not gone unnoticed. Her suggestion to Sarah was two-fold. She had no doubt Sarah's expertise would ensure the dress would be stunning, but more importantly, the idea provided an occupation for Sarah that might help in her recovery. 'Think on it, Sarah, it would be a lovely thank you to Bridie.'

The enthusiasm that Ellen's suggestion engendered shook Sarah out of her apathy but also filled her with trepidation. For the first time since the birth, she actively wanted to do something, but she was afraid to commit herself immediately. After a full week of vacillating, she came to a decision. The following Sunday as the three women strolled home from Mass, Sarah, tentatively announced to Bridie, 'Bridie, have you thought about your wedding dress?'

'Actually no, Sarah, I have to find someone but haven't had an opportunity to source anyone yet.'

Bridie gave no indication that she knew of Ellen's suggestion, and feigned innocence when Sarah muttered, 'I could make it, if you want? I would like to do it.'

A glow suffused Bridie's face and she patted Sarah's hand, as she responded, 'I would love you to make my dress, Sarah. I would be honoured.'

Sarah now beamed, while Ellen hid a smug smile of satisfaction.

Once Sarah had mooted the idea of making the dress, she was unable to contain herself. Excitedly, she busied herself with patterns and designs and she advanced suggestions for materials and accessories. Of necessity, she walked into the city to the drapers to buy needles and thread, buttons, and bows. She frequented the large department stores and stared endlessly at window displays, absorbing dress designs and memorising the minute details necessary to reproduce such creations. Although she was unable to relinquish her firm belief that her baby boy, Stephen, had not died, the incessant praying began to fade. A missing spark reasserted itself as she began to relax and focus on something other than herself. Endless hours were spent meticulously sewing the wedding dress and there was a barely discernible but definite, change. The wedding dress opened a small crack into the window of Sarah's bleakness and enabled some light to shine through.

Ciaran's letter notifying that he would be in Dublin for the big day before embarking for America, had another positive effect on Sarah. At times, snatches of the old girl glimmered through. Ellen was particularly sad to think Ciaran was emigrating but unfortunately, it was a well-worn path for those who needed to make a better life for themselves.

Danny's current problem was sourcing better accommodation for all four of them. He had no wish to start married life on his own in his cramped lodgings and with Bridie, came Ellen and Sarah. Their rent would be useful anyway. Housing was at a premium, but he did not intend they start their new life in a tenement block. They had all grown up in the freedom of Donegal and although they had known scarcity at times, they had never lived in a communal setting. They were used to their own space, surrounded by hills and mountains, and not people. He had never attempted to use his union contacts to further his wishes but in this instance, he realised the union had its uses and for Bridie, he would make an exception. He approached his boss, and with his assistance, Danny secured the lease on a small two-bedroom cottage in Clare Street, not far from where they all currently resided. It was in much need of repair, but its location would enable Bridie and Ellen to continue to walk to work. That summer, Danny spent every spare moment painting the rooms so it would be ready for occupation, come October. Bridie was delighted, as it was reminiscent of the cottage in which she had lived in London but fortunately, was a bit more spacious. A disadvantage was outdoor plumbing, but the scullery had running water and Bridie knew they were lucky to get it at all. The pending wedding and the preparation of the new house gave Danny some reprieve from the hostilities within the union.

There was tension and infighting within the trade union that employed Danny. His own allegiances were tested but he decided to remain, believing their direction was the one that best suited his own ideology. Those that broke away were focussed on a path that was too extreme for him with too much admiration for Stalin, and not enough critique. He had an intuition that power, as opposed to Marx, might prevail. Danny agreed that 'religion was the opium of the people,' but he was not averse to religious practice, per se, only the pervading influence of any one church in state institutions and its domination of social policy and its implementation. At every opportunity, he expounded his ideas, submitting articles, hiding his disappointment when they were rejected but never giving up.

His hopes of a political career had not disappeared but without the backing of the union, they had certainly dwindled. When he advocated a policy of equality regardless of gender or religious affiliation, others feared Communism. When he advocated freedom, opportunity, and choice for all, others feared the wrath of the Church. When Danny argued that a fair system did not put a limit on earnings, but that those who earned most should pay the most tax to aid those who were struggling, Socialism reared its head. The idea a safety net needed to be established that compensated those unable to work through illness or injury and assisted those who were unemployed until further work was available, saw business owners running scared. The idea there should be recognition that a worker contributed more than just his labour to the advancement of a company, that his knowledge and training were essential tools and a necessary asset for any business to thrive saw Communism, once more, in the headlights. The idea that recognition of that contribution should be steady, secure employment, which in turn, allowed a worker to plan for his future, signalled financial ruin. All agreed that a country, with a healthy, educated workforce, was a country that would prosper and develop economically, but it was currently too expensive and now was not the time. Danny raised flags whenever he spoke. An objection was always raised, whether it be from other union members, business owners, politicians, or the Church.

Danny accepted that his proposals would meet with resistance, not least from the clergy, who disliked State involvement in family life. He also recognised that the conservative thrust of Church policy was influential with voters and so it was an uphill battle for his own ideology to be heard and trusted. Ideally, the more pieces he managed to have published presenting his way forward, the more he felt he could persuade those on the fence to take a chance on supporting him. The Labour Party had 14 seats in the Dáil, or parliament and Danny advocated that there should be a concentration and determination in the coming years, to expand the Labour Party's influence and develop a Socialist Republic, through democratic means. It was only through the election of representatives to the Dail, representatives who would advance an agenda of equality, that progress would be made. He emphasised at meetings, in the workplace and in his writings, that voting and the exercise of franchise, was essential. Those who wished to be elected catered to the needs of those who voted. If only middle or upper-class constituents voted, then attention would only be paid to their needs. If the working-class population wanted accurate representation, they needed to vote for those who understood disadvantage and would work for its elimination.

He worked tirelessly, travelling the country, influencing the formation of unions against fierce opposition from employers, clergy and many workers, themselves. Danny despaired when he thundered to blank faces, faces with their vote already cast. Then there were those who would never change, embittered from the Civil War, and entrenched in its aftermath, adhered to the side with whom they had fought or supported, regardless of ideology. Once a priest spoke, all too many, followed his diktats. The danger that Irishness and Catholicism would become synonymous was all too apparent to Danny and with no place for diverse opinions or beliefs, the Irish people would remain fractured. The fact that he had served in the British Army was an unspoken source of suspicion for some, and undoubtedly hampered his progress within the union ranks. Yet overall, as the year progressed, and the wedding date loomed ever nearer, his ideas were better received.

The summer months drifted by according to a rhythm of their own and the three women were surrounded, for once, in a web of contentment. Bridie had found her niche in St. Ultan's Hospital, caring for women and their babies, hoping to ease their woes if only for a short while. For the few days they lay in the hospital, her dulcet tones, made them forget disease, hardship, and relentless childbearing. The poverty from which they sprang was not just a lack of material goods but an impoverishment of the soul, where all possibilities were banished, and choices stolen. Their expressions revealed an acceptance that life would never change so, rather than just being an endurance, they lived the best way they could. In so doing, they had unity and camaraderie with family, friends, and neighbours. The menfolk too, enjoyed and suffered in their own way. Finding respite in a few pints, aware, that without education and secure employment they were destined never to achieve their desires, but always, to live on the side-lines. Their masculinity, dependent on their ability to provide, was stripped, and they were humbled when they saw their family hungry and cold. Their emotions became blunted, out of necessity for their own survival.

The anecdote of the happy, capable, tenement woman was a myth, as far as Bridie was concerned but Ellen saw a different image of their life. She spoke to the women as they left the hospital, for once with hope, that this time, their baby might possibly live. They had had a few days of rest and were looking forward, once more, to the bustle of their lives. Whenever she could, on those summer evenings, Ellen escaped to St Stephen's Green with a notebook and pencil. Finding a comfortable nook, she scribbled the latest story and weaved her spell around their lives. Sarah too had changed. Freed, from the need to bend her knees in prayer, her nimble fingers danced around lace and silk, preparing a dress that Bridie could never have afforded. She revelled ceaselessly in the meticulous detail required, ensuring perfection. On her own initiative, with only two weeks to spare before the big day, Sarah managed to acquire material that eventually unfolded into two elegant dresses for herself, and Ellen. The extraordinary amount of midnight oil burned was well worth the expense.

The wedding day dawned, clear and bright, and the wedding party, now swelled to six with the arrival of Ciaran, and Danny's sister, Annie, made their way to Synge Street Church. The ceremony was to be held during ten o'clock Mass. The wedding dress was a testament to Sarah's gift, lavish in its beauty and elegance.

Ellen and Danny entered the church, while Bridie enjoyed her few minutes of fame outside. Sarah remained with her, preening with pride from the compliments emanating from those arriving for morning Mass.

The church in Synge Street was a beautiful structure, extravagantly decorated with gilt, and a fitting venue for such a happy day. Vows were given and taken and after the ceremony, Bridie, and Danny, sat high with pride as they were driven in a horse-drawn carriage to their new home. The wedding party undertook the short walk to Clare Street where Ellen prepared a wedding breakfast for all six. Ciaran had arrived with a dozen mackerel wrapped in salt and newspaper and combined with the rest of the fare, including a cake supplied by the hospital, a feast was laid on. Ciaran was to spend the night in the new house, only possible, because Danny and Bridie were having a short, two-day, honeymoon in Howth.

Annie had travelled from Donegal the previous day and was spending the night with a friend, in Dublin. By three o'clock, Bridie and Danny had departed, followed closely by Annie. Ellen and Sarah donned shawls and scarves and suggested a walk to St Stephen's Green. Ciaran agreed, but the trip was cut short as, without a proper overcoat, Ciaran was frozen. That evening, once the fire was lit and they had consumed most of the leftovers, they chatted about old times and their love of Donegal.

'New York will be so different from home, Ciaran. You must write regularly and tell me all about it,' sighed a wistful Ellen.

Although nothing was said, Ciaran did not fail to notice that Sarah, was not quite the girl he remembered. He recalled how a smiling and vivacious sister seemed to wither before she left for Dublin and the bubbly, irritating sister he recalled, was now a memory. Ciaran was not to know, that although Sarah still had a grey, gaunt demeanour, she was vastly improved on how she had been only a few short months ago. She was on the road to recovery and in a much better place since that fateful night and, especially, since the birth of Stephen.

'The most remarkable change was the slight sparkle in her eye, combined with an interest in her surroundings, which had been missing for too long. Ellen also noted the absence of that barely perceptible, hunch of her shoulders, visible, only to those who knew the old Sarah.

Ciaran said nothing, just hugged Sarah closely, awaiting the right time to speak to Ellen. From Ciaran's perspective, she was a different girl, but he could not quite put his finger on what had changed. Part of him wanted to ask Ellen, but he was reluctant to disrupt the comfortable ambience of the evening and decided to wait until morning and catch Ellen alone. This private chat was not realised as Ellen needed to work the following day and that evening, Ciaran was due to sail. Ellen was relieved because she was reluctant to discuss Sarah and all that had occurred, and she was aware it would hurt Ciaran if she refused to confide in him. Monday evening, they escorted Ciaran to the docks in good time for the sailing, at 8 pm. The farewell was emotional. Promises to write were easily given and easily kept, promises to visit were just aspirations and they all knew it was possible they might never meet again. Ciaran was also conflicted because he never mentioned the tension at home in Donegal, and the cause. Upsetting Ellen before he left seemed pointless, especially now that the Civil War was over. He fervently hoped the incident would be confined to history.

Chapter 19

Oblivious to the thunderous clouds that had hovered over "Droimreagh", Bridie and Danny returned from their short honeymoon and settled into married life, with ease. Ellen was content, but Sarah felt adrift without the focus of the wedding dress to occupy her. Danny was busy traversing the country and as Christmas drew ever near, he was hoping for a quiet celebration at home. This was not to be, as there was worrying news from Donegal that Josie was quite unwell. The three women, Bridie, Ellen, and Sarah felt it necessary to travel to Donegal for Christmas to check on her and young Kathleen. Danny's private longing for a restful festive season, was reluctantly relinquished as he helped organise the travel arrangements. Under no circumstance would he deny his wife the need to see her sister or Ellen and Sarah, their mother. Both Bridie and Ellen also felt it would do Sarah good to go home, believing that old maxim, that *"home air was healing"*.

From the day that Kathleen had received the letter telling their forthcoming arrival, she was exuberant. She had always been accustomed to Sheamus and even Ciaran, coming and going. The hollow emptiness on the day Ellen and Sarah departed lingered because she firmly believed, she might never see them again. The antagonism within the house, followed by the departure of first, Sheamus and then Ciaran, left a vacuum that her beloved garden could never fill. The bulk of care, despite Liam's help, now that Josie was sick, fell to Kathleen and she became both frightened and lonely. Exuberantly, she now prepared for Christmas by baking, cleaning, and decorating the house with holly.

Billy's son now operated the taxi cart from the town. It was the same old uncomfortable vehicle, but Billy Junior did not smell as ripe as his father, so the journey was a little more pleasant. At first glance, the farmhouse appeared unchanged. Still, despite Kathleen's attempts at Christmas cheer, no swathes of scattered holly branches could penetrate the pervading gloom inside or banish the sweet scent of sickness, permeating the atmosphere.

The small family group sat down with an urgency, anxious to hear about Josie. Kathleen looked strained, the awkward positioning of one leg, an indication of her utter fatigue, the continual entwining and uncurling of a lock of hair, a symbol of agitation.

'Liam is very helpful,' she explained, thoughtfully, 'but the private things, you know, I have to help with those, but he helps as much as he can, when she lets him.'

'Do you think she is awake now?' queried Bridie of Kathleen.

'Possibly, I will check. She so wanted to be up to greet you but today is not a good day. It varies all the time.' Kathleen looked away and a tear, probably of relief but also exhaustion, rolled down her cheek. 'Aye, I am so glad you are here,' she whispered.

Ellen had not witnessed such distress within Kathleen in years and guilt overwhelmed her as she realised her devotion to one sister, Sarah, had left a burden on her younger and possibly more vulnerable sister, Kathleen. As these thoughts tumbled through her mind, she almost missed Kathleen's next words.

'Sometimes Mary McNally comes in to help.'

'Mary McNally?' interrupted Bridie. 'Is she Seanie McNally's youngest, from up the road?'

'Well, she is about thirty,' responded Kathleen, 'not very young, but yes, it is her. She helps out from time to time, but Liam doesn't seem to like her. They just argue all the time and I have enough to deal with, without that. Yet if she is not here, he grunts like a bear, asking when she is coming next.'

Bridie glanced at Ellen with raised eyebrows and a smile. Ellen sniggered, unable to imagine Liam in any way under a woman's spell. Meanwhile, Kathleen looked disgruntled, whilst Sarah sat serenely lost in thought, possibly focussed on the upcoming anniversary of Stephen's birth which was not an omen for complacency.

Ellen and Sarah, followed closely by Bridie, now went into the bedroom to see Josie and it was quite clear she was, indeed, very unwell. Precisely what was the problem was not clear, but Josie appeared withered and shrunken in her bed, although she rallied slightly when she saw them all. That evening, Josie made a supreme effort and joined them for a short while by the fire. She was unable to eat much but made a feeble attempt to join the conversation. It was apparent that the struggle exhausted her, and after an hour, Ellen helped her back to bed. Kathleen was animated to have company and talked incessantly.

'I have been making her a drink with carrageen moss each evening. Liam collects it when he has his daily walk out along the seashore but most of the time, she is unable to have more than a few sips.'

'Carrageen moss?' said Ellen, taking her seat once more by the fire. Shuddering, she continued, 'That's awful stuff, I couldn't even drink it.'

'Aye, awful it might be,' interjected Liam, 'but you know she always swore by it. Anything that helps her feel better she can have as far as I'm concerned.'

'She has a bad cough as well,' continued Kathleen, 'she gave me instructions on how to make a poultice from goose fat, but it doesn't seem to help much.'

'Goose fat can work wonders,' said Bridie. 'Are you draining the fat and letting it cool down in a jar? Maybe rub it directly onto her chest, before covering it over with a cloth or a bit of a woollen shawl.'

Kathleen nodded, 'Aye, that's what she told me to do, but I don't see any improvement.' Kathleen prattled on as Danny rose and said he would stroll over to see his own family, before it became too dark.

'I'll wander along with you,' said Liam, stretching and getting to his feet to accompany him.

Bridie looked almost startled at this new amiable Liam, a man who some years before refused to utter Danny's name, now presenting, as almost congenial. 'I have never seen Liam so mellow. He must be in love!' joked Bridie.

'He is changed since the episode of the cross. All that anguish and the death of that man. And then the war ending a couple of weeks later,' replied Kathleen.

'What episode with the cross?' queried Ellen and Bridie, almost in unison.

Kathleen related the story of the ebony cross and the trauma of that night. It occurred to Ellen, with hindsight, that something had been amiss with Ciaran at the wedding. She assumed it was just natural trepidation at the journey to the States and the unknown future. He also expressed some worry over Sarah and for that reason, she had purposely avoided an intimate conversation. Now she understood there was a further underlying cause for his anxiety and motive for his departure to America. The distrust that ensued would have hurt all three brothers. Ciaran, and indeed Sheamus, were handling the situation by leaving but Liam would have been deeply affected and, she surmised, would not rest until his pride was intact once more. Josie had always held her head high in the area and the doubt and suspicion from some fair-weather friends and neighbours would have pained her and maybe contributed to her illness.

They all mused over the mystery of who could have deliberately moved the cross. All four women were unanimous that no one in the farmhouse would have touched it and, Danny, once he heard the story, totally concurred. Kathleen related how suspicion in the village still lingered and how the hostility engendered by the Civil War had still not abated.

'I think it's the same all over the country,' posited Danny. 'The war might be over, but memories can be long and bitter, and some deeds are never forgotten.'

Christmas, of necessity, was quiet. As per usual, all attended Mass where they met and greeted numerous old friends and neighbours. Joe and Brendan were home from Scotland and were also in the church. Although Brendan came over with smiles and outstretched arms, delighted to see them all, Joe hung back, barely nodding. Brendan promised to call in and see Josie once he heard she was so unwell that she was unable to attend the church on Christmas morning. He was not returning to Scotland for three weeks, so he had lots of time for visiting.

The priest had given Bridie a communion wafer with strict instructions on the care of the precious host. It took an enormous effort for Josie to swallow it, sapping her energy for most of the day. As a sincere believer in the healing power of communion, she was nevertheless delighted to have been able to receive it. She insisted on rising and joining the family at the dinner table. Despite everyone's best efforts, dinner was a sombre affair. Christmas was a time when loved ones were remembered and Josie's illness cast a cloud over the day with Donal's empty chair, a symbol of happier times. The absence of both Sheamus and Ciaran was also a poignant reminder that the family ties seemed irrevocably broken and Christmas would never again be quite the same.

That evening, Sarah took her turn to settle Josie in bed. As she turned to leave, Josie took her hand and whispered, 'My beautiful Sarah, what happened to you? Promise me you will find someone, and settle, maybe marry. I think your own home, with children, will make you happy once more.'

Josie closed her eyes and appeared to doze, as Sarah sighed softly in her ear, 'I will try, Mammy, I will try.' Josie's eyes flickered in response and Sarah gently patted her hand before turning to re-join the others.

For once, Liam did not leave the table as soon as dinner was over. He lingered instead, chatting in a surprisingly cordial manner, to Danny. He appeared inordinately interested in Danny's work and his attempts to unionise workers and fascinated by the ideas he expressed in his articles. Neither Danny, Bridie nor Ellen had ever heard Liam express an opinion with such balance before, almost, at times, able to see the other side of an argument. Leaving both men to continue to chat, Bridie, Ellen and Kathleen played cards, but Sarah went to bed complaining of tiredness.

Sometime later, when Ellen and Kathleen entered the bedroom, they saw Sarah slumped on the floor. Ellen guessed she had been praying but did not attempt to dissuade Kathleen of the notion that Sarah was somehow unwell. They helped her to bed, but long after Ellen heard gentle snores from both her sisters, she lay awake. It was the first anniversary of Stephen's birth the following day and Ellen worried as to how Sarah would cope. She also wondered, as she had many a time, if Stephen had died as the nuns insisted.

Sarah was so adamant that he had lived, but maybe that was just an inability to deal with her own anguish.

St Stephen's Day dawned wet and cold but there were still jobs to be undertaken on the farm. Danny helped Liam, the amicable atmosphere from the night before still in evidence. Once Josie was settled and the few household chores attended to, the blazing fire was a magnet, and the women sat down to relax. Josie seemed much brighter and, Kathleen, as fervently religious as her mother put it down to receiving communion the previous day. Whatever the reason, when Ellen went in to check on her, she patted the bed for Ellen to sit. Josie may have been sick, but she was still a mother, and not immune to Sarah's distress.

'Ellen, I need to speak with you in case I don't get an opportunity again.'

'Hush,' murmured Ellen, 'don't say that.'

'Please hear me out. I need to get something off my chest. That night, after the social, before you went away.' Ellen perked up, instantly alert. 'I saw the torn, wet clothes, I saw some blood, and I knew something had happened. Sarah was so distressed. I assumed some boy had forced her. I know I was weak but without your father, I felt helpless. She was so young, I thought if I let her go with you, over to Bridie, she would be alright, but I was wrong, aye, I see that now,' explained Josie. 'She is still not herself.'

Ellen had always suspected her mother knew what had happened to Sarah, but that she never guessed about the pregnancy, was now, a real possibility. It certainly was not the time to burden her with that news, not when she was so unwell. 'Mam, you did the right thing, she is okay. You made the right choice, me, and Bridie, we looked after her and we will continue to do so. It takes a while to truly get over something like that, but she is doing fine. She is so much better than she was a year ago. I know she may seem upset now but it is just with Dad gone and the boys away. She is sad for times past and with yourself not feeling too well, she is just worried.' Ellen forced a laugh, as she added, 'We are all worried, but you know Sarah, always the drama queen, insisting she feels more than anyone else.' Josie smiled weakly in response, seemingly satisfied. Ellen kissed her forehead and left her to sleep.

Sarah, meanwhile, had left the warm fireside and wandered to the ruined church without telling anyone where she was headed. It was apparent from Sarah's demeanour earlier that morning, that Stephen was on her mind. Ellen spent the afternoon checking the window for signs of her return, trying to hide her agitation from Kathleen. As dusk fell, she heard footsteps and Sarah appeared looking quite composed. She seated herself by the fire and once she had poured herself some tea and taken a sip, she calmly announced she was staying in Donegal. She requested that a few of her belongings, still in Dublin, be posted to her. Kathleen squealed, unable to contain her delight but both Bridie and Ellen locked eyes, unsure. Later, out of Kathleen's earshot, they tried to dissuade Sarah, but she had her mind made up. She was determined to stay and was implacable in the face of all arguments. She would return to Dublin at some point, but she wanted to be with Josie for now. Once Sarah mentioned Josie, it seemed churlish and unfair to attempt any further argument.

Three days later as they all settled down for a final evening together, there was a gentle tap on the door, followed by a soft voice enquiring, 'Is it alright if I join you for a few moments?' Mary McNally's round, pretty face, surrounded by a halo of bobbing curls, peeked around the door.

'Come in, come in,' responded a chorus of voices in unison.

'Aye, I will, just for a moment and maybe Josie might taste a piece of this.' Mary handed over some sweet pudding wrapped in a muslin cloth.

'Thank you, Mary,' replied Ellen, 'but sit, sit awhile. Kathleen has been telling us how helpful you have been.'

'Ah sure, 'tis nothing. What are neighbours for? Are you all away back tomorrow?'

'No, Sarah is staying on to help out. My heavens, just listen to that rain out there. You better stay 'till it eases, or you will be drowned going back home.'

'No, no, I'll be fine, it won't take me long.'

'I'll walk you up,' muttered a gruff voice from the corner and Liam stood up and grabbed a large blanket from a bench. 'You can shelter under this. Come now, if you're bothered coming.' He strode ahead to the door and Mary quickly followed, unaware of the number of bemused glances that watched the unfolding spectacle of a seemingly, pleasant, Liam.

Bridie, Danny, and Ellen left Donegal on the 30th of December but were only a few days back in Dublin when news was received that Josie had gone rapidly downhill and they were fearful she had not much longer to live. The price of three more train tickets back to Donegal, so soon after Christmas, was prohibitive. Resources were pooled and Ellen returned alone to "Droimreagh", to her mother's deathbed and funeral.

Liam enfolded Kathleen in his arms as Josie struggled over her final breath and whispered softly, 'It won't be long now, Kitty,' and Kathleen clung to him, the one steadfast in her short life.

Sheamus arrived from Scotland and joined the family around his mother's bed. He tightly gripped Ellen's shoulders, as much to console, as to control his own emotions. Except for Ciaran and Bridie, Josie, passed quietly away surrounded by the entire family. Joe and Brendan were still in Donegal and joined the family in their grief over Josie. Joe realised, now that she was gone, that she had been a stalwart, a steady rock that he had taken for granted. He hugged Brendan to him, belatedly understanding that Josie had been almost a mother to both himself and his son. As such, his grief was a well that ran deep.

The local community, as was the custom, were all in attendance at the funeral and among them was Kevin. His infatuation with Sarah had not diminished with her departure for London. Kevin had spotted Sarah at Mass on Christmas Day and his simmering obsession with her was now fully rekindled. As the funeral progressed, he watched her from the shadows of the church, drinking her in, revelling in the fact he was unobserved. As the funeral party moved down the aisle towards the church door, he sidled up alongside her, grasping her hands in condolence. Sarah did not shiver, as was her wont in times gone by whenever Kevin was near. Instead, she smiled in thanks, lost in grief, not seeing the face of the man still holding her hands. Realisation dawning, she turned swiftly away and noticed Patsy O'Hara embrace Ellen. Empathy and sympathy were apparent in his actions but also a barely perceptible antagonism that Sarah was unable to fathom, in her distressed state. Kathleen was next to receive a warm hug from Patsy before he finally clasped Sarah's hands, in his own. There was no acknowledgement for any of the McShane brothers, bar a fleeting glance of distaste, followed by contempt, in their direction.

Throughout the funeral service and graveside, Sheamus kept his head bowed, shrouded in deep sadness. Josie's three daughters clung to one another, with heaving shoulders and wet cheeks. Liam, to the casual observer, was a stoic figure, standing straight and tall with no visible sorrow. If one cared to look closely, the eyes of this severe man were glistening with unshed tears and his hands were tightly clenched to hold his emotions in check.

Mary McNally stood by his side and, for a few seconds, laid her hand upon his back in compassionate understanding of his pain. She had come to know this man well and the softness hidden within. She alone knew that even before the seriousness of Josie's illness was realised, he had given strict instructions to Kathleen to call him if needed, no matter the time. 'I will never be gone too far,' he grunted. Joe and Brendan stood, side by side, united in their anguish.

The steady drizzle increased to a torrent, and no one delayed once the final handful of earth resounded on the coffin lid. Mary followed Liam as he turned slowly away but he did not follow the family. Instead, he crossed over to stand solemnly by another grave.

'Sean O'Hara?' queried Mary. 'Did you know him?'

'Aye, I once knew him well. We were in school together and, for a while, we stood side-by-side with a united goal, a common cause. Times changed, as did sides. Sometimes we are called upon to act in ways that we can never forget.'

Once more, Mary took his hand. 'I have heard about Sean and how he died. You don't need to say any more.' Hand in hand, they left the graveyard, shrouded in an aura of mutual sorrow yet with underlying contentment with each other. 'I will see you tomorrow, Liam,' said Mary. Liam bent forward and gently kissed her before striding purposefully away and up the mountain track.

Liam stopped at his favourite spot, drinking in the all-consuming view of low-lying fields, brooks and boreens enclosed in the magnificent hills of Donegal, black and thunderous on this wet, January, afternoon. He had given his life and very soul to this country. Now, Liam felt all the pent-up anger and bitterness of the last years seep away dissolving in an instant, washed away by the torrent of tears that streamed, unrelentingly, down his cheeks. He was glad there was no one in sight to witness his distress, believing his display a sign of weakness. He had remained in control at his father's funeral needing to be strong for all the family. Josie was different, his mother and his rock.

The emptiness in the farmhouse that evening reinforced the family's loss. Josie, even when sick, had been a major presence, the centre of the home. Kathleen was distraught and there was now, no question, but that Sarah continue to remain in Donegal. Sheamus and Ellen both left the following day, and it would be many years before Sheamus returned. The rift with his brother Liam would still take a little time to bridge and, for now, Glasgow suited him very well. Sheamus travelled to Belfast and boarded the boat to Scotland, purposefully ignoring a mantle of loneliness that refused to shift.

Chapter 20

Sheamus was encased in a deep depression and barely noticed the waves as they thundered and tossed the boat on its short crossing to Scotland. His mother was gone and with her the last ties to his home. He was not so foolish as to discount his brothers and sisters, but the recent strain and the different paths each were now following, meant they were scattered, and the old closeness diminished. He intended though to keep in touch and had Ellen's address in Dublin tucked safely in his pocket.

Ellen, for her part, took the long, lonely trip back to Dublin. Bridie met her off the train, and together, they remembered and mourned, Josie, long into the evening in their cosy home.

Brendan had another week in Donegal before he too had to return to Scotland, and he resumed calling up to the farm most evenings for a chat with Liam. It was evident to all that he hated the thought of leaving Donegal and Liam told him he had a job if he decided to stay. Tempted though he was, Brendan knew it would enrage his father and felt obligated to decline. 'For now, Liam. Maybe, come next summer. I just don't want more bother with me, Da.'

Liam waved him goodbye and wandered into the kitchen. He sat down to have some tea but the continual chatter between Sarah and Kathleen grated on his nerves. Standing up, he muttered, 'Going out. Back later, don't wait up.'

Sarah and Kathleen sat by the fire, never stuck for words. Kathleen was relieved to have her sister home and the responsibility Sarah now felt towards Kathleen, served to distract her from her own woes. Kathleen was just fifteen, and although in rural Donegal that was considered reasonably mature, she was stunned by the death of her mother. It had hit everyone hard, but Kathleen had been so close to Josie that she was quite bereft. Consequently, Sarah's mothering instincts were positively coming to the fore.

Liam entered the local pub and ordered a pint. He sat quietly in a corner mulling over recent events. He had loved his mother deeply and it would be a while before he would be able to get used to her absence. He was glad Sarah was home to help with Kathleen, but they did get on his nerves a bit and from time to time, he needed an escape. A tap on his shoulder caused him to glance up. Old Jamsie McLaughlin was standing there looking as distressed as Liam felt. 'Ah, Liam, tá brón orm as do chuid trioblóide. I am so sorry for your troubles.'

'Aye, Jamsie, I know, I know, tá a fhios agam,' replied Liam.

'I only heard today about poor Josie, or I would have been at the funeral. I remember her well, aye, sure didn't we go to school together.' Jamsie paused, his thoughts returning to his youth shared with Josie and many others, now passed on.

'Jamsie, sochraid mhór a bhí ann,' brooded Liam.

'Liam, I know, I am sure it was a huge funeral, just wish I had known, but I was away for a few days to see my son in Dublin. Ar dheis Dé go raibh a h-anam dílís,' and Jamsie wandered away, his head bowed in sadness.

As Liam turned back to his pint, he noticed Joe in a far corner. He looked a little the worse for wear, probably from drinking in the pub most of the day. He glowered back at Liam before returning to empty his glass. Patsy O'Hara was on a stool at the bar. He smirked when Liam caught his eye before he raised his drink in mock salute. Their presence discomfited Liam, but he was determined not to allow them to irritate. In addition to his regular quota, he had three more pints and a whiskey chaser before he stood up to leave.

He breathed in the crisp, frosty air, as he began the short walk up the lane to the house. He had drunk more than usual, but in the circumstances, he felt he was entitled to indulge his grief. Nevertheless, he was a little unsteady and he cursed himself for over-imbibing to that extent. The first blow was struck from behind, without warning. The flash of the gnarled blackthorn barely registered as Liam stumbled and fell headlong into the ditch. Kicks came hard and heavy and further blows rained down, with such viciousness, that all Liam could do was curl up to safeguard his head from the continual onslaught. Almost as quickly as it began, the barrage ceased but not before serious injury had been inflicted. Liam's assailant disappeared into the darkness as Liam lay stunned and unable to move for several minutes. Slowly, he stirred, struggling to rise to his feet. He knew instantly his arm was broken but as he attempted to stand, his ankle could not bear his weight, and he almost collapsed again from the searing pain, shooting up his leg. It took some time to steady himself and the realisation dawned, that with no one around to help, he had better get home quickly before shock and cold did further damage. It required quite an amount of effort, and it was with extreme difficulty and quite a few failed attempts, before he managed to break a branch off a willow tree. Using it as a makeshift crutch, he hobbled slowly home cursing under his breath.

Sarah and Kathleen were both in bed when Liam arrived at the farmhouse, but he hollered loud enough that they both came running. 'Heavens, what happened?' screamed Sarah, taking his weight so that he could settle on to a chair.

Liam growled in reply, 'Attacked, bloody well attacked, wait until I get my hands on him, he won't be able to stand either.'

Kathleen rushed for a basin of water. Returning, she gasped when she bent over and saw the extent of his wounds. A large gash, seeping continuously, sliced the back of his head. 'I think your ankle is broken too, Liam, and so is your arm. You are going to need it set.'

'I know, I know, run, get Brendan, go, tell him I need oul Johnson, forget the doc, Johnson will do. Tell him to bring him back here immediately but for now, I need something to help me with the pain.'

'We only have whiskey from Christmas,' piped Kathleen, 'or some of Ma's tablets.'

'Get me some of them,' said Liam.

Sarah interjected, 'Don't, Liam, you don't know what they do, and you have had enough whiskey.'

'They are painkillers, and that's exactly what I need right now.'

Kathleen scurried to get them, while Sarah raised his foot, amid curses and roars, onto a stool. As he drank some water, Kathleen voiced what they were all thinking. 'Who did it, Liam? Who did it?'

Liam was gruff in his response, 'I'm not sure, but I have my suspicions and I am keeping them to meself, for now. It is the farm I am worried about. I will need help with the animals. I think Brendan. Yes, I will ask Brendan to come up in the morning. He is still here for another few days and he hates, Scotland.'

Kathleen returned from her errand, a little upset and shaken. Joe had reared in anger when he heard her request that Brendan fetch Johnson, the bonesetter. Red-faced at what he considered Liam's further audacity, he had ordered Brendan not to go near the farmhouse. Brendan was old enough to make up his own mind and had quietly donned his jacket and headed out into the night. He arrived at the farmhouse shortly afterwards with Johnson, as instructed. The wound to Liam's head was attended to first and Liam stridently demanded some medication for pain. Johnson confirmed what was obvious, Liam had broken bones in his ankle and arm. He set the bones as straight as was possible with expertise honed over many years in Donegal, attending to both people and animals. His instructions to move as little as possible were delivered unequivocally to Liam who was fuming at the pending incarceration.

That night Brendan lay awake undecided about what to do. He hated to argue with his father and had been content to return to Scotland, but now he knew, not just Liam, but Sarah and Kathleen needed help. Besides, they were all still grief-stricken over Josie. Without a doubt Liam would be incapacitated for some time to come, so Brendan strolled up to the farm the following morning after the attack. He ignored the scathing, verbal, assault emanating from his father, confident his decision was correct.

On the day Joe was due to return to Scotland, Brendan walked down to say goodbye. 'I can't go with you, Dad. Ye know that.'

Joe frowned, head bowed in contemplation, before muttering, 'Aye, I do understand, believe me, I do. This is your home, I know it is home, only too well. I don't mind you staying, I just wish it wasn't with that Liam McShane.' Joe's eyes swept the hills and mountains that surrounded their small cottage, a veil of sadness overshadowing his features. 'Aye, this is home, Brendan, this is home. You take care.' Joe raised his arms as if to embrace Brendan but at the last second abandoned the gesture, to grunt instead. 'I will miss you, ye know, but I want you to be happy. Look, wait here a moment, I have something for ye.' He returned, carrying a slean with an intricately carved handle. 'Keep this, but look after it, mind. When I was much younger than you are now, I carved it, meself. It was when I lived up in McShanes', in the old barn. Aye, it was the house at that time, I thought it would eventually be mine. Anyway, that is water under the bridge now,' he sighed. 'I needed my own slean for cutting turf and I spent one winter, carving that handle, bit by bit. I was so proud of it, but I thought it was well lost. I found it some time ago, so it is yours now.' Joe gruffly grasped his son in a rare hug and then climbed on board the waiting cart. He travelled back to Scotland and joined Sheamus without much expectation that life would improve.

Brendan duly arrived each morning from his cottage and saw to the needs of the farm, enjoying the regular tea and bread throughout the day and hot stew at one o'clock. Liam recognised the turf slean from the barn and had noticed it was missing, but for once, did not comment. He was a dreadful patient and drove both Sarah and Kathleen to distraction, shouting instructions and moaning at his helplessness. He was only silent on the few occasions Mary McNally strolled down and Kathleen and Brendan gasped in astonishment, when she made him apologise to Sarah for his abrupt manner.

Liam's boredom drove him to reflect on his conversations with Danny and to consider viewpoints other than his own. He became engrossed in reading about the political machinations necessary to form the new Irish Republic and how Civil War rivalries still dominated many editorials. Regularly, the daily newspaper was late arriving, and Liam instructed Kathleen to search Ellen's belongings for 'the stuff' she used to read. He was at pains to point out that she was to tell no one that he sometimes read *The Irish Citizen*. If anyone knew he read feminist claptrap, he would never live it down. She was permitted to mention Jim Larkin's, *The Irish Worker and People's Advocate*, as there was no shame in a Socialist newspaper. Otherwise, when he was alone with his thoughts he pondered over his assailant. He believed it was Patsy O'Hara, but he never felt Patsy was into fighting, too afraid to dirty his clothes, but then a cowardly attack from behind would not be beyond him. Also, he was sure the weapon used was a blackthorn stick. Aye, an attack in the dark with a club, that could easily be Patsy O'Hara alright, sneaky to a fault. He pondered could it have been Joe, but he had seemed too drunk to have been able to inflict such blows. For all he might think about Joe, he was his half-brother and had always been upfront with his anger, confronting him to his face with his rant and his venom. It might also have been someone who held a grudge since the Civil War, but Liam felt that was too random. In the end, he settled on Patsy, although the idea that Patsy could best him, even in a surprise attack, was a sore point. He decided for the moment to let things go. In time he would know what to do, but for now, he closed his eyes and allowed his thoughts to drift to Mary.

Chapter 21

Kevin's delight when he spied Sarah on Christmas morning was amplified when he heard she had not returned to Dublin. She was always on the periphery of his thoughts, but he presumed she was gone from Donegal for good and he was unlikely to see her again for many a year, if ever. He attended Josie's funeral as expected but bided his time afterwards, so as not to seem too pushy while she was grieving. His insatiable hunger for Sarah had returned as soon as he laid eyes on her once more, but he recognised it was a mistake to rush. Now each Sunday at Mass, as though magnetised, his eyes were instantly drawn across to where Sarah was seated with head bowed. Never sure which Mass she would attend he showed up at each one until he spotted her. Such was his obsession he was blind to the gaunt features and dejected appearance that had become part of her demeanour, and instead, he revelled in the beauty he remembered and the sparkle that had beguiled. When he heard how Liam was incapacitated, he offered his services on the farm. It was now spring and there was a lot more help needed so both Liam and Brendan, gratefully accepted another pair of hands.

Sarah still shrank when he was around and was forced to listen to Kathleen, her baby sister, admonish her sullenness. Unable to be any way pleasant, she contrived to keep out of sight most of the time. At other times, she gritted her teeth and tried her best to show her appreciation for his help. Unfortunately, Kevin viewed this as encouragement. He was not a stupid man and knew Sarah had never had much time for him, but he was determined to overcome any unwillingness, with his patience and persistence.

Kevin lived in what had once been his grandfather's cottage at the edge of what was now, his father's land. The cottage was originally constructed from local stone with a central hearth, but time and weather had reduced a portion of the outside walls to rubble. Kevin had added a wooden structure enlarging the cottage from one room into two. An external spring provided fresh running water. The general appearance was ramshackle, so he set about making it more attractive. The mismatched planks of wood were whitewashed and if one did not look inside, it appeared quite charming. This outward appearance belied the fact the dwelling was little more than a bothán, half-buried, in the earth. He had a seasonal job in the local quarry, and interspersed his hours there, with working his father's smallholding and hiring his labour to other local farmers. He now spent a few hours, three times a week, helping Liam and Brendan. Liam's ankle was slow to heal so he was not yet mobile. Kevin was a diligent worker, and his services were invaluable with the resultant pressure on Sarah from Liam and Kathleen, to be more civil.

'Will you come for a stroll with me, Sarah?' was a daily request, from a persistent Kevin.

The eventual urging from Kathleen, 'Go on, Sarah. I can manage here,' forced a reluctant Sarah to agree.

'Yes, come and see the house,' insisted Kevin. 'It won't take long.'

Kevin proudly displayed his cottage and Sarah, although not overly impressed kept her counsel, but steadfastly refused to go inside. She remained aloof but Kevin was just content to be making progress and never expected, that a prize worth having, was easily won.

'Glad you are more pleasant to Kevin. He likes you a lot, and he is a great help here,' approved Liam.

The walks gradually morphed into a regular occurrence. Kevin did his best not to touch Sarah but sometimes her nearness was too much for him. If he took her hand, she jumped as if scalded and if he stood too close, just to inhale her scent, she moved quickly, as if stung. At night he drifted to sleep imagining her beside him and dreamed of how it would be when she became his. When Sarah went to bed, her dreams were invaded by visions of the night she was attacked. Her attacker had Kevin's face, his cloying hands, grasping at her body. Every morning she awoke in a sweat, heart pounding, and then sighed with relief knowing she was safe in her bed. For so long, she had deliberately blocked the details from her mind, a necessary protection to deal with the trauma. The more nights she sweated and relived the horror, the more her suppressed memories resurfaced.

It was Kevin who first broached the subject. 'Sarah, do you remember that night?' Sarah gasped in surprise, as he continued, 'I relive that night, over and over, you know the night I mean?'

'Don't talk about it, it's over, forgotten,' replied Sarah, shakily, her uneasiness apparent from the quiver in her voice.

'No, Sarah, it is not forgotten by me. I was always worried I might have hurt you, but you know, I did think you wanted me, and you were, are, so beautiful, I just, couldn't help myself.' Sarah went quiet, unable to answer, accepting he was right but knowing he was wrong. 'But you disappeared after that night, and I didn't know how to contact you. I just heard you went to London but now you are back, I want to be with you. Marry me. We belong together if only because you and I have known each other already.'

Sarah returned to the farmhouse in a state of shock. Mary was inside chatting with Liam, but Sarah barely acknowledged her, going straight to her room, and firmly closing the door. Sarah's old habit reasserted itself and she dropped to her knees but there was no solace in the answers she believed she received.

Where possible, she continued to avoid Kevin as night after night for three weeks, she prayed for guidance. The answer was always the same and Sarah finally acquiesced, in silence. She understood the penance she now must undertake for being an *occasion of mortal sin*. Such piety in Sarah was a mystery to Kathleen who was even more perplexed when Sarah announced she was going to marry Kevin. When Liam was informed, he frowned, and looked quizzically at her for a few minutes before nodding in agreement. It was Mary who took Sarah aside and queried if she was making the right choice. Her soft demeanour and understanding words almost undermined Sarah's resolve but, in the end, she stood firm.

Kathleen immediately wrote and informed Ellen that Sarah was going to be married and to whom. Ellen was astonished, knowing how she used to be repulsed by him, and replied instantly to Sarah to attempt to dissuade her from a course of action that she was perceptive enough to realise, would be disastrous. Ellen knew how Sarah had struggled, the despair she had battled and the feeling of worthlessness she had attempted to overcome. Her letters were to no avail and Ellen was unable to gain an inkling of what was going through Sarah's mind. The complexity of her reasons, quite incomprehensible. Ellen's development, wrought by her discussions with Bridie, her reading, and the strength she had garnered to care for Sarah, had created a maturity that still eluded a fractured Sarah. Sarah was almost stuck in a time-warp, moulded by her experience and religion, reinforced by the nuns and the trauma of losing Stephen.

Sarah realised that neither Ellen nor Bridie would understand. She alone knew how she had, perhaps unwittingly, enticed a young man to sin and that this marriage was a form of reparation for that offence. Marriage to Kevin was not the life she had envisioned. Most of the time, all he engendered was a profound loathing but Josie's wish and advice that she marry were uppermost in her thoughts. She also had a need again to be part of life, to feel, to penetrate the numbness that encased her. Besides, Kevin was also Stephen's father and if there was a possibility, however remote, that being married to Kevin aided her quest for her little boy, then there was no other option. Her twisted logic gave her confidence that, for once, she was making the correct choice.

The wedding went ahead as planned although Sarah did not wear a dress anything as sumptuous as the one, she made for Bridie. Out of respect for Josie, the ceremony was small with only Kathleen, Liam and Brendan in attendance, and of course, Kevin's parents and family. Kathleen laid on a wedding breakfast after the ceremony for the few guests, before Kevin took Sarah's hand for the short walk to the little 'tigín'. Her imperceptible wince did not go unnoticed by Kevin, but he held her hand firmly as if to announce to all, she was now his.

An attempt had been made to tidy inside the cottage, but Sarah was still appalled and sighed with dejection. The scattering of crudely painted boxes in place of furniture, was no problem. She had always lived with a variety of crates utilised in numerous ways, for storage and comfort. A few cushions and a tablecloth would make them attractive. There was a fire smouldering in the grate but even her inexperienced eye could tell there would be a problem with smoke, come wind and winter. The most depressing aspect was the dirt floor. Cold and damp already permeated through the soles of her cheap shoes, and at a glance, there was already an abundance of insects in residence. She shivered, disappointed, as she had hoped for something a little better prepared to start her married life. Before she could voice any thoughts, Kevin, unable to wait any longer, grabbed her and hauled her onto the bed. She endured his advances which were passionless and speedy but lacked any love or gentleness. Her one experience of sexual intercourse was almost a forerunner of her wedding night.

When he left for work the next morning, Sarah lay in bed without moving until she heard his footsteps recede down the lane. Scrambled and confused thoughts raced through her mind. *What have I done?* So insistent was that question, it was almost a physical effort to banish the thought before it needed an answer. *It will get better, I know. In time, it will get better.* She repeated the mantra several times, before adding. *It is my atonement and once fulfilled, it will get better.*

Awkwardly, she rose from the bed, conscious of a stinging sensation between her legs and along her thighs. She hobbled outside, gulping the cold, fresh air, before she bathed herself in the chilly water from the spring. Sarah spent a few more minutes scanning the landscape, gathering her resolve, before returning to the cottage to make it a bit more habitable.

Chapter 22

Sarah's struggle to make a home and a life with Kevin isolated her and despite her determination, she had yet to put pen to paper and write to Bridie or Ellen. Ellen was especially worried about Sarah, but Bridie had another issue on her mind.

Bridie still loved her job but had an ache inside as month after month, there was no sign of any baby on the way. 'I cannot understand it, Ellen. I see women every day, with ten, twelve or even more children. Some even come in to deliver, with a ten-month-old in their arms. I just want, one.'

Ellen had no answers and just held her when she cried. She also had a restlessness and a desire for some transformation in her own life. Her short stories of tenement life were rejected by one publication after another. The usual response was no one was interested in misery, readers wanted happy stories of rags to riches. Ellen did not believe her stories were necessarily sad, just real life, depicting how strength and community helped women battle adversity and still have hope. A response that particularly galled suggested her stories were only *'women's writings,'* denigrating, she believed, the lives of many women implying they were less important than men. Both Ellen and Bridie, in different ways, were searching for a new meaning.

It was through Amy, one of the nurses at the hospital, that Ellen was introduced to "The Irish White Cross". "The Irish White Cross" was set up with funds from America but administered by a Quaker businessman, James G. Douglas. Amy's family were Quakers and heavily involved in charitable works and she wondered would Ellen like to assist once a week.

'Just a few hours on a Saturday, Ellen. There is so much hunger, especially among the children.'

Ellen had no hesitation and cheerfully agreed. Amy was gentle and kind and distributed food to the needy with no hint of condescension or expression of judgement, however vague. Her attitude indicated that she was the privileged one, and over time, Ellen felt humbled by her actions.

Each Saturday morning, Ellen walked to her allotted area, often Summerhill, but usually, Thomas Street or the surround. Sometimes, she recognised a face from the hospital and often was recognised herself. Despite the destitution, there was always hilarity, a lot of banter, but overall, an appreciation of the help provided. Saturday and Sunday evenings were spent documenting her experiences and adding wealth to her increasing stock, of "Tenement Tales".

Ellen now shook the rain from her umbrella and opened the front door with a sigh of relief, glad to be home. She was soaked through and planned to venture no further than the fireside for the rest of the evening. She removed her coat and scarf and was a little disconcerted to hear an unknown voice emanating from the kitchen. The kitchen was the source of fire and heat and, as such, her destination, so she carefully opened the door in case she was intruding.

'Come in, Ellen, come in, you look frozen,' welcomed Danny. Ellen ventured further and paused as the stranger with Danny rose from his seat, and pinpointed her with a regard of such intensity, she was unable to fathom what to think. Although his scrutiny was but seconds, she found it discomfiting. 'This is Jack, Jack Wallace,' introduced Danny.

'How do you do?' he responded, but rather than outstretching his arm to shake hands, he kept his right hand firmly in his pocket, a breach of etiquette Ellen found baffling.

Feeling a little uncomfortable, she sat in the chair indicated, but within minutes, fervently wished she had gone to her room when she first heard the strange voice. Jack Wallace stood close to her, tall and angular, with black hair slightly curled over his collar. 'Where have you been on such an awful day?' he enquired, in the warm, soft tones of the Midlands.

'Up in Thomas Street with The Irish White Cross.'

'Oh, a "*Lady Bountiful*", I see,' he gently mocked, while Ellen felt herself bristle.

'You can sneer but those people are glad of the help they receive,' was her indignant answer.

'My apologies,' with a slight, imperceptible bow. 'I know what you and many others undertake is sorely needed. Suffice to say, it is a sore point with me that our so-called "Free State" has so many of its citizens depending on hand-outs.'

Danny intervened, perhaps to somewhat defuse the increasing tension. 'Jack intends to run in the next election under the Labour Party banner.'

'Yes, I am hoping Danny will help to organise my campaign, but he is a little reluctant, at the moment,' was the wry response.

'No, Jack, not quite accurate,' interrupted Danny, 'I said I would think on it and when you come back next week you will have my answer.' Shortly afterwards, Jack left.

Ellen breathed a sigh of relief. 'He is an odd character, Danny. I can see why he might be difficult to work with.'

'Well, it's not that, Ellen, that gives me pause. A lot of his proposals are admirable, and he seems to be part of that rare species, a politician who means what he says. His candidacy will also appeal to many Sinn Fein voters. No, my hesitation stems from his history. I believe he was heavily involved on the anti-Treaty side during the Civil War, not unlike so many of our prominent public figures. It is rumoured, and in fairness, we all know rumours are not always true, that he operated in Cork, in 1922. You may remember reading about a dreadful sectarian atrocity in that area, and that is my hesitation with Jack. I am unsure if he was involved, but if he was, I do not want to associate with that mindset. You also may have noticed he kept his right hand firmly in his pocket. That is because his hand was shattered from a bullet, and he lost some fingers as a result of the injuries he sustained. My concern is whether he has renounced violence from conviction or because he can no longer engage in military activity. He does appear a bit volatile, so I am not entirely sure what to make of him.'

Jack left the warmth of the house with his mind made up to return. Initially, he wanted Danny to lead his campaign because of his expertise but also his standing. He had heard Danny speak, encouraging workers to unionise, and he admired his clarity of thought and his vision. Aware his own reputation was frowned upon by many in the Labour movement, he thought Danny's imprimatur would help his chances. Danny's questions about his activities during both the War of Independence and the Civil War were irritating, to say the least. His demand that he further pledge to forsake any form of violence was foolish in the extreme. How could anyone make that commitment with six counties still under British rule? If the opinionated Ellen had not appeared, Jack felt he would have walked away. Her presence had eased the tension with Danny, and he left with an agreement to return the following week. Despite himself, Jack was intrigued by Ellen. He failed to recall the last time he had found a woman's face quite so arresting, but more importantly, from his short conversation with her he could gauge she had a social conscience and her opinion had value. He might disagree with her, but her viewpoint was worth his attention because it differed so much from his own. Jack knew he had irritated her with his comments and realised he was sometimes too abrasive, but that did not mean he was unwilling to hear other assessments of a situation

Jack's accommodation was sparse. Formerly one room, now divided in two, his section was windowless and always chilly. His earnings as a union official and organiser were not so meagre as to prevent him from renting anything more comfortable. The surroundings, however, did not affect him as all he needed was a roof over his head. Settled in his lodgings for the evening, he intended to spend the time organising election literature. Yet, he found his thoughts straying from time to time, pondering Ellen, distracting him from his purpose.

Surprisingly, Ellen found Jack occupying her own thoughts from time to time. Danny's comments indicated he had a chequered past but her own family had not been immune from involvement in the horrors of conflict. She could not fathom why he had been so ill-mannered. The effects of his abrasiveness lingered long after he departed. Such an abrupt manner could only hamper his prospects in any occupation that needed interaction with the public. His acerbic comments to herself did not bode well either and would make for discomfort if she were to meet him regularly at the house. Yet, whether through design or chance, she was in the house on the following Saturday when he called once more. His 'Lady Bountiful' comment continued to rankle and his opening address when he saw her did not help.

'It is lovely to see you again, Ellen, and you are obviously not out helping the poor unfortunate today. I hope you skipped your charitable works in order to see me!'

Ellen felt a surge of irritation inside but kept her cool. 'No, Mr Wallace, I am not required every week and am about to leave for my walk, in St Stephen's Green. It is unfortunate I was delayed leaving. I am sure you have a lot to talk about with Danny, so I will say goodbye now and leave you to it.'

Jack watched her thoughtfully as she walked sedately away from the house, regretting his flippant remark, wishing he could start the conversation again. His reverie was interrupted by Danny, impatient to resume discussions.

With some misgivings, Danny had agreed to assist Jack in his attempt to get elected. He explained later to Bridie and Ellen, 'More violence is probably inevitable, but a certain way to ensure it continues, is to prevent engagement in the political arena.'

The enormity of the task ahead was not lost on Danny. For a newcomer like Jack, a good showing, paving the way for future success might be a more realistic goal. However, a by-election often provided those lesser-known candidates with a better chance of electoral success. He decided that if Jack's campaign began early, then with maximum exposure his face would become familiar, so ensuring the final result would be the most positive that could be attained. Why Jack had joined the Labour Party, considering his anti-Treaty history, was also problematic.

Jack explained, 'It is the James Connolly connection. The Labour Party encompassed the whole island and there are still many in the Northern counties who believe in his ideals. I want to battle for the final six counties from a position of strength. How better to persuade others to join our Republic than by showing them we have a truly egalitarian society, worthy of Connolly?'

'Fine, Jack,' nodded Danny. 'Just remember, questions will be asked about your past activities and your new-found commitment to the Party. Be sure you are sincere when you give your answers.'

It surprised Danny when he heard that two candidates had been chosen for the by-election and he was even more than surprised that one of them was, Jack. Jack's opponent had tremendous support within the Party, so Danny surmised that it was a deliberate political strategy. Jack might garner transfer votes from a more radical electorate but that would not be in his favour. Danny further suspected the support for Jack was more to "blood" him as a candidate for the next general election, and that no one really expected him or even wanted him, to take the seat. This was not the kind of information that was easy to impart to a serious, single-minded, and passionate candidate, such as Jack. However, the following few weeks, saw Jack Wallace become a fixture in the house, regular meetings with Danny a necessity, to devise a plan of action for the forthcoming by-election, in November.

Ellen found herself gradually drafted into the position of note-taker as Danny and Jack plotted the election strategy. On occasion, Danny was missing, as his own work commitments had to take precedence, and Ellen and Jack were thrust together. They worked companionably enough, and an ease developed between them. Ellen's knowledge of elections was limited but she had an innate understanding of people. Jack listened respectfully to her suggestions even if, most times, he ignored her advice.

'Jack, calm the rhetoric a little. In that area, food and shelter are more important than regaining our cultural heritage. Remember also, the Catholic Church offers a haven and hope for many people. Tone down the criticism.'

'I know, Ellen,' responded Jack, 'but isn't it sad, that life for so many is just struggle with the hope of a fairy tale ending when they die?'

'Jack, don't say that. If you want their vote, give them a hope they can aspire to but don't denigrate their belief.'

Jack's caustic manner was still in evidence, yet the growing attraction between Ellen and Jack was apparent for all to see. Inevitably, he engineered an opportunity to meet her alone in St Stephen's Green, her regular haunt. Once the weather was fine, Ellen went for a stroll after work each evening before heading home. When she saw Jack in the distance, sitting comfortably, at ease with himself, she was excited but also confused. For a moment, she was tempted to turn around before he saw her. The moment passed, as he waved, stood up, and strode purposefully in her direction.

'Ellen, may I join you on your walk and take you to tea afterwards? I promise to be on my best behaviour.'

This mannerly approach was so unusual she just mumbled agreement, inexplicably for her, quite tongue-tied. She was attracted to this tall, thin, intent man, who varied between teasing her and purposeful questioning. He made her nervous, unsure of herself, how she looked, what she felt, what she believed. Listening to him debate with Danny, she could readily see him standing in the Dail, bamboozling all those who dared to question him with facts and figures. In many ways, he reminded her of her brother, Liam, with his absolute certainty that only his opinion was correct and valid.

The summer of 1925 was wrapped in magic and happiness for Ellen and Jack. They walked in the evenings, drank coffee and tea in numerous cafes and on one occasion went to the Abbey. Ellen wanted to see Sean O'Casey's play, *Shadow of a Gunman* and, to her delight, Jack produced tickets for the Saturday night performance. Ellen had never been in any establishment remotely as glamorous as the Abbey Theatre and dressed with special care that evening. Sarah's gift at alterations would have been useful for the event but nevertheless, complete with bonnet and gloves, she was as stylish as her wardrobe would allow. Jack, likewise, dressed in his best and Ellen felt they were both elegant as she entered the theatre on his arm.

However, Jack seemed ill at ease throughout, and although the depiction of Dublin life and the down–to–earth characters fascinated Ellen and held her enthralled, Jack was unsettled. He could never rest easy at the best of times. Sitting still for even a couple of hours while there was political work needing attention was torture, and his agitation and constant motion took somewhat from Ellen's enjoyment. His apology on the walk home only partially mollified her, as he explained, 'I was never at the theatre before, to me it seems such a waste, all that play-acting. Hope I wasn't a distraction but sitting there for so long gets a bit boring.'

Ellen grinned and relaxed. A half-hearted apology it might be, but she realised that this was Jack, and she was just content to be by his side, and after he kissed her goodnight, she felt happy enough to forgive him anything.

There was no more mention of the theatre, but weather permitting, each weekend they wandered along Sandymount Strand or headed out to Dollymount Beach. Jack originally hailed from the Midlands, and he was fascinated by the sea. He always carried a rug and Ellen packed a small picnic. It was sitting together, listening to the soughing of the breeze or the gentle swish of the waves that they came to know each other well. This new-found knowledge was not easy for either of them.

Ellen regaled Jack with stories of the tenements. She admired the strength that shone through such adversity, how she felt satisfaction in playing her part in alleviating some of the stress caused by extreme poverty. She gave him the gift of her vision of the future. Marriage with children, a garden for them to play in, enough money to enable them to stay in school and the hope of a niche for herself as an author or even a playwright. Most of all, a husband who would love her and support her. He smiled in wonderment at Ellen's ambitions and aspirations and felt chilled at the realisation he could not be a part of them. How could he ask her to share his life of agitation, maybe of poverty, definitely of continual uncertainty? Jack's vision of the future was more daunting, and he gave Ellen not a gift but a presentiment, of turmoil. He could not rest, he explained until there was a 32 county Ireland. He was supportive of whatever means necessary, but because of his injury, his only effective avenue was in furthering the political route.

'I thought you promised Danny you were finished with violence?'

'I did, and I am, sure, look at this hand,' and Jack held up his right hand as though displaying something new to Ellen, implying, she had not previously seen the mutilation and discarded it as unimportant. 'This hand is fairly useless now but that does not mean I would not assist those engaged in military action, if necessary.'

'Were you not dissembling with Danny then?'

'Wow, such a big word, Ellen,' he lightly teased, in an attempt to ease the growing tension. 'No, I don't think so. Danny is not stupid, and he has sussed me well. He just needed to hear me speak the words to give himself permission to help me.' To still further questions and remove the frown from her face Jack bent over and attempted to kiss Ellen on her lips.

'Don't, Jack. Do not treat me like an idiot. I am not a child to be pacified with a smile and a pat on the head. I am a woman who needs to understand you, and to believe in you.' Ellen marched away and Jack hurried to catch up with her.

'I am sorry, Ellen. I did not intend to demean you. That is the last thing I want to do. I love you and admire you.'

Ellen was taken aback by Jack's declaration of love, something she had wished to hear, but a statement that was out of kilter with the strain that had now arisen between them. 'I love you too, Jack,' Ellen responded quietly. As they walked silently back to the house, a coolness persisted between them, despite their admission of love.

As the hazy weeks of summer flew by, Danny was worried about the blossoming romance between Ellen and Jack and conveyed his apprehensions to Bridie. He did not dislike Jack, as such, but he feared he would hurt Ellen. Whereas Ellen viewed Jack as having a dedication to the pursuit of an Irish Republic, Danny saw a man with a compulsion that was all-consuming and left little time for family. He was also anxious in case Jack's previous activities came to light and in so doing, reflected unfavourably on Ellen. He had no doubt the Labour Party investigated Jack's background thoroughly and most were satisfied, but there were always skeletons that the opposition could unearth. If there was a serious possibility that Jack might take a seat at the next by-election due in early January, in-depth searches into his previous activities would be automatic. Personally, Danny thought, although he did not voice it, Jack had little prospect of winning the seat. More and more Danny had concluded that there was a strategy at work and Jack was being used by the Party to secure the seat, but not for Jack.

Every weekend, at Jack's insistence, they travelled to the constituency and they both pounded the pavements canvassing for votes. As a seasoned campaigner, Danny surmised, Jack's prospects were becoming increasingly more limited due to his intractable stance on a variety of issues. Despite his good looks, his appeal was compromised by his intensity and argumentative nature. His abrasive response to many general queries was far from diplomatic and regularly a door was slammed. His heart was in the right place, demanding change in social conditions, but Danny knew from old that these promises were viewed as freely made and more easily forgotten. The promise of a pint down the local pub, with a verse of an oul ballad thrown in, worked wonders with some of the electorate and was the only campaigning necessary for some of Jack's opponents. Danny's attempts to discuss Jack's intransigence was met with a terse response.

'Jack, soften your tone a bit. If someone disagrees with you, try and show a bit more restraint and agree there is room for everyone's opinion.'

'Never, Danny, never. Anyway, those people won't vote for me, and I can't just let them rant at me at the door without giving a proper answer.'

'Most won't vote for you, but some might. There is always someone who likes a discordant voice to shake up the establishment, but if you set their backs up...' Danny's voice trailed away as he could already see, Jack was not listening.

As the summer months waned, and the autumn chill and creeping darkness stole their seaside cocoon, the proximity of the election was a catalyst for sustained activity. Jack became so busy that walks and, even time spent over a quick coffee, seemed to irritate him. The glow that had surrounded Ellen started to dim. She hid her disappointment well, knowing the election was paramount, but questions niggled at the side-lines especially alone in her bed at night. Regardless, Ellen, Bridie, and Danny spent a very quiet, but enjoyable Christmas in the city and even Jack managed to join them for a few hours. However, continually preoccupied with the upcoming election he displayed a disdain for the holiday, that bordered on rude. He left early to everyone's relief, and it was some days later before he reappeared again.

Chapter 23

Whilst Ellen vacillated, switching from disappointment to revelling in her new relationship with Jack, Sarah was finding life with Kevin increasingly difficult. At the start, there was a genuine effort on her part to make the marriage work and she acquiesced to his attentions without objection. Yet, as the weeks passed, each subsequent night became more abhorrent, and Kevin was not slow to be just as demanding in the morning. His features flushed with indignation if she demurred but her passive submission appeared to incense him even more. He did not intend to be an unpleasant man, but he had no knowledge beyond what he had learnt on the farm. His every touch now made Sarah's skin crawl. Kevin had always known that Sarah had little interest in him, but when he saw her flinch, anger reared inside, akin to hatred. He wanted her with such intensity, such passion, that his obsession clouded all common sense. His inability to make her want him was a canker, eating him inside. His original hope was that, over time, she would at least be content but within weeks he knew it was not to be and this incensed him even more. He felt he was an irritation in his own home and what he saw as his husbandly rights, she endured with a face of disgust.

Sarah did not deliberately decide to limit his access to her body despite his continual demands. The first time she said no, she was just unwell with a heavy cold and wracking cough. Reluctantly, Kevin left her alone, sleeping on a chair for a week. That alone hardened Sarah's resolve. It was as if she had no meaning for him beyond the physical. He had no desire to hold her because he loved her and wanted her close. She knew, beyond a doubt, that the power she had over Kevin was held solely in the beauty of her face and body and nothing else. That knowledge initially stripped her of herself, but strength quickly followed. The first morning she felt well enough, she rose early and made his porridge. He took that as a sign.

'Aye, you're looking well again, come here.'

'No, Kevin, not yet. I am a bit better but not ready for that yet.'

He glared contemplatively at her for a few minutes, then stood up, muttering, 'Well, I am off to work now, so be seeing you.' Kevin did not come home until much later that evening and had evidently stopped on the way, for he smelled strongly of beer, and the pungent, stale stench of sweat.

Once he had eaten, he pulled at Sarah, but she paused him with three words, 'Go, wash first.'

His fist caught her by surprise, painfully splitting her lip, and she reeled backwards bruising her hip. Kevin stormed out, and it was the early hours when Sarah heard his stagger outside the door. She feigned sleep but there was no need. Kevin passed out, almost before he sank into the chair, and stayed comatose until morning. When Sarah roused him for work, he avoided looking at her, instead he mumbled an apology, before awkwardly making his way out the door.

Prior to his marriage Kevin never drank heavily and just enjoyed the odd glass on Saturday evenings. Now, as the weeks progressed, a habit developed to stop for a few pints, maybe a whiskey or two, most nights. Afterwards, he meandered slowly up the laneway preparing himself for rejection. He soon realised, that with a few drinks taken, the better able he became to force his attentions on Sarah. The more this happened, the further apart they drifted, and the more Sarah loathed him and knew she had made a serious mistake. When Kevin overdid the drinking, he would pass out in a chair the instant he arrived home. She welcomed the awkward lurch that heralded a drunken coma. If his steps were reasonably sturdy, she prepared herself for the onslaught of hot, fetid breath and rough hands. Sarah endured those nights with a newfound stoicism, a precursor to an evolving maturity. As she would later tell Ellen, the return to Donegal had revived that long-ago night and the forcibly suppressed images resurfaced in her dreams.

Since Stephen, she had felt hollow inside and unable to connect with anyone or anything. Irrationally, she thought that any type of sensation would help but she had been wrong. The renewed stress brought about by her dreams, had also rekindled the senseless praying and, absurdly, made her believe she should marry Kevin as a form of reparation. Conversely, confronting the detail of what had occurred, and its aftermath, eventually made her see events in a more balanced light. The maturity which followed enabled her to realise the foolish mistake she had made, but by then she was well married to Kevin.

Slowly, as the weeks passed, the time Kevin spent in the pub did not go unnoticed by his family and many a neighbour and he knew, both himself and Sarah were the subject of intense speculation and gossip. Sarah was not immune to the questioning looks, particularly when she sported the odd bruise, but she no longer cared and made little attempt at concealment. She had made a grave error in marrying Kevin and all she wanted now, was to hammer out a workable relationship with him. They were four months married and Christmas was once more on the horizon. She dreaded spending the day with Kevin's parents and family, but, apparently, there was no way to avoid it. She decided to try anyway. Unfortunately, she chose the wrong moment to broach the subject. Kevin had arrived home earlier than usual. He had not missed stopping at the pub, but he seemed in good form, complimenting her on the stew and warm fire.

'Kevin, what would you think if I spend Christmas at the farm with Kathleen?' suggested Sarah. 'The first Christmas without our mother will be sad for us all but especially Kathleen.'

The blow caught her unawares with its speed, slamming her against one of the boxes and sending her senses spinning. Kevin was on her before she could move, hands grappling and clawing at her clothes. A white-hot hatred surged inside her. If she had been able to grasp any weapon, she would have hit him. Instead, she went limp, enduring his assault yet conscious enough of such a violation that, even in her terror and helplessness, she vowed he would never touch her again.

When Kevin saw Sarah the next morning he felt a twinge of guilt, which he quickly quenched. She was making a laughing-stock of him in the neighbourhood, even his father had mentioned that all was not as it should be. Wanting to spend their first Christmas away from him was an insult and would bring disgrace on him and his family. Inwardly, he quaked though, because if her brother Liam got wind of any speculation about the source of her bruises, there would be trouble and a day of reckoning that harboured no good for Kevin. By all accounts, Liam was back on his feet but regardless, he had some dangerous friends who would do his bidding. The blame would be placed on Kevin, yet their troubles were all Sarah's fault for denying him. He worked hard, provided a home, at the very least she should submit to him. Yet, guilt gnawed at him, and the next two weeks saw long evenings spent in the pub, tottering home, unable to do more than collapse onto a chair.

Sarah ignored him. She made meals and cleaned as before but refused to engage with him. The only time she spoke was to wake him for work so he would leave the cottage in the morning. She had another reason for wanting him out of the way. She believed she was pregnant and if Kevin saw her getting sick in the morning, he would know. This was going to be her secret for as long as possible until she sorted out what to do. She worried about how she could fend him off the next time he approached her. She had a poker by the bed but knew it was unlikely she would be able to use it.

A week before Christmas Sarah went early to bed. Her morning sickness had been severe, and no amount of firewood seemed able to heat the cottage. Temperatures had plummeted and ice had remained on the windows all day. She left some food heating for Kevin, but by nine o'clock, there was no sign of him. Relieved, she expected he would not return until the early hours of the morning and drifted comfortably off to sleep.

Kevin was in a quandary. He sipped his pint slowly. It was his third of the day. He knew he was drinking too much, and the quarry foreman had told him he had better sort himself out or he would not be hired anymore. 'Lots looking for work here. We don't want slackers and drunken ones, at that.'

Rage had thundered through Kevin at these words, but he had been sensible enough to hold his tongue. There was no doubting it was all Sarah's fault. Every time he looked at her, he wanted her with such a hunger, it frightened him. If she could just act like a normal wife, things would be fine. Maybe, if they had a baby she would settle. He would like one too, it was what marriage was about and the Church expected it.

'Hey there, Kevin.' Disturbed by the greeting, Kevin looked up into the smiling face of Patsy O'Hara. 'How are things, eh? How's that wife of yours?' Kevin felt like punching him, but Patsy just laughed and placed another pint in front of him. 'Drink that up, it's Christmas.'

Kevin mumbled an ungrateful thanks, but nevertheless, quickly downed the drink before a short while later ordering another one for himself and, reluctantly, a drink for Patsy. The night wore on in the usual vein and Kevin finished up with a few whiskies. 'G'night, everyone. Happy Christmas,' he slurred, as he stumbled towards the door and the traipse home.

The freezing night air took Kevin's breath away, surrounding him like a cloak. He bundled his thin jacket tightly around him, surprised, at the carpet of snow underfoot. The wind whistled through trees of white blossom that blew into his face as he stepped, uncertainly, onto the laneway to his cottage. The moon lit his way, while the alcohol made him sway. His well-worn boots slithered on the slushy ground unable to find adequate grip, as he trudged slowly up the rocky path. Senses dulled, barely focussed on each step, he stumbled along, too close to the ditch. The fall itself only stunned him but combined with his copious intake of alcohol, that was enough to render him into a stupor. Kevin lay still, overcome by fatigue.

When Sarah awoke the following day, there was no sign of Kevin. She surmised he either had never come home or had left early for work. Either way, she did not care. The uneaten food was congealed in the pot, but it was still welcome on such a cold morning. Outside, the mountains and valleys were blanketed in heavy snow and ice had formed on the privy and speckled the spring water. Sarah stepped outside cautiously, anxious lest she slip, fascinated by the sun, sparkling, on a silent white world.

The impact of the death of both parents and the conflict between her brothers had a maturing effect on Kathleen. She gained a wisdom about the unpredictable and arbitrary nature of life and relationships, which is usually reserved for an older person. Support from Sarah had helped her through the first difficult weeks and even the necessity to help Liam, after his attack, had helped her cope with a grief that had threatened to overwhelm. She had hoped Sarah's marriage meant she would always have a sister close by, but she was astute and could recognise that all was not well, and that Sarah was miserable. The little cottage was not welcoming, and Kathleen avoided calling in as much as possible. She knew she was powerless to help her through whatever difficulties had arisen. As contact with Sarah was now minimal, the extent of abuse was also not realised.

Christmas was approaching, and to Kathleen's surprise she set about Christmas preparation with her usual vigour. Memories would make the occasion very poignant as the recollection of happier times would be interspersed with a deep sadness. Yet, she planned on decorating the farmhouse as per usual. Ellen wrote regularly but Kathleen knew no one from Dublin would join them that year. Ellen's letters never mentioned Jack, and, in retrospect, Ellen could never understand why.

Kathleen was unsure where Sarah would spend Christmas Day but assumed it would be in her parents-in-laws' home. As such, the farm would have a party of five. Liam and herself of course, plus Brendan and, not surprisingly, Liam had announced that Mary McNally and her father would join them too. Kathleen liked Mary, and they had developed an affinity between them and grown quite close. Sarah's preoccupation and undeniable difficulties had generated a gulf and Mary filled that gap. She was a regular visitor to the farmhouse and Liam's awkwardness was now both a source of amusement for Kathleen and an irritation. She was a romantic and wished he would just ask the obvious question. At times, despite her affection for her older brother, Liam made her cringe. He supervised all aspects of the farm, ever critical of those who offered help due to his incapacity which, fortunately, was now much improved. Kathleen recalled the day Mary hauled buckets of milk from the barn.

'Whist, woman, you will spill those. No wonder, you're not married yet.'

Mary placed the buckets at his feet. Small, dark, and fiery, with feet planted part and hands on hips, she was a spirited opponent to Liam's usual stark and stern visage that, this time, held a hint of humour. 'Aye, and you can do better, can you?' she snapped. 'No man yet who asked me, has been worthy of me. You do well to remember that Liam McShane.' Mary marched off and it was a further week before Kathleen saw her again.

Liam was never easy to live with, but during that week, he was impossible. These fleeting thoughts floated through Kathleen's mind as with Christmas preparations now completed, she finalised the stew and lit candles to offset the deepening, December, gloom.

Holly sprigs festooned the fireplace and she had fashioned a wreath of berries and leaves for the front door. Her well-tended garden had produced a selection of vegetables and Liam had promised a goose. She was startled out of her wistful reverie by a surge of cold air as the door swung open and a dishevelled Sarah, rushed through gabbling incoherently, spraying snow all over the clean flagstones.

Less than an hour had passed since Sarah heard the news. It had been early morning when Kevin's father first came hammering on her door. 'Where is he? Where's Kevin?' Sarah just shrugged which incensed Kevin's father, and he roared, 'When did you see him last?'

'Why?' queried Sarah. 'What has he done now?'

Spitting impatience, he demanded, 'Has he gone to work in the quarry?' Without waiting for an answer, Kevin's father turned on his heel, marching away, shoulders heaving with anger. Kevin had been due to arrive at the family farm early that morning and assist with a difficult cow. Assuming his son was either at work or possibly once more the worse for wear, his father tramped back home. With some help from a neighbour, he managed to sort the sick animal. As the day wore on, and Kevin had still not appeared, his father went to the quarry, only to learn Kevin had not turned up there, either. Reluctantly, he trudged the short trek back to the cottage. 'When did you last see Kevin? He has not been seen at the quarry all day.'

'Last night,' muttered, Sarah.

'Last night?' echoed Kevin's father. 'Last night? Aye, and you, his wife, and you can't keep him at home.'

The news that his son had not been seen since the night before alarmed Kevin's father. Despite knowing things were not going well with the couple, he was concerned at such a long absence. He now gathered some of the locals together and, between them, they made enquiries in the area. When no result was yielded, they formed a search party with urgency, now the night was closing in around them. The snow hampered the quest, but it helped visibility. The first route was the track from the pub to the cottage and, before long, Kevin was found lying in a ditch, frozen, on a bed of snow. They did not carry the body back to his wife but brought Kevin straight to his parent's home. No one thought to inform Sarah, but the wife of a kindly neighbour called to check on her. When she realised Sarah had been left in ignorance, it reluctantly fell to her to relay the news. Sarah sat in shock, unable to absorb what the woman was saying.

'Ye will be alright, love,' she murmured reassuringly, 'let me get you something strong for the shock, and I'll stay with ye.'

'No, no I will go to my sister, Kathleen.'

'Well, alright, but wait until my Johnny gets back to bring you up.' Sarah nodded but did nothing of the sort. Once the neighbour had left, she donned her shawl and rushed up the laneway, so familiar, it posed no threat or danger of her slipping. She hurled herself headlong into Kathleen's astonished arms.

Kevin's parents, brothers and sisters closed ranks, excluding Sarah from most of the funeral arrangements. She said nothing, knowing it would be hypocritical to don the mantle of grieving widow. The mass and burial were quite traumatic as it was recognisable to all she was side-lined from the family. Sarah bore the indignity with her head high. Although she was sorry that Kevin had died in such an ignominious manner there was no denying she was suddenly looking forward to a future alone with her child. No one knew she was pregnant, and she planned that few in Donegal, least of all Kevin's family, ever would.

When Sarah returned to the cottage after the funeral, she set about packing all her belongings. Kevin's family had given no indication, but she knew they would want her gone from the cottage, very shortly. It was while she was tidying Kevin's meagre possessions that she found a box, and within it, was almost £4.00, a fortune to Sarah, which she instantly packed away in her bag. She had arranged for Brendan to collect her the following morning as she was going to spend Christmas Day with Kathleen, after all. Before Brendan arrived, Kevin's father appeared at the door. He declined her invitation to enter and abruptly, announced, 'I'll be wanting the cottage back. You can stay until you're sorted, for a week or two, but then I'll need it.'

'Aye,' Sarah responded, 'I figured that.'

'He loved ye, ye know, and because of that I'm leaving you this, but I never want to see you again. You made him a drinker, and that's what killed my son.' He stomped away, having dropped £5.00 on the dirt floor. Pride made Sarah want to leave the note where it lay, but common sense made her retrieve it. His words had stung, not least because she felt they held a grain of truth. In his own way, Kevin had loved her, but it was without understanding or tenderness. He had stolen her youth and was both the perpetrator of her greatest joy but also greatest sorrow, her baby Stephen. He had made it impossible for her to reciprocate his love in any way. Her few months of marriage had taught her something else. She had been a carefree young girl that night, innocent and naïve, and not responsible for Kevin's actions. She had not been to blame and, the realisation released her from a weight that had crushed her, for the past few years. The knowledge that we all must take responsibility for our actions, and the hurt we inflict on others, gave Sarah the courage to look towards her future with equanimity tinged, with anticipation.

Chapter 24

Ellen was conflicted. Since autumn, her relationship with Jack appeared to be floundering. She could understand his objectives and therefore the need to put his whole heart into campaigning, but his focus was all-consuming. The attention she received was minimal at best, and she felt diminished. The cold nights pounding the pavements were a prelude to heated discussions with Danny. Each evening they were closeted together for hours with Danny's reasoned tones interrupted by Jack's strident demands. By the time Jack was leaving, Ellen was either already in bed or too tired to deal with a combative Jack. Now he had lost the election Jack seemed to be blaming Danny, accusing him of not giving it his all. The few times he had called to the house since the election result, had ended in further argument. Danny wanted him to bide his time and listen more to what people wanted. There would be a general election before too long and Danny was willing to work to obtain the full might of the Labour Party behind him.

'Jack,' cautioned Danny, patiently, 'soften your stance and if you manage to take a seat, you can then put forward your proposals, but you need to first get elected.' Danny did not suggest that Jack give up on his ideals but merely tailor them, to suit the beliefs of the people. Danny knew all too well that people did not want an Ireland that abandoned the Church in favour of a

Soviet-style republic. The Church had been a rallying call for nationalism and was part of the people's psyche. 'Representatives are supposed to reflect the electorate's viewpoint,' he reiterated.

Jack viewed this as dishonest and the problem all along with politics and politicians. If his beliefs were so malleable and he was so flexible as to promote one ideology, and then once elected, purport another, then he was no better than those he despised. He wanted to be elected on his own terms. Consequently, the debate between Danny and Jack went around in continual circles.

'The problem with Jack,' Danny explained to Ellen, 'was that he wanted people to vote for his ideals but was not willing to give any compromise. It is all very well to promise education and health care but if that included discarding the Catholic Church, then Jack was not going to have success with the electorate. Add to that the bitterness still festering since the Civil War and Jack's further objective of a united Ireland by whatever means necessary, made Jack unelectable in the present climate.'

Murmurings from a few members within the Party indicated Danny was not alone in his opinion, with some venturing to say the choice of Jack Wallace had been a mistake. Listening to Danny reflect on the difficulties with Jack, Ellen reluctantly interjected, anxious not to appear to betray Jack, 'You know, Danny, it often appeared to me that the name on the ballot paper should have read Danny Walsh and not Jack Wallace. Don't misunderstand me, I have the height of respect for Jack and his principles. I truly admire how steadfast he is in his beliefs, but you are twice the politician he will ever be.' Ellen paused in consideration for a moment. 'Jack,' she continued, 'has a divisive nature, no matter how honest and sincere he is in what he believes, but you, on the other hand, are a unifier and will always seek out common ground.'

Danny laughed heartily, 'Maybe I am now, Ellen, but it wasn't always so. I learned to tone down my rhetoric and I think that is what Jack needs to do now. I think Jack, at times, is his own worst enemy. The lesson I learnt is that change is not achievable from the side-line. One must be pragmatic and get elected first. After that anything is possible. What the future holds for Jack, or even me, well, who knows, but I never say never, to anything.'

This changed Jack was a different man to the one with whom Ellen had fallen in love. On the surface, he bore no relation to the Jack who lay by her side on the beach the previous summer. She recalled him nervously twisting some seaweed in his mangled hand, while guaranteeing to be always faithful, his black hair, falling across his forehead, obscuring the tenderness in his deep brown eyes. The softness and tentativeness of his tone was the opposite of the strident demands he made of Danny. It was impossible to imagine the hands, and torn fingers that softly traced a pattern on her palm or gently stroked her cheek, firing a weapon with intent to kill. She was no church attender, but her roots were in Catholicism, and she understood how belief, inculcated from childhood, was not easily discarded. She agreed with Danny that anyone suggesting abandoning the Church in favour of a totally secular republic would have difficulty getting elected. Yet, she loved the strength in Jack, his unwavering principles, because that courage and tenacity embodied the Jack whose love would never falter.

Jack himself was utterly dejected. After months of treading pavements and trekking up and down laneways and byways promising reform, he had barely kept his deposit. The months of happiness with Ellen were forgotten, swamped in his despondency. He knew he was a fractious person, but that was born from a need for his viewpoint to be correctly understood. He looked around now at his lodgings, a small room off Mountjoy Square, in central Dublin. He had never ventured to bring Ellen to where he lived, and forcefully rejected any sense of shame at his home. He knew he could afford something better but, most of his neighbours were not in that position. Perhaps that was why he was so critical of her Irish White Cross activities. No one should have so little they needed hand-outs from those who were not much better off but had buckets of compassion. The state should provide for those in need, and if that meant radical reform, then so be it. To compromise, as Danny and the Labour Party wanted, was anathema. It was dishonourable to suggest he run on one platform and change tack once elected. It was that type of dishonesty in public representatives Jack most despised.

He was due to have dinner in Clare Street that evening with Ellen, Bridie and Danny. Another round of political discussion would follow between imself and Danny with no ensuing agreement. Jack visualised Ellen's face and how it would be suffused with waves of confusion, concurring with Danny's viewpoint but wanting to agree with him. Her beautiful face and gentle nature, too good for the likes of him. If he had been elected, he would have proposed marriage, but he had nothing to offer her now but more angst. He would not bring her to live in his one-room flat but neither had he the time to look for more suitable accommodation. He currently felt he could not present any vision of an engaging future. Despite his extreme left socialist leanings, Jack was a product of his time believing a man's duty was to provide.

The table was set and dinner almost ready, but there was no sign of Jack. Ellen had expected him earlier, as there was a vague understanding, they would have a walk or coffee together, before the meal. Once dinner was over, she knew Jack would be ensconced with Danny for more campaign review and future planning. By 6.30, Danny insisted they all eat. Used as he was to dinner midday, he was starving.

'Jack was due at the latest 5 o'clock. No excuse. We eat now.'

Ellen wanted to wait but duly sat down with Bridie and Danny. Ordinarily, she would have cleared her plate of boiled bacon and cabbage, within minutes, but tonight she found it impossible to swallow more than a few forkfuls. She alternated, between anger at Jack's non-appearance and worry that he might have met with an accident.

It was well past 9 o'clock when there was an insistent rap on the door. A dishevelled and incoherent, Jack, was leaning against the frame, obviously in need of support to remain upright. Danny hauled his dead weight inside, depositing him roughly in a chair. Jack mumbled all the time, of his heartfelt love for Ellen, his apologies for missing the meal, his shame and worthlessness. Eventually, his voice trailed away to be replaced by thunderous snores. Ellen, Bridie and Danny went to bed, and by morning, Jack was gone.

Almost a week passed by, and Ellen had still not heard from him. She was tempted to look for him but realised she was unsure where to start. They had always made prior arrangements of where to meet, and she now realised, Jack had only given her the vaguest idea of his address. Danny, of course, would know, but Ellen's pride held her tongue and prevented the simple question from forming on her lips.

The following Friday evening when she left the hospital, Jack was waiting outside, leaning against a low wall. He was contrite, but the old fiery Jack was once more in evidence. 'Can we go somewhere and talk, Ellen?' She nodded agreement and they strolled to one of the many cafes they had frequented that unforgettable summer. Once seated, and after his first sip of the steaming brew, Jack took her hands in his and smoothing her fingers one by one, he began, 'Ellen, my beautiful Ellen. How can I say this without hurting you? You are a part of me. I know I have been distracted lately but you are always there, in my thoughts and in my dreams and in my future. I love you, Ellen, but I cannot offer you the life you want and deserve, not yet anyway. I want to make a difference and I need to first find my own direction and purpose. Can you be patient for a while longer? I always want to be a part of you and your life. I promise to write regularly, and I hope the time will come when we can be together.'

Ellen's eyes were dry, conceding defeat, hiding the well of sorrow that now nestled deep inside. Her response was slow and thoughtful but realistic, acknowledging her understanding of this complex man. 'I love you too, Jack, and I will wait. I know the time is not right for us, not at this moment, anyway. But I will expect you to write, and often.'

Hands held, they gazed at each other for a long time, before, by mutual consent, they rose and with a final goodbye, he left her at the corner of Clare Street.

Once the festivities were over Sarah wrote to Bridie and Ellen. She knew she would not be staying in "Droimreagh", and was gratified to see Kathleen at ease, and apparently in charge, of the domestic side of the set-up. She had a maturity for her young age that Sarah both admired and envied, wishing she had been that way herself. Kathleen pestered Liam and Brendan with a soft smile, reminiscent of Josie, and all three settled into a pattern that currently worked well for them all. From the interaction between Liam and Mary McNally there were bound to be changes in the future, but that boded well, as there was a comfortable dynamic between Kathleen and Mary. The letter to

Dublin was challenging to compose as Kevin's death and funeral were awkward issues to comfortably outline. However, she explained as well as she was able and requested to stay in Clare Street for a short while. She emphasised it would not be for long as she had plans of her own. In Dublin, the letter was a real source of conversation for days. Arriving shortly after Christmas, it was intriguing to say the least and provided much speculation and a break from the constant conjecture about Jack.

When Sarah stepped off the train in March 1926, the first thing Ellen noticed was the absence of the brooding demeanour that seemed to have become such a part of Sarah. Ellen had felt such dejection over Jack that Sarah's contented pose gave her a lift, despite herself. Sarah's composure, although welcome, did not invite questions so details of her life with Kevin were never revealed. Ellen and Bridie were satisfied to let her be, knowing in her own time Sarah would confide in them, if she felt the need.

Space in the little cottage was always tight, now, it was once more at a premium. Sarah outlined her plans enlisting help, particularly from Danny. She did not reveal she was pregnant believing she would face opposition if they knew. Her idea was in many ways, quite simple. She would work as a seamstress altering dresses and, hopefully, designing and sewing new ones. She required a small premises, one perhaps with a storefront onto the street, nothing fancy, but somewhere she could also live. This dream necessitated money for a lease and weekly rent, never mind a sewing machine and materials. She explained how much money she had to Danny, and he set about seeing what he could do. March was not the best time for such an undertaking and in vain, for three weeks, he valiantly roamed the streets. All this time, Sarah managed to hide her pregnancy despite how sharing a room with Ellen left little space for privacy.

Ellen, however, paid Sarah little heed, reading and rereading each letter from Jack, residing in a bubble of her own, fully engrossed in the plans Jack outlined. He had only written a few times, interesting letters, but letters that were hopeful rather than positive about his future. His latest letter, although quite optimistic, meant travelling abroad. Miners in Britain had suffered massive wage reductions and coal output was at a low ebb. Jack had applied and was accepted into the 'General Council of the Trades Union Council' to assist in organising miners against more proposed wage cuts. His enthusiasm shone through the letter, his belief he had a worthwhile purpose to pursue, reassuring Ellen he was now finding his direction and path.

In late April, Danny burst through the door beaming. He had a possible place but needed Sarah to come immediately and have a look. 'We can walk to it. It is just on Camden Street. Come on, come on,' he gestured excitedly. All four were infected by his enthusiasm and walked speedily to a small, mid-terrace premises in need of repair but solidly upright. Danny stood back with a bow for all three women to proceed inside. 'It needs some work doing but I'll help. You will only have one room, but it has street frontage. You can get a curtain to cordon off where you live from your customers. There is no fireplace but there is a heater. You share water in a back scullery with the rest of the tenants and there is an outside lavatory for everyone.' Danny looked at Sarah expectantly, his gabble slowing, excitement waning, noting how dismal it now seemed in comparison to Clare Street. 'You don't have to take it. I can continue looking, but it's just a good price…'

His voice faltered and trailed into the ether, at the same time as Sarah clapped her hands and exclaimed, 'It's wonderful. It's ideal. I will get some boxes and materials. I have been looking at adverts for sewing machines. Aye, it will be perfect. A sign in the window onto the street. Oh, thanks, Danny, thank you.' Sarah danced around the room, kicking dust into the air and laughing.

Nothing, however, is ever easy and eventually Sarah had to borrow a small amount of money from Ellen. It was given good-naturedly, knowing it would be repaid, but it put Ellen's burgeoning plans on hold. In many respects, Ellen had lived vicariously for the past two years. The trauma of the barn and witnessing her three brothers take a man's life was still deeply buried in her subconscious although the therapeutic effects of writing had helped her cope. She missed Jack every day and the poignancy of her memories of their wonderful summer left an ache inside. He was busy in England and Wales, but his latest letter spoke of a pending trip to the States. Details of his new job were vague, but he seemed content. Looking back over the last number of years, Ellen concluded that the necessity to assist Sarah and depend on Bridie and Danny had generated a hiatus. Her personal wishes and desires were suspended, thus hampering her growth to independence.

Another few months won't be any bother, she comforted herself. *My time will come soon, and Sarah will be settled before I leave.*

Meanwhile, Sarah set to work with an energy and diligence that amazed Ellen and Bridie albeit, very welcome. She cleaned her new residence thoroughly, and with Danny's help, painted the walls white, careful not to overstretch. A large curtain divided the room, separating her living and work areas. Her bed was a straw- filled mattress, the same as Donegal, and would do perfectly for a while. Two butter boxes and an orange box completed the furniture. In pride of place, in the large window facing the street, was an old Singer sewing machine. Overhead was a large board, hung prominently, advertising her dressmaking and repair services. Once she was settled and ready for customers, she announced that she was expecting and hoped to deliver in St Ultan's Hospital. Bridie agreed enthusiastically, although not quite speedily enough to hide a shadow of envy that flitted, for a second, across her features. There was immediate consternation, of course, that Sarah was alone, but she was a different woman now. She had come to terms with her history, with the absence of Stephen and the deaths of her parents and Kevin. Determined to be independent and make her own way and put past conflict behind her, Sarah smiled and assured confidently all would be well.

Business was slow, and it was only with careful management that Sarah made ends meet and paid a weekly few pence to Ellen. In some respects, it was her location. It was not a wealthy area, so most women altered and repaired their own clothes. The wealthy preferred somewhere with more cachet and a known name. Most of the work undertaken by Sarah was the renovation of old clothing to fit a new owner. But for the moment she was content, happily singing to her unborn child and revelling in her swollen body. When, which was often, there was little to do, she set about making a christening outfit in preparation for the ceremony after the birth. She loved most of all interweaving intricate designs, and Bridie's wedding dress had displayed how meticulous needlework, artistically crafted, could stand alone enhancing even the most inexpensive material. When the christening shawl was completed, she displayed it in her window and surprisingly, it was sold the next day. Thereafter she advertised as a speciality, christening shawls, soon joined by communion dresses, all outfits, where money, if available, was handsomely spent.

The baby was due in August, and Bridie came to see and examine Sarah as she had done most weeks, of late. 'I have been quite sick myself the last few days, Sarah,' intoned Bridie. 'I don't want to give you anything, but I do think you should come to Clare Street and stay until after the birth. I'll get Danny to call for you this evening.'

Sarah agreed. Nothing was going to happen to her child and if that meant giving up, what she now considered her home, for a few weeks, then that is what she would do.

She awoke in Clare Street the following morning as Ellen bade her a cheery goodbye before heading off to work. 'Check on Bridie when you get up. She is sick again.'

Sarah looked sideways at Ellen. *Surely a midwife and someone who works in a hospital have considered Bridie is pregnant?* ruminated Sarah. She lumbered out of bed to the music of Bridie's retching and knew without a shadow of a doubt, that Bridie, their stalwart bastion, was the last to know her own body. That night, Sarah went into labour and in the early hours delivered a baby girl whom she named, Deirdre. She glowed, as she held her daughter tight. It would be a tough road ahead, but for the first time in many years, she was happy and content.

Over the past year, Ellen had been in constant contact with her brother, Ciaran, now settled in New York. She had sent him some of her short stories on tenement life and surprisingly, he had managed to have a few of them published in a local journal. Although she enjoyed her job in St Ultan's Hospital and appreciated the opportunity it had given her, she now seriously contemplated moving to America. The hospital was no longer sufficiently satisfying, and change was required. Jack was moving on, and she had too as well. The future might well connect them once more, but for now, she had to make her own life. Her title was now "hospital administrator", no longer "maid" or "cleaner", and she would have a useful reference and should easily ind work. Joining Ciaran seemed like the sensible route but also, a big step. However, the good news, now confirmed, that Bridie was expecting a baby in March put Ellen's plans further on hold. Bridie had done so much for her. Ellen wanted to be there with her throughout the pregnancy and delivery.

The pending birth was a catalyst for change as the house would certainly be too small for all of them. It cemented Ellen's plans to move on and excitement began to build at the thought of joining Ciaran in America. Once her mind was entirely made up, she approached Sarah to see if she would like to accompany her. 'Think of all the opportunities for Deirdre if she grows up in New York, Sarah.'

'I cannot go, Ellen,' was Sarah's quick response when Ellen spoke of her plan. 'I am actually content here. I can look after Deirdre and still work at my dressmaking. My little business keeps me going, but more importantly, I have never given up hope that at some point I will find out what happened to Stephen.'

That statement alone said it all for Ellen. Sarah would never leave while there was the remotest possibility of finding the whereabouts of the little boy, she still maintained was alive. Ellen resolved to go to Ciaran and explore the challenges of the New World, alone. Bridie's baby boy, Martin, named after Danny's father, was welcomed into the world on the 20th of March 1927. On the 30th of May, Ellen set sail for America.

Chapter 25

Ellen anxiously searched the crowd for Ciaran. The requirement, however necessary, to endure endless questions after tedious hours waiting around, had been exhausting. At long last, permission had been received to leave Ellis Island and enter the United States of America. Now she had taken her first few steps on American soil, all she wanted was to find her brother Ciaran, and get back to his apartment where a promised bed awaited. A tap on her shoulder and she turned around, to be enveloped in a loving, and welcoming hug. They both took a step back, simultaneously, the better to see the other. In Ellen's mind, there was no denying Ciaran looked well but had gained quite a few pounds. He also appeared quite prosperous, smartly dressed and to her surprise, sporting highly polished shoes adorned with spats.

For his part, Ciaran thought Ellen looked beautiful and held her tightly, savouring his only connection with home. He imagined he could smell the wild fuchsia and the smoky scent of smouldering turf.

Ciaran hauled the cases to a waiting taxi rank and within thirty minutes, they were at his apartment, in Brooklyn, with Manhattan easily accessible. It was more spacious than Ellen had expected and surprisingly, quite smartly decorated with some very tasteful furniture. The only downside was the fact it contained just one bedroom. Ciaran had kindly vacated that room for Ellen and cordoned off space in the living room for himself, but it was clear that this arrangement could only be temporary. Ellen had enough savings for a deposit on her own place but sensibly, she wished to procure employment before committing herself to a rental agreement.

The first time Ellen ventured into Manhattan she felt an instant buzz, a quickening pace, a grasping at life that she had never previously experienced. She could see it in Ciaran also, and although he said he hankered after Ireland, particularly Donegal, she sensed that the slow pace of home would no longer be enough for him. He now worked for Tammany Hall and the local "ward". Tammany Hall was a political machine that exerted substantial control over politics in New York and assisted, in the main, those of Irish descent and new immigrants to obtain work and achieve positions of political power. Business interests were varied with tentacles extended, to insinuate into a variety of areas. The prevalence of the influence of Tammany Hall was apparent in construction, social clubs, and various other activities.

When Ciaran arrived in New York, akin to most immigrants, he gravitated towards the Irish community. He had been instructed to locate Jackie O'Shea, the older brother of a friend from Donegal. Jackie was a labourer on a building site and introduced Ciaran to the foreman, Mick O'Connor. Mick was a heftily built, Mayo man, unshaven and intense, his manner intimidating or affable depending on his mood. He emanated a constant sour odour from sweat that beaded his forehead and ringed the underarms of his shirt. He studied Ciaran for a moment before barking, 'Can you handle a saw?'

'Aye, I can,' was the quick response.

'Grand so, be here tomorrow at 7.30 and no later.' Mick marched off without another word.

'See,' said Jackie, 'I knew I would get you sorted.'

Ciaran's skill with a saw was very basic but the work did not require a whole lot of knowledge, and he quickly mastered the necessary competence. Besides, he was steadfast and diligent, and Mick nodded approvingly at him from time to time. It was not easy to get along with Mick, but Ciaran's natural charm complemented Mick's brashness and they developed an unlikely friendship. Mick introduced Ciaran to some of his more "connected" friends and Ciaran soon found a new niche assisting in the procurement of votes for up-and-coming political hopefuls. After a year, Ciaran began to settle in New York and feel he belonged.

Ellen applied for a position in St. Columba's General Hospital and her experience in Dublin guaranteed her success. Her wages were small and for the time being, she had no option but to continue living with Ciaran. The apartment was comfortable enough, but his constant stream of acquaintances was an irritation and, most of all, worrisome. These "acquaintances" had a presence that held sway and subtly altered, Ciaran.

'A few friends are coming tonight, Ellen. Tidy up a bit, be nice to them, they're important. Might help you advance.'

'What do you mean, Ciaran? Be nice to them? Who are they anyway?' queried Ellen, as she gazed thoughtfully at Ciaran. The change in him was barely discernible but Ellen could spot a brittleness, even a certain pandering note, in his tone. This was particularly true around Christy. He stood apart, almost a spectator, and that was all the more unnerving. Dressed in sober, well-cut suits, he issued instructions with little more than a nod. His gaunt features were overshadowed by bushy brows that hid perceptive but impenetrable, eyes. Ellen had only met him twice but more than the others, he compelled her to voice her worries to Ciaran.

'Ciaran, Mick is fine, but who are these other people, especially Christy?'

Instantly shuttered, Ciaran retreated into the alien world in which he was now encased. 'Business, business, Ellen, no worries, eh?' Ciaran refused to engage in conversation and later that evening, totally unsettled, Ellen rooted in her purse for the letter from Maisie O'Reilly.

Bridie had given Ellen, Maisie's address before she left Ireland, and her words resonated clearly as Ellen hunted through her belongings for the scrap of paper. 'Ellen, do you remember Maisie O'Reilly? Here is her address. She was a nurse here in the hospital and I have kept in touch. She lives in Toronto and might be able to help you get a position. Sure, Toronto can't be that far from New York.'

Ellen had previously written to Maisie out of respect for Bridie but now she put pen to paper for much-needed advice. 'You will easily find employment here, Ellen,' responded Maisie. 'We are always looking for good workers in Toronto General. Let me know if you wish to come here and I will assist you, whatever way I can.'

Three weeks later, Ellen received a further reply to her request. 'Ellen, good news. There is a job here for you provided you meet with the approval of Miss Morrison, and I am positive that is just a formality.'

A further three weeks later, Ellen was packed for departure to Toronto. Ciaran was surprisingly agreeable to accompany her to Canada. Perhaps her questions about his "friends" were becoming uncomfortable or maybe living together had lost its sheen and he needed his own space. They were to travel from New York to Buffalo and from there to Toronto.

'It's a route I travel now and again, for business,' he explained. 'I know it well, and you can avoid a lot of the checks now prevalent at the ports, for incoming migrants.'

The journey was both exciting and arduous. Ciaran was asleep almost before the train moved from the station. Ellen was glued to the window determined to relish the majesty of a trip across New York State. Yet the endless terrain, combined with the hypnotic oscillation of the tracks, induced a languor and she herself dozed, intermittently, for much of the journey to Buffalo. They spent the night in a small boarding house where Ciaran was evidently a well-known patron, before continuing to Toronto the following day.

The next morning, Ellen's excited anticipation gave way to anxiety and a fear, that if she were unsuccessful at the interview, she would have to return to New York with Ciaran. All tension soon vanished, replaced by wondrous awe, as their journey got underway. She gasped at the magnificent spectacle of Niagara Falls in all its stunning glory on an August morning. Wispy clouds floated lazily overhead, as the powerful cascade of water thundered into the river below on its journey to Lake Ontario and the Atlantic Ocean. Donegal's mountains and barren landscape had its own beauty, but Ellen devoured the splendour spread before her, as the train sped towards Toronto. Eventually, the train clattered into the station and, true to her word, Maisie O'Reilly was waiting for her.

Introductions were barely completed before Ciaran announced, 'I'll take you both to lunch tomorrow after the interview. See you at the Gladstone Hotel, do you know it, Maisie? It is near the train station.'

'Yes, yes, I do. We will see you there, at 1 o'clock.'

Ciaran then disappeared so quickly, it was barely polite, but Maisie made no comment. The two women spent the day, quietly, in her small apartment. It was not much more than one room and although near the hospital, was in quite a depressed area. Setting aside any misgivings, Ellen concentrated on preparation for her interview the following morning, which went smoothly. Her typing was always a little suspect, but her knowledge of hospital systems and the numerous forms that needed deciphering was excellent. She was to start two days later.

Saying goodbye to Ciaran after the promised lunch was not so difficult. She was glad to be away from an atmosphere that seemed to border on the intimidating, as each day passed by. Also, he was no longer so far away and was a frequent, if irregular, visitor to Toronto.

Although the hospital was extremely large, catering for men, women and children, with all types of ailments, the work was pretty much the same as that undertaken in Dublin and Ellen settled in relatively quickly. Procuring an apartment was not so easy but Maisie was easy-going and suggested pooling their resources. As such, they found a larger apartment with two bedrooms. It was on a street that, perhaps, had seen better days but it was quiet and only a fifteen-minute walk to the hospital. Maisie was about ten years older than Ellen, single and quite content. Her flaming red hair was always a source of conversation with the patients and her happy freckled face invited much laughter. She was now a senior staff nurse in the Toronto General and hoped to one day save enough money to purchase her own home.

'Probably never happen,' she mused. 'Between the cost of living and being a "woman". However, sharing with you helps me save a little more so maybe someday…' Maisie's voice trailed away, her eyes focussed inwards, on some faraway spot. The only blight on Ellen's horizon was the fact that she had not heard from Jack since before she set sail from Dublin. She had written to him, giving him Ciaran's address but the letter was returned a few months later with "not known at this address", scrawled across the envelope. There was nothing he could do but hope he contacted Danny, in Dublin. Putting her disappointment aside, she helped paint the apartment and together with Maisie, bought what furniture they could afford. It rapidly became home and a sanctuary after long hours at work.

Ellen now had space and freedom to indulge her passion and soon she was writing once more. A proper outlet for her anecdotes was not readily forthcoming, an avenue apparently as elusive in Toronto, as in Dublin. By now, she had a vast accumulation of short stories, funny, poignant, sad, and taking up too much space. Maisie introduced her to the city, bringing her to the notorious St. John's Ward. The first stop for many immigrants, it was an area raucous with a multitude of accents, including a variety of Irish. Ellen, quickly pinpointed the exact source of many accents from that, far away isle.

'The area is changing and for the better,' informed Maisie. 'Our hospital was built here in 1909 and there are plans to erect more civic buildings.'

Their stroll brought them to St. Paul's Basilica, a beautiful, but poignant reminder of Ireland with so many victims of the typhus epidemic of 1847 buried in its grounds. Automatically, both women paused and bowed their heads in silent prayer and thanks. The still air, disturbed only by the fluttering of numerous birds, gave a testament to the saddest period in Irish history. Thousands fled their homeland from famine and destitution knowing they would never return. Canada's open arms gave sanctuary and hope to countless numbers who survived the hazardous, Atlantic crossing. Maisie was first to disturb their silent reverie. 'This is the most wonderful country, Ellen. I hope you will come to love it as much as I do.'

Ellen's arrival, in the autumn of 1927, had enabled her to enjoy the long hot days of early Toronto Fall. The advent of the biting cold of winter was a revelation. She had never encountered such freezing temperatures and the apartment took hours to heat up. Maisie invariably worked late, often staying in the hospital overnight. Once a week, if possible, but whenever funds allowed, Ellen relished the opportunity to eat her evening meal after work in a local café, with a young colleague named, Jenny. There they revelled in the heady aromas steaming from the various Italian dishes, but most of all, the warmth within the cosy cafe, before facing the trudge home. Now and again, Jenny was unable to accompany her, and it was on those occasions, with icy rain or sleet pouring from a grey thunderous sky, that Ellen sometimes wrote her best. Sitting at a table alone she felt more comfortable with an activity to occupy her, so she would write another "Tenement Tale", from the endless supply in her memory.

One early December evening as an elderly gentleman passed by her table, he tripped and fell forward. Ellen jumped up immediately and helped him to his feet. 'Are you alright? Shall I call for help?'

'No, no, thank you, I am fine, just slipped. If I can just lean on you for a moment.'

Ellen helped him to his feet as the owner of the café came rushing across. 'Oh, Mr Harrington, sit here, I will get you a drink.'

Ellen quietly left, and it was another two weeks before she saw him again.

'Am I interrupting, may I join you?' Ellen looked up into a vaguely familiar face. 'I hope I am not disturbing you, but I so wanted to say, "thank you" for assisting me the other evening.' Ellen instantly realised it was the gentleman who had tripped and indicated he should sit down at her table and join her. He insisted on buying her a glass of wine in appreciation and as he sat down, commented, 'I have seen you here many evenings, scribbling away, and I am fascinated by how you can endlessly write. My name is Jeremy by the way, Jeremy Harrington.'

Ellen inclined her head and outstretched her hand, 'Ellen McShane, nice to meet you.' She assessed her new companion as she packed away her writing pad and pen. *He must be near seventy*, she thought, *although his hair is not yet fully grey*. He was well dressed and spoke with, what seemed to her, a cultured, Toronto, accent.

'I see I have disturbed you,' he said. 'That was not my intention. I just wanted to say thank you for your assistance the other day. I am also intrigued. I have always loved to write myself, so, when I saw a young, fellow advocate of the written word, I felt compelled to make your acquaintance.'

Ellen smiled at this distinctly genteel and perhaps interesting, man. 'What do you write?' she enquired. 'Have you ever been published?'

'I worked as a newspaper reporter and assistant editor for many years, so I suppose you could say, I was regularly published. When I retired, I decided to write a book, the plot had plagued me for years and, yes, it was published although it did not sell that well. I then wrote a play, based on the book, and that was an exciting challenge. We travelled to the United States, and it was even performed in New York, off-Broadway, but, unfortunately, not for long. So, tell me, what do you write about? What is your inspiration?'

Ellen gave him a brief outline of the provenance of her short stories and, before he left, he asked if she would bring one for him to read. This she duly did, once Christmas was over.

Christmas 1927, in Toronto, was tempered with sadness. Dedicated Maisie had volunteered to nurse that day, but Ciaran had travelled, as promised, from New York. The morning together was spent reading cards and letters from Donegal and Dublin. Sarah's little business appeared to be thriving and Deirdre was now toddling around. They were both joining Bridie, Danny, and baby Martin for Christmas and Ellen felt tears welling at the thought of the little group in Clare Street.

For Ciaran, it was the best Christmas he recalled in years. Ellen was with him, so he did not spend hours wistfully romanticising about Donegal and family, reminiscing, and drinking too much. Jenny, Ellen's friend, dropped by for a quick Christmas drink and ended up staying until the early hours. From time to time, Ellen's thoughts turned to Jack. She wondered how he was doing, was he finding his own path, just as she was. She had not heard from him and neither had Danny. Danny did tell her that he understood from some colleagues that Jack was in the United States, in Colorado, where there was a major strike underway for better pay and conditions. He was heavily involved in the Labour movement and was often on the move. Danny had attempted to locate an address but was unsuccessful, but as he gently pointed out, if Jack wanted to keep in touch, he knew the address in Clare Street. There was also no word from Sheamus. His letters, if his minuscule communications were worthy of the name, had been sporadic at best after Josie died and then, faded away, altogether.

Kathleen's Christmas card and enclosed letter generated a few tears from Ellen and suspicious sniffs, from Ciaran. Mary and Liam were to be married in early January, but neither Ellen nor Ciaran, would be in a position to attend. On the first free day, after Ellen returned to work, she spent an enjoyable hour searching for a suitable wedding present, one that was easy to post without getting damaged.

It was a full four weeks after the wedding before the parcel arrived in "Droimreagh". Showing an unusual amount of self-control and despite prompting from Kathleen, Mary fore-bore opening the parcel until Liam returned home. Before long, she could hear Liam outside, rinsing the day's dirt off himself, while humming contentedly. He was instantly alert to a buzz and excitement when he entered the farmhouse. A quick hug for Kathleen and a tender kiss for Mary followed by, 'What's going on here? Why all the excitement?'

'This package arrived today from Canada,' was the response from the women, almost in unison.

To tease Mary, he grabbed the parcel and in so doing she saw his knuckles, skinned, and raw. 'What happened, Liam? What happened to your hands?'

'Whist, Mary, nothing. Just scrapes from mending fences. Now, what do we have here?'

Wrapping paper was swiftly ripped away and Liam held aloft embroidered bed sheets and pillow slips. Throwing his arms once more around Mary, taking hold of Kathleen's hands, he grinned as he tunelessly, warbled, 'Aye, sure isn't life grand.'

As they all sat down to eat in "Droimreagh", a morose, Patsy O'Hara shuffled into the pub. He did not choose his usual spot at the bar, but instead, sidled into a corner not wishing to be seen as he lingered over his pint. His new, grey, suit jacket was speckled with red droplets of blood, the entire suit, spattered with mud. One eye was half-closed, and an array of rainbow colours would surely be visible over the coming days.

'Someone teach you a lesson, Patsy? Not so dapper this evening, eh?' roared a voice from the other side of the bar.

'Feck off,' Patsy murmured and standing, he painfully limped his way out the door.

It was almost a year, since Ellen had left Ireland and she had become very settled. Her job was going well, and she had made a few friends. They were all enthralled with the movies and, each weekend, they went to a different cinema. She wrote to Ciaran at least once a week and, on his last visit, had been introduced to Jill, his new girlfriend. Ellen was disappointed his friendship with Jenny had waned but felt it was not the distance that had seen it, founder. Although pretty enough, Jill had a brashness about her that seemed to appeal to Ciaran, an attraction Ellen failed to understand. However, he was a grown man and evidently, she must have some alluring traits that eluded Ellen. Ciaran had noticed Ellen's quizzical look and understood she was not impressed by Jill.

'Jenny is more your type,' she quietly hinted, but he ignored her.

What Ellen would never understand was the depth of self-hatred, that consumed Ciaran. It was only with a supreme effort he kept Sean O'Hara's terrified eyes and pathetic pleas from haunting him, daily. A vision he could not hide from, was the sudden spray of blood as his throat was slit, a rainfall of red, emitting a shower, that could never cleanse. He recalled Liam hissing orders, 'Ciaran, put the ebony cross on the door so no one comes near. Then get Billy for the injured lad, he will know what to do, where to bring him.' Ciaran raced away, as strident tones echoed behind him. 'Sheamus, help me with him.' Together, Liam and Sheamus discarded the body of Sean, a shameful and dishonourable end, to their one-time friend and neighbour. The horrific night was still far from over. Ciaran helped Billy load the now, almost lifeless body, into the cart and spent the next few hours, as dawn crept in spurts through the darkened sky, cleansing the barn. Crimson streaked hay was hauled away and burned. Walls, flecked with droplets now turning to brown, were scrubbed, and rinsed, as the uneven floor, puddled and slippery, was washed and washed again. His once calm nature was replaced by a restlessness and destructiveness, that he could not control. Whenever he was touched by gentleness or by the possibility of happiness, he kicked back. Only through his own destruction, could he keep going, make reparation, and thereby expiate his guilt.

Dispelling the disquieting thoughts about Ciaran, Ellen marched quickly along the pavement. She was slightly irritated at herself as she was somewhat late for her meeting with Jeremy but had been unavoidably delayed at the hospital. She was relieved to see him still sitting at his usual table with a bottle of red wine and two glasses, awaiting her arrival. He also had a large notebook in front of him and a folder containing her stories. Jeremy Harrington had been the assistant editor of a well-renowned newspaper for many years and believed he was a decent judge of good writing. Since his retirement, he enjoyed a comfortable lifestyle and was able to indulge his passion for the written word, but he also edited the odd book for a publishing company. The earnestness visible in Ellen and the fascinating way she depicted tenement life excited him. He was amused at how the world could collapse around her, and it seemed she would barely notice, so intent was she on her writing. Such was the absorption in her thoughts, she might have been sitting anywhere in the world and not a small, Italian café, in Toronto. Ellen, as requested, had duly given him a couple of her short stories. He found himself admiring how she wrote, the approach she took to the depiction of poverty and how laughter and life thrived, in such deprived conditions. As their unlikely friendship progressed, Jeremy asked her to bring him some more of her "Tales", and he sat many an evening in his garden, fragrant with spring flowers, pondering how best to proceed. He eventually resolved to meet her in the café and put an idea to her.

Jeremy went straight to the point. 'Ellen, I want you to collate your "Tenement Tales" into one book. You will need to write an introduction and a conclusion, so they blend well together.'

Ellen was taken aback with delight at the idea but frightened at the surge of apprehension that immediately coursed through her mind. 'Jeremy, I don't know if I am able to do that.'

'Of course, you can, Ellen. Anyway, I will guide you and help edit but you already have the bulk of the stories written. I think it will be a "must-read" for many of our immigrants, reminding them of all they left behind, the good, and the bad. By bearing witness to the desperation that so many people endure, you not only have been inspired to become a writer but ensure their story is told. Overall, however, I think you are talented and can do this. The stories are so active and lively. It will be a terrific book and an anecdotal history of the times.'

Ellen glowed, astonished, delighted, emotional and overwhelmed, but most of all eager to embrace the opportunity. 'Jeremy, I so want to do it and as long as I can depend on your help, I will give it a go. Thank you so much for your belief in me.'

'If I could make one more suggestion, Ellen, I think, if you are agreeable, and if your efforts prove as successful as I firmly believe they will, a percentage of the profit from sales should go towards the relief of poverty in Ireland. There are so many charities attempting to alleviate hardship, but as I am sure you are well aware, funds are always needed. You could choose one yourself that focusses on assisting the poor of Dublin.'

Ellen's book took almost a year to complete between rewrites and the addition of new material. Jeremy had been as good as his word, offering advice, reading, and editing. With many contacts at his disposal, he was able to coordinate all elements so successful publishing was assured. The launch was organised in a well-known bookshop with a small reception afterwards. Ciaran and Jill, and many friends from the hospital, were all invited, but initially, the public would have open access for book signings. Interest from the general Irish immigrant community was unprecedented and a large crowd was expected.

Ellen's apartment was full of flowers and cards from well-wishers and, as she dressed, she felt rightly proud of her success. The dress she had purchased for the day gave her a frisson of shock when she thought of the price but also anticipation at donning something so spectacular. It was blue and white with intricate, embroidered detail and, as she fingered the delicate material, a rush of nostalgia washed over her. She longed for Sarah, and how she would appreciate such finery. Her reflection told her she looked stunning, and she walked carefully down the stairs to the waiting car, and Jeremy.

The bookshop was busy, with sales steady all afternoon. Ellen sat for about three hours continually signing her book, barely registering the faces or the steady stream that passed by the desk where she was seated. As the crowd thinned and reduced to a trickle, she raised her head and gratefully accepted a welcome cup of coffee, from Jeremy. It was at that moment Ellen saw Jack, standing with his usual amused glint, watching, and assessing her.

'Definitely *'Lady Bountiful'* this evening, Ellen,' grinned Jack as he slowly bent forward to kiss her cheek.

Printed in Great Britain
by Amazon

85402162R00140